CLAW HAMMER

A GATHERING OF STORIES

CLAW HAMMER

A GATHERING OF STORIES

Chris Helvey

Hopewell Publications

Published by Hopewell
Publications, LLC
PO Box 11, Titusville,
NJ 08560-0011
(609) 818-1049

info@HopePubs.com
www.HopePubs.com

International Standard Book Number: 9781933435510

Library of Congress Control Number: 2015952931

First Edition

Printed in the United States of America

DEDICATION

This book is for my readers.
After all, these stories were written for you.

CONTENTS

THERE IS A SEASON

"PUT ON THAT GREEN BIKINI, you know, the string one, and let's go," I hollered, easing back in my chair. I was sweating like a pregnant hog on the 4th of July and I wiped the sweat of my face with a purple do-rag that smelled like the ass end of a mangy dog.

I noticed then my hands were shaking so I folded them and put them in my lap.

It was going to be another hot one. Sunlight glittered off the chrome on the junked cars out in the yard where the grass had browned and gone to seed. The river birches at the corner of the trailer had already shed most of their leaves. Those leaves lay like small brown wrinkled animals. Dead animals.

No rain for almost three weeks is hard on the living. A hot dry wind rustled the dead leaves and carried yellowing newspapers across the gravel drive and impaled them on what remained of the picket fence I'd put up back in the spring.

The only item of real value out in that yard, or in the trailer for that matter, was my '67 Camaro. Last year, when I got Daddy's insurance money, I'd got some body work done and a paint job. The original paint had faded almost down to metal and primer and there were rust spots that looked like bullet holes. Actually, there was one of those. But that's a West Virginia tale. Making, West-by-God-Virginia, to be exact.

After Freddy Powers got through the Camaro was so blue in the sun that from a distance you think you're looking at a pond. And all that chrome sure does glitter.

Junior Evans installed new seat covers for me back when I was working and semi-straight. Well, straighter than I am now. The radio is only AM, but what the hell? Enough songs are playing inside my brain to keep me happy. Besides, I can pick up local news and weather from

WSIP over in Paintsville and, in the summer when the weather doesn't act up, I can get the Reds on WLW.

The son-of-a-bitch has a 396 cubic inch, big block V8 that pushes 375 horses. Not much short of the Kentucky State Police can keep up with me. And even those brick brains won't take half the chances I do.

Tommy Preston has been after me for years to sell it to him. Ever since he won the Lotto. Offered me twenty thousand one night when he was drunk.

I told him to go to hell. Yeah, he's got the money but he's a stingy bastard. My brother asked him to loan him twenty-five hundred dollars to slip into Judge Newsome's robes. Tommy turned Benny down flat. Now Benny's ass is in LaGrange doing three to five.

Besides I've seen classic Camaros in Auto Trader not a whole nicer than mine bring big money, over fifty thousand dollars. One dude was asking seventy-five for this '67 red and black SS. God, but it was beautiful. Made my dick hard just looking at it. But seventy-five big ones? I mean, come on. Course that old boy was from Texas, so I figured he wasn't quite right. George W sure cured my ass of thinking anything from Texas was legit.

I shook my head and turned back to the television. Up here at the head of Big Blaine we don't get cable and since old man Philpot had let me go down at the tipple I'd had to quit making payments on the dish. Mountain Satellite cut me off last month. Now the only stations we could get were those that came in on the rickety antenna I'd pilfered from the McAllister place. Not that anybody would ever miss it. Nobody had lived there since the old man died right before Christmas. Only the girls had come in for the funeral and neither of them had stayed. Figured somebody might as well use what was left around the homeplace before the Whitmore boys got to nosing around.

We really get only two channels good. Couple of others come in fuzzy when the atmospherics align. I can't even get Braves baseball.

At the moment a fat guy with a shiny toupee was giving the weather. He talked funny, working the words out of the side of his mouth like fishing worms.

"And today it will be hot enough to fry eggs on the dashboard of your car," he said and laughed. Actually, it was more of a snicker, as phony as his hair.

Just watching his fleshy lips twist themselves all around aggravated my nerves, which between the kids crying and Doreen's whining and the heat were about shot. I got out of the chair and changed channels the old fashioned way. Batteries for the remote had quit back before the hot spell.

I sat through a commercial featuring a monkey playing with dynamite and a fat sister selling hemorrhoid salve. I was hoping for a cowboy movie or maybe NASCAR or the Roller Derby, but instead an old guy who called himself Revered Micah flickered on. I groaned and reached for my beer before I remembered that I'd finished it off an hour ago.

Reverend Micah was one of those old-timey mountain preachers who liked to tell everybody else how to live. Think he was from Martin County. Anyway, he preached at the Mountain Tabernacle of the Holy Word. Was on the Hazard station about three times a week and gave the name of this church at least a dozen times every sermon.

Thirty years ago Reverend Micah would have been a Sunday afternoon radio preacher on WEZJ out of Williamsburg or WCCT out of Corbin where he could rent a half hour cheap, preach hell for twenty minutes, salvation for three, and beg like a leper for seven. Radio had been taken over by the big-money, self-righteous Republican wingnuts and the Pentecostal preachers had started begging harder and migrated to local television.

I got up and switched channels again. The weather dude had given way to a beefy Australian selling weird kitchen devices that would chop up all kinds of food nobody I knew had ever eaten on purpose. Dude had one of those grins that I wanted to smack off his face. I turned back to Reverend Micah.

Today, the old fart was reading from Ecclesiastes. "Chapter 3, verse 1," he intoned, his voice dropping until it rattled around in his cadaverous old chest. "To everything there is a season, and a time to every purpose under heaven."

"Right," I said, and got back up and walked into the kitchen, which looked like a tornado had hit it a glancing blow. My hands were shaking worse than before and my guts felt like I'd been eating barbed-wire.

The little one was hollering in the back like a bee had stung him on his weenie. "Goddamn it, Doreen," I shouted, "hurry up and get that bikini on and those kids dressed. We need to roll."

I could hear the stress, or anger, or hatred, whatever the right term was, vibrating around in my voice. Didn't like it, wasn't proud of it, but it was there. Reality was reality, whether or not a man chose to admit it.

"Can't you help me a little, honey? The baby needs changing and I can't do that and get me and Bobby ready at the same time."

She was using her whiney voice this morning, the one that makes me want to hurt something, and I yelled back, "Alright, Goddamn it." Nerves in my legs were starting to wriggle.

I'd have to get a fix soon.

Reverend Micah was still blabbering on about everything happening in a season for a reason and the Lord working in mysterious ways. I gave him the finger and kept walking.

The little one had crapped his diaper and wouldn't hold still and my hands were sorta shaky and it took me a long time to get the dirty one off, wipe his hind end, and get the new one on. The whole time I was wondering who his daddy was.

Doreen swore it was me. But then she never told a hard truth when a soft lie would do. She'd been sleeping around for a couple of years before the kid came along. Sure, I guess he could have been mine, but I wasn't betting my welfare check.

He was so young that it was hard to tell much. But those blue eyes bothered me. Mine were the color of an old hound dog's, and Doreen had Melungeon blood and her eyes were ebony. I'd thought about taking one of those DNA tests I'd read about at the Health Department, but had never found the money, or the nerve. Still, every time I looked at those blue eyes I wondered.

Finally, I got him changed and hauled him out to the kitchen. The television was still on and I was starting to sweat. Outside the turkey vultures were back. Three of them had been parking on the picket fence most of the summer. They reminded me of the Three Stooges.

"Hurry up, Doreen."

"Here I am."

I twisted my neck and looked at her across the kitchen. A horse fly buzzed between us. Flies had been bad all summer. Guess I should have fixed the screen door. She was wearing one of my old t-shirts and a pair of cut-off jean shorts.

"Hope you've got that bikini on underneath that garb."

"Oh, honey, I can't go out wearing that. I'd just be hanging out everywhere."

"Damn, Doreen, you are dumb. That's what we want. Old Cardwell can't take his eyes off you anyway and with you in that string bikini he wouldn't know if Muslims were blowing up his store."

I walked over and cupped her chin in my hand. "That's the whole point, you big dummy. Let me explain it to you again, slowly, so you'll understand. Ready?"

She blinked her eyes rapidly. I took that for a yes.

"Okay then, listen. Now here's how it works. You go in the store first in that bikini with your tits and ass all hanging out and in sixty seconds old Cardwell won't even know his own name, let alone who else might be in the store.

"Now you lead him way in the back, where they have all the heating pads and knee braces and shit."

"What will I say?"

I wanted to smack the stupid right off her face. Instead, I put my hands in my pockets. They fluttered against my leg muscles, making me think of baby rabbits.

"Damn it, Doreen, you don't really have to say anything. Just wiggle that fat ass and bend over a lot so he can get a good look at the twins. Got that?"

Her eyes were glazed with confusion, but she nodded. One thing about Doreen, she tries real hard to be agreeable.

"Alright. Now while you've got Cardwell's attention I'll be hitting the safe where he keeps the good stuff. There's enough OxyContin in there to take care of both of us for six months. I swear it."

"But it's a safe. Don't Cardwell keep it locked?"

I closed my eyes and took a deep breath. Pain had started to creep into my bones now and I was half sick at my stomach. Trying to have a conversation with Doreen was a pain-in-the-ass when I was feeling good. When I was feeling the pain talking to her was almost more than I could stand.

If I hadn't needed her to distract Cardwell I would have hopped in the Camaro and headed for West Virginia. Had friends there. Huntington and Wheeling and Buckhannon and Barboursville. Friends who wouldn't let me down. Maybe I'd go there anyway, just as soon as I got old Cardwell's stash and had another session or two with Doreen. The woman might not be the brightest bulb in the pack, but she would do anything you asked and she had a body that refused to quit. You had to give her that.

I opened my eyes and tried to smile. She cries sometimes when I yell at her and I didn't want that pretty face all messed up this morning. Had me a plan. A sure one this time. So I wiped the sweat off my forehead and ignored my stomach that was cramping like somebody had jammed a tire iron inside my bowels and started twisting.

"No baby, he cracks it open. Just a red hair, but he cracks it just the same. Seen that last time I was in. Dropped a quarter and pretended to look for it behind the counter just so I could scope things out. Don't worry, that safe will be open. Guess he does that early so he can get into it easy all day without having to twist the dial."

I kissed her then. Her breath smelled like she'd been eating roadkill. Or maybe that was just mine blowing back in my face.

"Now, have you got that bikini on underneath?"

"No."

She looked like she was going to cry. I was sweating real heavy now and cramping like my guts were trying to pass an anvil. I swallowed hard.

14

"Alright pretty baby, just go put it on, okay? You can wear that t-shirt over until we get to Cardwell's. Now go change."

I patted her on the ass. Even with the cramping she felt sweet. "Hurry up, baby. I'm gonna step outside and smoke one. Just bring the kids when you come."

I turned then and hurried on out. I was cramping too bad for her to see me. She would get to worrying and wouldn't want me to drive. Shit on that. I pulled a long butt out of the soft pack and fired it up. Generic crap.

I farted, blew smoke out my nose, and meandered over to the Camaro. While I was waiting for Doreen I wiped the body down with a soft cloth just like my daddy taught me. He'd be proud. At least of the way I was taking care of his vehicle.

Just as Doreen finally stepped outside hauling the two kids along, I noticed a bug smear on the windshield and I hustled back inside and grabbed the Windex. By the time she had the kids in their car seats the windshield was clean.

My hands were shaking as I buckled up and my stomach kept wanting to turn over, but I couldn't afford to get sick on the side of the road. Cops around here were real pricks; they'd just as soon write you a ticket as eat lunch.

Speaking of eating, I couldn't remember the last time and I was sort of hungry, only a stronger hunger than the desire to eat was driving me.

Inside the Camaro it was hotter than what I figured for hell. Sunlight poured through the windshield until it felt like my chest hairs were starting to catch fire. The AC sucked too much gas, so I rolled down my window. Doreen bitched about what the wind would do to her hair and I told her it was fine with me if she wanted to melt like a plastic doll, which, if you looked at things a certain way, she was. When her mascara began to run she rolled her window down.

I turned on the radio, but all I could get was that same damn preacher. Reverend Micah was preaching the same sermon on television and radio. Seemed greedy to me. I showed him there was a season for turning off greedy, annoying preachers. After that I just listened to the wind and the voices inside my head.

All the way to town I kept one eye out for the police and the other on the asphalt that squirmed before me like a dark, unhappy snake. Sweat coated my shirt to my back and ran down the crack of my ass. The kids cried and Doreen pouted. If I hadn't been aching all the way to the marrow of my bones, I'd have pulled over and busted all their asses.

It was the first of the month and traffic was thick as flies swarming fresh horseshit. Circled the square three times before some old biddy pulled a Chrysler as big as a boat out of a parking space right in front of Cardwell's.

Jackie Maculey, who used to be the preacher down at Main Street Baptist before Sue Ellen Grider joined the choir, was signaling for the spot but I goosed the gas pedal and cut him off. He gave me a dirty look as I wheeled by and I laughed at his ugly face. We went back a lot of years.

I switched off the engine and just sat there for a minute sweating and breathing through the pain. My body was betraying me again; I was trembling too hard to move.

"Are we getting out?" Doreen asked.

I nodded and swallowed. "Yeah, in a minute."

Closing my eyes, I leaned back and listened to the cars roll by and the squeaky voices chattering inside my skull.

"Honey?" Doreen rubbed on my arm like it was the toe of Abraham Lincoln's long lost boot. I wondered what kind of luck she thought I'd bring.

"What?"

"It's getting really hot in here. Can't we go in now? The kids are getting fussy."

"Alright, alright," I said and unbuckled my seat belt and popped the door open. I wasn't sure I could stand, so I leaned on the door frame and watched Doreen get out. The dummy was still wearing one of my old t-shirts over her bikini. She had a body that wouldn't quit and a brain that never quite got into gear.

"Take that goddamn t-shirt off."

"But..."

"Take it off, Doreen, or do I have to whip your ass right here on Main Street?"

She started to tear up, so I showed her my fists and she shrugged the t-shirt over her head and flung it back inside the car. Just then the little fartknocker started whining and Doreen's mouth popped open like she was a ventriloquist's dummy.

"What about the kids, baby?"

I'd forgotten about the kids. I licked my lips and thought about the situation.

"I'll just roll the windows all the way down." I grinned at Doreen. "They'll be okay. We won't be but a minute."

They'd be fine; I was sure of that. I could remember my daddy leaving our dog, Tonga, in the truck with the windows cracked plenty of times. Even in the hot of summer. Why one time we'd even gone in to the Lane Theater and watched a John Wayne western while old Tonga sat on the seat, panting and staring out the window, watching for us. Sure he got hot and maybe he howled a time or two, but it never really hurt him.

"I don't know," Doreen said, putting that worried mother look on her face. "It's awful hot, honey. You heard that weatherman."

So it's hot, I thought, and my bones feel like they're cracking apart. Be able to suck the damn marrow in a minute.

I felt like slapping the shit out of Doreen. Made myself take a deep breath. "It'll be okay, Doreen. I promise. Come on, let's roll."

She stared at me across the hood of the Camaro and for just a minute I thought she was going to make a scene. I hate scenes.

It was her turn to take a deep breath. Her rack rose and fell. With that lousy t-shirt off the plan was going to work better than a blind mule being beat with a tobacco stick.

After a minute she let it out and turned and stomped in the store. The kids weren't fussing too bad. I wiped the sweat off their little faces with one of my shop rags and followed along after Doreen.

Walking up the steps to the old store the sunlight brutalized my bare head. For a second I wondered about the kids. Then I pulled the door open and never gave them another thought.

After the heat outside the store was dark and cool. Cardwell was an old fashioned guy and never had installed central air. However, he had the three huge ceiling fans churning and a few years ago he'd hired the Upton boys to come in and put dark filmy stuff on the windows. Stepping into the drugstore was sort of like stepping into a cave, or back in time.

For once Doreen was minding. She had old Cardwell clear back at the ass end of the store and was jabbering away about some skin care product. She sounded like a damn TV commercial and I figured that's where she'd heard the patter. Even from where I stood it was easy to see that that green string bikini couldn't begin to contain anywhere near enough of Doreen's flesh. I figured Cardwell was about ready to have a stroke, or cum in his underwear.

I could see the safe where Cardwell kept the good stuff and he was plenty occupied. His wife had died last year and she'd been his only employee. He'd never replaced her. My legs were trembling again and I leaned against the counter while I took a long look around the store. The setup was perfect—except for two things.

First, Gladys Carter, the mayor's wife was in the next aisle, studying the hemorrhoid remedies.

Second, Cardwell had the old Philco radio up behind the counter on and that damn preacher was still ranting about Ecclesiastes. If there was a time and a season for everything it sure as hell was time to turn his mouth off.

Out of the corners of my eyes I caught the mayor's wife studying me and I pretended to read the back of a Colgate box. Doreen's voice rose and fell like the buzzing of bees. The old fans groaned as they stirred the air and my stomach made gurgling noises. The words on the Colgate box were blurry, but I kept on pretending.

After a couple of minutes I heard the mayor's wife clomping down the next aisle and I waited until the door closed behind her before I began to work my way behind the counter. Kept moving slowly and carefully. My legs weren't working quite right and I didn't want to bump up against a rack of bottles and send them tumbling.

Plus, I was keeping an eye out for the old man. Once I saw him patting Doreen's bare shoulder and it made me a little sick, but maybe that was just because I hadn't had a fix in almost forty-eight.

Took longer than I expected but I finally made the safe and eased the door open wide. I was having trouble catching my breath and my spine felt brittle.

The contents of the safe were disappointing. Plenty of fixings if you wanted to cook up some meth, but that wasn't my poison. All he had were a few Oxy's and some of those blue pain killers that Tommy Whitaker swears by. Plus there were a few little numbers to help you sleep and some for nerves. I took all the Oxy's and the blues and a couple of handfuls of the sleepers.

How long all that took I couldn't say. Had to go slow so I wouldn't make any noise. Even Doreen's tits sticking better than halfway out of the bikini wouldn't hold the old man if he heard pills rattling around the floor.

By the time I had my pockets full my legs were barely working and I crawled behind the counter until I got to the wheelchairs. Pulled myself up real careful. Then, I tiptoed to the front of the store, half-expecting to hear the old man screaming at me.

He never made a sound. Doreen giggled once and I turned with the door in my hand, but all I could see was the top of her head on the other side of the suntan lotion. Easing the door open I stepped outside.

For a minute I was blinded by the light and I stood still, blinking. Then I could see. Then I wished I couldn't.

Two cops were standing by the Camaro. Actually, one of them was leaning inside. I was tempted to turn and walk in the opposite direction, but the cop that was standing outside was Bud McCoy. He was the one that arrested me a couple of years ago just because I'd given him some lip. McCoy knew my car. Trying not to think about the pills in my pockets I started strolling toward the Camaro. People were milling around the car. I don't like strangers around my Camaro.

Halfway there I could sense McCoy eyeballing me. After a while, especially when you've done time, your nerves get real sensitive to cops. Instincts, I guess; self-preservation or some shit like that.

McCoy nodded. He had his reflector sunglasses on and I couldn't read his eyes. Not that it mattered. I'd seen them before. They were blue and cold. I wished I was back with Doreen.

"Help you, officers?" I tried to sound real polite.

"This your car?"

"You know it is, McCoy."

He said something then, but I couldn't hear because the little one really went to squalling.

"Sorry," I said, "couldn't hear you."

"I said, you want to step around here and put your hands on top of the car for me?"

My blood turned to ice. What the hell? I mean all I was doing was walking down the sidewalk. There weren't any parking meters and my tags were legit. What the hell? I couldn't stand for a search. Not with me being a two time loser. I was looking at more time than I could stand.

But what was I supposed to do? In the shape I was in I couldn't outrun my grandmother. My bowels started to loosen. I wanted to cry. Anywhere but here is where I wanted to be. Hell, I'd be damn glad to be sitting in Doreen's nasty trailer listening to that old fool of a preacher.

I stopped on the bottom step trying to figure the angles. It was sort of like a bank shot on a pool table. Only I was shooting left handed and blindfolded. I am screwed, I thought, but royally.

My only hope was that Doreen would come along in that green bikini and distract McCoy enough so that I could ditch the pills. Relying on Doreen for anything was a piss-poor plan. Better than any man I knew that. Trouble was she was my only hole card. Looked like my flush was about to get busted.

"What?" I asked, just to stall for time.

"You heard me. You're only stupid, not deaf. Hands on top of the car."

"What for? I ain't done nothing. Hell, McCoy, all I'm doing is walking down the sidewalk minding my own business."

McCoy only grinned. It was the sort of a grin what chills a man off considerable. His left hand rested on his Taser.

"Don't make me use this."

I twisted my head around like a hoot owl, looking for Doreen. Where the hell was that stupid cunt?

McCoy didn't say anymore. Guess he wasn't in one of his patient moods.

Electricity shot through me like a waterfall. Thought I was going to die. As I was falling I wondered if this was a little bit of the way the electric chair felt. Remember promising someone I'd be good. Only, I'm not sure if it was McCoy or Doreen or my Dad.

Old addicts I've talked to, the few that survived, tell me the first seventy-two hours are the hardest. At least until the next seventy-two.

Afraid I can't confirm or deny. All I can remember about those first few days is the barbed-wire twisting inside my guts and the alive darkness and the little green men without eyes and all those whispering voices.

Vaguely, as though I was looking back through a hall of mirrors in some smoky spook house, I can remember the concrete floor against my back and the smell of stale piss and sweat and day-old vomit and rotting flesh. Voices I do recall, but all in a jumble, or a babble as the Bible calls them. Sometimes I thought I heard laughter. Five minutes later I was sure it was crying.

It was a Saturday. I could tell because a couple of the guards had been talking about football earlier out in the hallway. Probably a shift change. Which in this lousy jail meant the youngest Blevins boy was replacing Tom Cox.

Tom was a year ahead of me in high school. Back then he was Tommy. And I was, well that's harder to figure. All I can truthfully say is I was a different man then than I was later.

21

And now I'm different again.

Some nights in here I lie awake thinking I'm some sort of snake, say a copperhead, shedding my old skin and coming out a different man every seven years.

No judgments, see. I've given them up in jail, along with OxyContin, eating fresh vegetables, and giving a rat's ass who sees me take a shit.

Lots of folks say jail changes a man, the guards and the newspaper reporters and the preachers, even some of the dudes who spent time on the wrong side of the bars. Guess they're right. Only some men come out a better person, some a worse one. I just aim to come out.

I've about served out my ninety-days for child endangerment. They've back-filed the possession charge. That's in case I fuck up in their town again. That won't happen. Guaranteed.

How can I be sure? I'll tell you. The minute I walk down the jail-house steps I'm headed west, as far west as my money and willpower take me.

It was the day before Thanksgiving when I pushed open the jailhouse door and walked down the steps in a cold drizzle. Bud McCoy was standing up on the landing, under the overhang, watching me. I felt like a field mouse but I kept walking and never looked back.

My Camaro was down at J.R. Whitaker's Auto Salvage, in the side lot. They'd given me my keys at the jail and I jammed my right hand down in my pocket and rubbed on those keys until I rubbed up a blister.

As I turned the corner onto Montgomery Street the rain started coming down harder and I wished I had a coat, even a long-sleeved shirt. But all I had was the clothes I'd been wearing the day I got arrested. When the wind shifted I could smell myself.

Doreen had come to see me a couple of times early on. Her and the court appointed lawyer, a curly-haired Jew by the name of Abramson who'd grown up in Louisville, were the only two. Except for the preachers on television, that is.

The jailer had got religion last year after his wife caught him screwing around with his only female deputy. Word is he got right with God just in time to keep his old lady from squeezing off a few rounds in his general direction. As a result he had the jail TV hardwired so all we could get was the Religion Channel. Worse than the damn Weather Channel. Nothing but praying and gospel singing and Pentecostal preaching. All kinds of preachers on that station (think it was out of Hazard): young ones with lots of hair, black ones who looked like Chicago Bears linemen, a few women who read scripture through their noses and pointed their breasts straight at the eyes of the sinners.

Even heard that old fool that was always on Doreen's television. The one who preached about everything having a season. Reverend Micah.

Heard him so often I sorta got to wondering if maybe he'd latched on to one of those Biblical truths. Won't claim that he converted me or nothing like that, only that maybe I'm more open minded.

More open-minded and fatter. Jail food is lousy, full of salt and sugar and grease, and it tastes like crap, but it's all you got in there, unless you've got money on account—which I didn't (not one damn dime), so you eat it. Eat whatever's on your plate and whatever else you can bum off the guys in the cell with you. Lots of fattening shit and it all settles in the middle of your gut. Course, I'll admit I could have stood to gain a few. Man don't eat right when he's on Oxy. Like them preachers said about the Lord, He doth provide.

Swinging into J.R.'s lot I wished he'd provide me with a poncho and a ball cap. Didn't pray mind you. Did a helluva lot of that inside and it never did me one ounce of good. Just wishing, that's all I was doing.

It was raining so hard now that J.R. was a big fat blob on the dry side of the single window of what he called his office, but what really wasn't a thing more than a shed putting on airs. He was staring at me and I started to wave, but he sorta looked like he was playing with his pecker and besides I was cold and wet. So I just nodded to let him know I knew he was there and stepped quick to the Camaro.

For a minute I sat on that vinyl with my eyes closed, letting the rain drip off me, trying to make up my mind. Then I rubbed the water out of my eyes, dug the keys out my pocket, eased them in the ignition, crossed my fingers, and cranked.

Maybe somebody was praying for me. Or maybe Diehards really did die hard. Anyway, the motor growled and then roared. I buckled my seatbelt, just for luck, and shifted into drive.

For a long time when I was behind the bars I'd told myself the first thing I'd do was drive on out and pay Ms. Doreen a visit. We had a few matters to settle, starting with why in the hell she'd quit coming to see me. Then, I thought I'd swing over to Culver Creek and pick up a six-pack from a bootlegger I knew. Last night, I'd decided to drive to Ashland and have me a steak dinner. Just enough folding money in my wallet.

In the end I didn't do any of those things. What I did sorta surprised even me, despite the fact I had studied on it during some of those long nights when I fought off fear, bedbugs, and the gay dude from Portsmouth who wanted me to suck his cock.

It was seven curvy miles to Tommy Preston's place and I must have changed my mind seven times seventy. Still, when I got to the gate I swung between the two concrete lions on guard and drove on up the blacktop in second.

For a good five minutes I just sat in the Camaro, revving the engine, thinking about my dad and what he would have done and what I figured I had to do. Had to for a lot of people, including myself.

Almost without thinking, I leaned on the horn and in a minute Tommy came out wearing cowboy boots and one of those dusters you used to see on Westerns when they were still showing them. He popped the door and slid inside.

For a little we just sat there, listening to him drip rain and sniffing each other like a pair of mongrel dogs. Finally I took a deep breath, swallowed, and said, "You still want her?"

Something harder was mixing with the rain when I slogged up in front of the trailer. You could hear it pecking at the fallen leaves in the dark like some creature trying to get underneath. The picket fence had fallen down and a big dog on a steel chain paced back and forth in front of the steps.

That dog and me had us a little staring contest before I finally got up my nerve and walked around him and climbed up the steps. Two steps from the top I heard him growl and the hair on the back of my neck stood up. Right before I knocked I remembered I still had a key to the front door in my pocket. I wondered if she'd thought of changing the lock.

I fished the key out and it slid in like a Bowie knife through soft butter. The door screeched as it swung open and her head came up and one hand snaked into a drawer on the end table and came out holding a twenty-two. I didn't say a word, only held both hands up, palms facing her like I was under arrest again. That shit I had down.

Hadn't come to ask her to forgive or forget. Despite my wanting forgiveness so bad I could taste it, it seemed to me that nobody ever really forgave, and they sure as shit never forgot. Not even God, if He was still hanging around.

For a couple of heartbeats I thought she was going to shoot me right there in the doorway. Then the fire went out of her and the gun came down. I lowered my hands real slowly.

The television was on. Thank God it wasn't that old preacher, only some woman trying to sell auto insurance. Well, I surely didn't need any of what she was selling. When she quit talking a man with a deep voice came on rumbling about the desperate need to vote for some jake leg lawyer over in Pike County running for the state senate in the special election. What the hell, we were all running for, or away from, something.

I pulled the roll of bills out of my pocket and palmed it. Then I walked over to Doreen, close enough to smell the bath soap she used and see the light reflecting in her eyes.

Those eyes kept staring at me, half afraid, half expectant. Back in jail I'd thought of at least ten thousand words I wanted to say but when it got down to it there wasn't any need. Actions speak louder anyway. So I smiled and nodded and dropped the roll of bills in her lap.

"That's for you and them kids," I said and turned to go.

When I grabbed the door handle she spoke. "Where you going?"

I turned back around and looked at her one last time. I looked a long time, real hard. Like I was taking a picture with my eyes.

Finally, I just said, "Away," and smiled as sweet as I could to let her know I wasn't harboring no hard feelings. Hell, we both knew whose damn fault everything was.

"Travel safe, baby," she said and I nodded and turned and stepped back out into the rain.

I jumped off the porch and jogged around the dog. I could hear him growling behind me in the rainy night but I was a good piece down the lane now, hurrying. If I hustled I could just make the midnight bus to Paducah.

I jogged on right steady through the rain. After I hit the highway I started hearing the voices again. In a little while they settled into one voice and it was that of the old preacher, with Doreen mixed in, and now and then my dad. Even Bud McCoy.

You could smell fall in the air and feel it on your face. The seasons were changing. Guess the old preacher had something after all. Only I didn't stop to listen to the voices, only kept running, going harder now.

After a while all I could hear was the sound of the rain against the black asphalt and the wind worrying the tops of the cedars and the rise and fall of my own breathing.

INHERITANCE

LICKING HIS LIPS, HE rolled over and peered at the clock.

10:14.

The day felt older, as though it had grown up while he slept. Saturday was his day to sleep. During the week he cleaned toilets at the college. On Sunday he walked five miles to the President's home and, depending on the season, cut grass or raked leaves or shoveled snow.

Belinsky rolled back over and closed his eyes. During the week he got up at 5:30; on Saturday he often slept past noon. Dreams bothered him some nights, but this morning he couldn't recall even a fragment.

Forty-one years old and cleaning toilets for a living. He hadn't planned for his life to unfold like it had. It was just that ever since he'd left home for college things had slipped away: jobs, friends, wives. It had been like trying to hold ice cubes in your hand.

He'd traveled a hundred roads to a hundred lousy towns, kissed women from eighteen to eighty, and worked jobs without beginning or end. Texas, Kansas, Arizona, Idaho, he'd seen them and a dozen more. Seen snow knee-deep to a big Indian and heat so fierce you could sizzle an egg on the hood of a dumpster. All those miles and all those tears and all that sweat and for what? Blisters, a bad back, sunburns, and the clap. And now he was cleaning toilets for college kids.

The old man would be disappointed. Not that such disappointment should be surprising. As far as he knew Belinsky had never pleased the old man.

Still Belinsky had to admit his father had sacrificed to send him and his sister to college. Paying double tuition couldn't have been easy for a farmer plagued by droughts and locusts and snows that came too late in the spring. Moaning and cursing and rising before dawn the old man had persevered. He had beaten Belinsky out of a warm bed with a hickory stick and worked him like a mule, but he'd paid the tuition like a trooper.

Nancy had made a nurse. Belinsky had flunked out of three colleges and made a well-educated hobo. Now Nancy was cold and dead in Kansas and he was cleaning toilets at a second tier college in Kentucky. Last he'd heard the old man still held down the fort at the farm.

Belinsky passed gas and rolled over, pushing his face down into his pillow. He hadn't talked to his father since the day he left the farm. His uncle Ira had given Belinsky an update when they'd crossed paths several years before in Pocatello, where Belinsky had worked briefly for the railroad. He wondered if his father ever thought of him.

He should have written his father. A postcard at least. Then Belinsky shrugged. Crap on that, the old man could just as well have written.

His mind began drifting away from consciousness. Then it shifted and he rolled over and sat up and looked around the room, trying to imagine that it was all new and different and exciting to him.

Belinsky slipped out of bed and pulled on his pants. Walking to the window, he ran his fingers through his hair. On Saturdays he didn't always shower.

Except for a Mustang that hadn't run since he'd been living there, the parking lot was empty. Most of the men who stayed there didn't have cars. Since March, when the sweet old lady who couldn't leave wine alone had been driven off by the priest, no woman had lived at the motel. Weeknights Belinsky was too tired to think much about women. Weekends however were tinted around the edges with a pale indigo loneliness. For perhaps the five hundredth time he wondered where Joyce Glenning was now.

A robin hopped across the asphalt, flapped its wings and floated up to the lowest branch of a scraggly locust. Its eyes glittered in the sunlight. Shadows drifted across the asphalt. Grundy, who lived in number 5, had his radio on. All day long the old man listened to news. Grundy had wrinkles that looked eighty years old and was nearly deaf. After almost two years Belinsky could recognize the announcers.

He stood listening to a report on poppies in Afghanistan and watching the robin. His stomach growled. A police siren wailed and Belinsky listened to it fade away. The robin took wing and flew toward the sun, a dark wedge heading west. Belinsky's stomach growled again and he turned and put on his shirt and socks and shoes. As he tied the laces there was a knock on his door.

For a moment Belinsky just sat there. Since the day he'd moved in no one had knocked on his door. He had halfway convinced himself that he had imagined the sound when it came again. Belinsky pushed out of the chair.

Outside the room a kid was sitting on a bicycle. He was wearing a yellow baseball cap and there was writing in a slanting script on the brim. Western Union. He held a yellow envelope in one hand. The kid tilted his head. His eyes were the color of a clear October sky.

"I'm looking for Dave Belinsky."

"That's me."

"I need some ID."

Belinsky dug his billfold out and flipped it open. His driver's license was expired, but the picture was clear and the name legible.

The kid nodded and handed Belinsky the telegram.

Belinsky jammed the telegram into his shirt pocket. He stuck his wallet back in his pants. Then he remembered and said, "Thanks."

The kid nodded, but kept his palm open. Damn, Belinsky thought, the tip. Making a face, he dug his wallet back out and peered inside. One five and a pair of ones. Seven dollars to last until payday. He tugged a dollar out and handed it to the kid.

Old man Grogan's radio was giving the weather. Eighty-seven and getting hotter. Belinsky fingered the envelope. Sweat tattooed his checks. He shut the door. Then he turned on the fan he'd found at the Goodwill and drug a chair over to the window. Cool air blew across his face, then oscillated away. Belinsky stared at the envelope. Curiosity gnawed at his insides. Belinsky slit the envelope open with a finger.

His eyes focused on the thin lines. Then his throat went raw and the room turned blurry. He tossed the telegram on the windowsill and shut his eyes. His heart was hammering. A chill swept through him. Belinsky opened his eyes.

It hadn't been a mirage. There were no mirages. Belinsky had discovered that in Arizona. There were only different exposures of reality. He read the telegram again. Then, just to hear the sound of a human voice, he read it aloud. His voice sounded high and far away, as if it belonged to a different man.

DAVE:
YOUR FATHER PASSED AWAY THURSDAY. HE DIDN'T SUFFER. FUNERAL SUNDAY.
SAM CRAWLEY
STOP

Sam Crawley owned the farm north of the home place. When Belinsky had been a kid Sam Crawley had milked a herd of dairy cattle. Crawley had been a good man, but his wife got cancer and died young. For six weeks Belinsky had carried a major crush on Crawley's daughter, Linda. Finally Linda had taken him aside one Saturday night, gave him a hug and told him she only liked girls. That had been the last time Belinsky had cried. He'd been sixteen.

Once his growth had come on he'd helped Crawley with the milking. After two years of working together in the old barn, Crawley hinted that he wanted Belinsky to buy him out in a year or two, but all Belinsky could think about was leaving.

Crawley hadn't been young when Belinsky had gone off to college and he hadn't left yesterday. Without warning, he remembered a vague uneasiness on the bus the day he'd left for college. He had never quite been able to define it; the closest he could come was a sense of leaving something unfinished. Tears began to run down his face.

Gradually he became aware of cool air washing across his face. Belinsky looked out the window. The light was going. Old man Grundy was listening to the national news. A sparrow had flown down and was pecking at a dried hamburger bun in the parking lot.

Belinsky stood and folded the telegram and put it in his wallet. He got a clean glass out of the cabinet and filled it at the sink. The water was lukewarm but he drank three glasses of it before he sat back down.

A river of memories was flowing across his mind. A roaring filled his ears. It was like standing on the beach as a typhoon swung to shore.

By the time he heard the birds chirping the air had gone dark. The wind was still rising, worrying the locust leaves and whining under the eaves. Belinsky sat and watched the security lights flicker on. Moths swirled around the lights. A talk show came on the old man's radio, but the wind was up, turning the voices into fragmented murmurs.

Leaves tumbled across the parking lot. Belinsky wished his memories would blow away like the leaves. He watched the leaves until silver rain began pummeling the asphalt. Deep in the night the wind began to fall. Before daylight the rain stopped. A disembodied voice selling used cars drifted across the night.

The bus started overheating just after crossing into Nebraska and gave up the ghost two miles short of Grand Island. Belinsky had borrowed the price of the ticket from the college president and it pissed him off to think he'd wasted the money.

Since the Mexican family had gotten off in Kansas City, only seven other people were still on the bus with Belinsky, and the bus company hired a couple of taxis to haul them to the station at Grand Island.

The relief bus was being serviced and they sat around the station all afternoon. The guy behind the counter promised the second bus would leave Grand Island by dark but at five he came around and advised it wouldn't leave before daylight. Something about the brakes.

Belinsky strolled outside. All the hassle of going to the home of the college president on Sunday afternoon and wheedling his way into an advance on his salary and what did he have to show for it? Another nowhere town where he was going nowhere. Grand Island sprawled before him, flowing west until it was swallowed by the wild grasses.

He'd been in a hundred just like it, always leaving one headed for another that sounded more promising. He was like the October leaves, he thought, going where the wind blew him. When the air grew dark above the high plains he turned and went back into the station. The big sky full of winking stars somehow made him feel lonesome.

The guy who ran the station had brewed a vat of coffee and scrounged up a bag of mushy apples. Belinsky drew himself a cup of coffee and grabbed two apples. As he ate the apples he tried to read. All he had was a novel he'd found in an empty college locker at the start of summer. It was about a girl growing up in South Africa. She lived in a farm on the veldt and she sounded as lonely as Belinsky felt. He shut the book and stuffed it in his bag. Then he carried them both out into the night. Behind the counter the agent was nodding in his chair.

The moon was up now and looking west he could see the land sloping upward. A jet was blinking its way south and he followed until it was lost in the stars. Mexico, he guessed. He'd planned to go to Mexico after college. Word was living there was cheap. But that was before he'd met Delores, and that bad time in Vegas, and that muffed chance in Roswell, and to hell with it. Remembering all those years wandering in the wilderness made his head ache.

Belinsky sipped coffee and stared at the moon and listened to the trucks rolling west. The rhythmic sound of the rubber whirling against the asphalt was like an old song he'd heard years before. The tune was familiar but he couldn't remember the words.

The night slid west as he stood in the moonlight, drinking coffee and listening to the rigs rumbling across a darkness so vast Belinsky couldn't fathom it. It was like being marooned on a tiny planet in deep space, an island in the alive darkness that ran to the edge of the universe and beyond. He wished Joyce Glenning was there with him.

The urge to keep moving was growing inside him. His body was so awake that it was tingling. All the people in the bus station were asleep. Let the dreamers dream he thought as he gazed at the sky, looking for an omen. All he saw were stars and the drifting moon.

He crossed the parking lot and sat down on the sidewalk in front of all night café. Dropping his bag, he stuck out a thumb. The smell of bacon hung in the air. A bob-tailed cat walked by like he owned the sidewalk. Belinsky felt a nerve jump in his cheek.

Forty minutes later a man with a droopy mustache and a pick-up truck full of cattle headed west rolled down a window as he chugged out of the parking lot. He yelled through the window and Belinsky grabbed his bag and ran and jerked the door open.

His last ride had put him off at Bean Lake just after daylight. A fine drizzle, hardly more than a mist, had been falling from the furrowed gray clouds and he'd waved at the hare-lipped guy hauling cantaloupe to the coast, pulled his baseball cap lower and started walking. His legs were fresh and it felt good to be moving.

The road was just as he remembered it, curving, sunken between banks covered with cedar and brambles. Ferns fluttered in the wind like green feathers. Birds chirped in the thickets and the scent of the pines drifted on the wind.

By midmorning the clouds had begun to break apart, streaming south like ancient sailing ships, revealing glimpses of a pale sun. Belinsky kept marching north, eating a candy bar he'd bought somewhere down the line, wondering what awaited him.

He hadn't slept right since the telegram and wasn't thinking straight. Belinsky climbed a cut bank and lay on his back on a patch of grass, thinking again about sailing ships. When he had been twelve he'd known the names of a half dozen of the most famous. Now all he could remember were blurry artists' sketches from books.

Time does things to a man, he thought. Time does things. The sun popped out from behind one of the streaming clouds and warm light bathed his face. Sleep drifted over him like a benevolent tide.

He woke up, soaked in sweat, feeling he'd missed something. His back ached and he was uncertain where he was. Then a crow called from across the road and his mind cleared and he knew what he'd missed. Missed by three days. His father's funeral.

He struggled upright and picked up his bag and started walking. For the first time in years his legs were tired and the bag seemed as heavy as one of the loads of firewood that he'd hauled into the old farmhouse.

By mid-afternoon the land began to buckle as though a giant had run his fingers through still forming soil. When he came around the blind corner and saw the old stone church Belinsky smiled. Abandoned for years, falling in on its foundation, the church marked the spot where the road forked. Evergreen lay to the west, the home place five miles to the east.

Without thinking, Belinsky stepped off the road and wandered between the tombstones, pausing now and then to read names, working his way toward the stone shell.

His grandparents had worshipped here. Standing there in the ruins with the wind brushing against his skin, carrying the scent of pines and farms hidden by the hills, Belinsky felt like the lone survivor of a holocaust. All around lay the scattered stones of what he had been promised was God's house. Either those people had lied to him, or God was a feeble exercise in futility. Belinsky kicked a stone and sent it tumbling. A sourness filled his mouth. He spat, but the acidic taste lingered.

Crows were calling from the fields beyond the trees. Sunlight slanted through the trees, painting mosaics on the ruins. Belinsky drew in a deep breath and started for home.

Going to the funeral home would have been a waste of time. Without asking, he knew the old man was buried on the hill behind the house. Three generations of Belinskys were buried there. Swinging the heavy farm gate open, Dave wondered if he would be the fourth.

Just inside the gate he sat down on one of the pine stumps that lined this end of the lane. During his fifteenth summer he and his dad had cut down an entire row of pines. They'd been old and hollowing out and one had fallen across the road the winter before. Belinsky could still remember the force of that July heat and smell the freshly cut pine and feel the sweat trickling down his thighs. For a moment he thought he heard his father's voice, but that was just his mind playing tricks.

In the overgrown field before him a covey of quail rose and whirled into the timber lot beyond. Seconds later an animal trotted out of the tall grass. At first glance Belinsky thought it was a tawny dog. Then the animal cocked its head and he could see that it was a coyote. He'd heard that they were moving north, but hadn't expected to see one here.

Apparently unconcerned, the coyote stared at Belinsky. A crow cawed from beyond the trees. Sunlight colored the road. The coyote's ears twitched as it trotted off into the timber.

Belinsky wished he had someone to talk to about the coyote, but there was only the sun and the wind and the cloud shadows dancing across the open fields. He scuffed a toe in the dirt and pushed off the stump and lugged his bag up the lane. The lane was longer than he remembered. Topping the rise, Belinsky saw the house and felt his throat beginning to close up.

The old barn was leaning like a drunkard and the hen house roof had fallen in. The grass in the yard had gone to seed and a shutter on the front of the house hung askew. The front porch steps creaked under his weight. His mother's rocking chair still sat in its corner of the porch, but cobwebs bound the legs together.

The front door was locked. Belinsky checked the windows. He sat down clumsily on the front steps and stared at the wren's nest under the eaves.

Darkness was seeping into the sky and the air was tinged with lilac. The wind was out of the northwest, carrying scents of aging manure and moldy hay, chilling the air. He'd forgotten how cool it got here in the foothills at night, even in summer.

Belinsky had always prided himself on his memory. It was a private vanity. Now, within the first hour of returning, he'd discovered something he'd completely forgotten, or repressed.

Over the years he'd developed a theory that a person remembered everything that ever occurred in their life, at least after a certain age. Every fact, event, emotion they'd encountered was somewhere in the protean sludge that flowed slowly through the brain, drifting for years, submerged, only to bubble to the surface in response to some stimuli that the person might recognize, or perhaps intuit dimly.

The wind was whimpering in the sugar maple in the front yard, rattling the hanging gutters, and smacking a barn door against the frame of the barn. Above his head the chimes his mother had bought on a trip to the Grand Canyon tinkled.

Suddenly a light arced on in the darkness and Belinsky jerked his head toward the glow. He'd forgotten the security light attached to a corner of the barn. In the next breath he remembered the light and walking back from the barn on a windy night with his hand in his father's.

He strained to remember more, but all he could recall was the security light popping on as he and his father had exited the barn that smelled faintly of hay and grain and warm animal hides. Another filament of memory tickled along the outer rim of his mind. Had his mother been calling to them from the porch?

The wind rose another notch and Belinsky eased off the porch and strolled toward the old barn. Only a shimmering of coral so faint that it wasn't quite light clung to the western sky, but the clouds were broken and the moon was rising, fat and saffron, and he followed the path to the barn, telling himself he could have done it by memory alone.

One of the two big barn doors was unlatched and banging heavily against the slats. Pulling it to behind him, Belinsky wondered if his father had forgotten to close it that last day or if hobos had wandered in. Hobos had come around when he was a kid. If his father wasn't home his mother had fed them.

He stepped inside, half expecting to see a raggedy man hunkered down in the hay. But all he saw was worn harness hanging from the rafters and empty stalls. Spider webs as big as the bottom of peach baskets occupied the corners. A moldy, dank smell filled the air and he could hear rustlings in the hay and, more faintly, the chirping of sparrows in the loft.

Belinsky stood listening to the birds. They sounded like distant voices, or voices from the past. Without warning the entire night seemed to settle on his shoulders and he turned and hurried back into the windswept moonlight. For a stride or two his father was with him. Then he was gone and Belinsky trudged alone toward the house, white and solid in the darkness.

Halfway there he remembered where they had hidden the extra key. As he passed the lilac bush, something small and dark jumped out and scurried up the steps. In the poor light it looked like a slender raccoon. Then the clouds shifted and he could see that it was a cat.

For as long as he could remember cats had lived in the barn. Unnamed and rarely petted or fed, they had lived primarily by their wits. Mice and birds and spilled milk had been their diet. Funny, he'd never before considered how the cats had survived. Not the barn cats and not other people. He climbed the steps and crossed the porch and ran his hand along the top of the doorframe.

His fingers closed on cool metal and he lifted the key from its hiding place and unlocked the door. The cat rubbed against his legs. The door screeched open and he stepped into the hallway.

Elk antlers still hung in the hallway and the black dial telephone was still affixed to the wall. He picked up the receiver and listened to the dial tone. Wondering when the phone had last rung, he eased the receiver onto the cradle.

Only narrow bands of moonlight fell through the windows, revealing bulky, mysterious shapes. Without conscious thought, Belinsky flicked the light switch just inside the living room. High in the ceiling a single bulb crackled on, revealing a worn green couch Belinsky didn't remember, a pair of mismatched chairs, and a coffee table littered with newspapers.

A small television sat on a stand in the corner and Belinsky crossed the floor and twisted the on knob. The old house was too quiet to suit him. Never had it been completely quiet before. Always there had been sounds—his mother singing to herself or his father stomping around in his work boots, or the low murmur of voices from the electric radio atop the refrigerator.

From four-thirty in the morning when his father had risen until the last person went to bed at night the radio had always been on. News, weather, price reports on canners and cutters, who had been born and who had died, the voice had spoken out against the silences, an invisible shaman's chant against the great aloneness, the silent, pervasive aloneness. Aloneness gets into a man's bones, Belinsky knew, wondering how his father had stood it the last few years. Surely he had played the radio deep into the night.

But it wasn't on now and the silence felt heavy. His ears ached with the holding of it. Why wasn't the television coming on? Belinsky's eyes followed the power cord across the wooden floor to the socket. "Everything is dying around here," he mumbled as he began to walk toward the kitchen, welcoming the echo of his footsteps.

Stepping around a stack of National Geographic magazines, he glanced out the window, the one he had broken once throwing rocks at barn swallows. From the thickening darkness a pair of lights glowed and began drawing closer, rising and falling.

A car was coming up the lane, wallowing in the ruts. He stepped into the hallway, tugged the door open and stepped out on the porch. When the driver's door swung open Belinsky almost called out, but instead pressed his lips together as the man walked across the yard.

At the bottom of the steps the man stopped. He was wearing the kind of hat men had worn when Belinsky had been a kid. The brim cast shadows across his face. Still, something in the line of the jaw and the tilt of the head looked familiar.

"That you, Dave?" the man asked, his voice raised a little to carry over the wind.

"Yes," Belinsky said, "who are you?"

"It's me, Bob O'Hearn. From the funeral home. Remember me?"

"Yeah," Belinsky said, "but I figured you'd be a lot older."

The man laughed. "That would be my dad you're thinking of. He turned sixty-seven in May. I'm only a couple of years older than you. Used to see you at school. Remember?"

"Vaguely."

"Can I come up? I've got something for you."

"Sure." Belinsky stepped to one side and nodded toward the hall. "Want to come in?"

"Sorry, I can't stay. Got to get to a school board meeting." The man lifted his shirtsleeve and peered at his watch. "Matter of fact, I'm late now." He stuck out a hand. Belinsky shook it once and let go. He didn't like touching other men.

"Sorry about your loss."

Belinsky nodded.

The wind rattled the chimes and the man looked up. "That's a nice sound," he murmured and turned his head and peered across the yard, toward the barn and the field beyond where the tops of dying corn stalks showed white in the moonlight.

"Bet it's really pretty out here, especially in the spring."

"Used to be."

O'Hearn cocked his head and studied Belinsky's face. The wind died into silence, then rose again. "That's right," the man said, "you've been gone a long time."

Belinsky gnawed on his lower lip.

O'Hearn's face twisted up like he was going to say something else. Instead, he nodded and his hat slipped, revealing his bald spot.

"Guess I'd better go. The other members are probably wondering where I am. Well, see you around."

"See you."

Halfway down the steps O'Hearn turned, reaching inside his sports coat. "About forgot this," he said, pulling out a long white envelope. "Your father had this in his suit jacket when we received him. Died in church, Sunday morning. Wasn't sure if you knew."

Belinsky's face felt flushed. There was a buzzing in his ears as he reached for the envelope. His father in church—some things were beyond understanding. But then it had been a long time and he honestly couldn't claim to have known the man his father had become.

"Thanks," he mumbled. A vein throbbed at one temple and his left eye twitched. A moth fluttered up out of the darkness. Large and gray in the pale light spilling from the house, it beat its wings rapidly, flying in circles.

"You're welcome," O'Hearn said and strolled down the steps. At the lilac bush he turned and called back above the wind, "Welcome home."

"See you," Belinsky said. In his hands the envelope felt like a cool smooth stone.

The night was starting to age. Belinsky didn't have a watch and there didn't seem to be a clock in the house. Time must have ceased to matter to the old man, he thought, turning and looking out the window, trying to get a fix on the moon. Clouds were in the way and all he could see were the top branches of an oak that had been ancient long before his birth.

Bedsprings squeaked beneath him. He was lying on his parent's bed, the only one in the house. Where in hell had all the other beds gone? A line of sweat began to slide down behind Belinsky's left ear and he wiped it off and sat up, fumbling in the darkness before he found the switch on an old horsehead lamp his mother had bought when he'd been about five or six. It must have been expensive. Belinsky could still remember his father shouting at his mother.

The envelope was propped against the base of the lamp. Inside the envelope was a single sheet of paper. Belinsky wasn't sure what he had been expecting when he slit the envelope open. Money, perhaps, or a key to a lock box, but never a letter from his father.

He hadn't even tried to read it. The sight of his father's scrawl had chilled him. Letters from the dead. He wished he had some whiskey.

Beyond the light a mosquito whined. Belinsky wished he'd left the radio on. Part of him wished he had never left Kentucky. The envelope seemed to stare at him. Sweat rolled down his back. The window was jammed shut and the air was stale, as though all the oxygen had evaporated years ago.

The stale air was saturated with aging odors. Belinsky could smell his sweat and the mothballs in the dressers and dust and, just at the edge, another scent, indefinable. He stretched out an arm, noting with a clinical dispassion that his fingers didn't tremble. He picked up the envelope and shook the letter out.

It fell open onto the faded wedding ring quilt. Blue ink meandered across the page. The letters were shaky, ill-formed. The mosquito whined again and the wind moaned in the oak leaves.

Dave:

When you see this I'll be dead. You probably won't be sorry and I sure as Hell won't be. I've lived a long time and most of the years have been lonely. A man gets lonely without a family, you know. Or maybe you don't. We sure haven't kept in touch over the years. Guess that's my fault as much as anybody's. One thing I've learned is that there's always plenty of fault to be passed around, and fault is one thing I've thought a lot about lately.

Haven't really decided anything, though. We never got along like a father and son should have, and your mother and I sure never got along. Probably never should have married, but there was you to consider. Not that I'm blaming anybody. Blame enough for all the way I see it.

I do want you to know a couple of things. Don't worry about me. A year or so after my first stroke I got right with God and now the grave don't scare me.

Looks like I've started to wander. Sorry. Do more of that every day. Better say what I aim to and not get sappy. What I want you to know is two things, like I said. First, I never really loved your mother, but I never cheated on her. Holy truth is I was glad to see her gone. Never tried to find her. Heard now and then from someone who thought they'd seen her. Last word I got was about ten years ago. Supposedly she was running a cash register in Gallipolis, Ohio. Maybe you'll want to look her up. Won't matter to me.

The second thing I want to tell you is something that has been inside me for years. Wanted to say it a thousand times, just never could bring myself to speak. Pride can be an awful thing, son. But that's not what I want to say. What I want you to know is that I'm sorry for the way I treated you. I wasn't a good father and never gave you a chance to be a good son. Thought about that a lot since you left. You may remember I didn't want you to go, but you always were a stubborn little son-of-a-bitch. Maybe that was our trouble. We were just too much alike.

Anyway, I figure you were too proud to show me the respect I wanted. Not that I blame you. Way I see it now pride runs in a family, just like a big nose or brown eyes. Guess the main thing you inherited from me was pride.

This place is yours now. Do with it what you want. Won't matter to me if you burn it down. My time is up.

Know it's just old man sentimentality but I hope you think of me now and then, and not too badly. Don't make my mistakes, son.

Your prideful old man

P.S. I always did love you

P.S.S. Joyce Glenning is living over to Tacoma. Think she's back to teaching school since her husband died a couple of years ago. Cancer, I think. Saw her in town right before Christmas and she asked about you.

Belinsky looked at the paper until the words grew blurry. Then he lay back on the old bed. Downstairs a board creaked as the house cooled. Down by the pond a whippoorwill started up. In the distance cattle called to each other. Belinsky reached over and turned on the radio he'd lugged from the kitchen. A Vancouver station was playing dance music. He wondered if his father had ever lain in this same bed and listened to music that reminded him of when he was young and love still seemed possible.

Outside the air was full of filtered starlight. The radio reminded him of old man Grundy and Kentucky. He twisted the knob and listened to silence reclaiming the room.

He turned off the lamp. Far away, beyond the line of hills to the west, a dog barked. Then he could hear the cattle again. He could place the sound now. It was coming from the old Jamison place, which lay to the south of the Crawley farm. Surely old man Jamison was dead. He'd been stooped with age long before Belinsky left home.

Almost everybody he'd known from before was dead. Belinsky thought about Joyce Glenning. He wondered if she ever lay in her bed in Tacoma thinking of him. Maybe he would fire up his Dad's rusty pick-up and drive down to see her in a day or two. Or maybe he just should just roll out at first light and drive straight into the sun.

The moon smirked at him from the top of the windowpane. All the rest of the light in the world seemed to have died. The wind had fallen away and it was so quiet Belinsky thought he could hear the night breathing. He held his breath and listened.

He'd been wrong. It had only been his own breathing. An owl hooted in the night. Owls had lived in the barn all his life. He remembered his father telling him that the owls helped the barn cats keep the mice down.

Belinsky thought of all the things he could remember his father telling him across the years. Then he thought of the words in the letter.

The owl hooted again and the wind rose and rattled the glass in the window frame. Belinsky stood and took off all his clothes and pulled the old quilt back. Then he lay down on his back, naked as the day he was born, with the sheet cool and smooth against his flesh and moonlight liming his body.

Belinsky wondered if his father, knowing he was dying, when sleep wouldn't come and the nights wore on his nerves like a plague, had thought of his son, lost and wandering in the great darkness, half-wanting to come home, yet never making the effort.

Scents of new mown hay and the barnyard drifted to him. Belinsky turned his head and gazed at the moon. It had floated across the dark sea of sky like a lost ship. He felt hollow inside and he closed his eyes with the sense of having missed something.

Moonlight and the wind and old hobos in the barn wait for no man, he thought. Then he rolled over and pressed his face against the sheet and tried to imagine what Joyce Glenning looked like after all the lost years.

CLAW HAMMER

JUST BEFORE DARK THE wind blew me in off the road. The sun had gone down behind the Kentucky hills and all I could hear was the wind and the cardinals in the underbrush. Humping hard, I was trying to make Big Blaine Creek before dark. Up at the head of Big Blaine there were people who still felt like they had to care about me and wouldn't let me down. Leastways they never had.

I was hurrying because I was cold and tired and hungry and my feet ached the way a bad tooth will. Flat out of money, I was wore out of being on the road. That, and the fact that the law was looking hard for me.

Six days ago I'd walked off a work gang in DeKalb County. Georgia cops get real serious about escaped prisoners. Even use bloodhounds. Last man who I knew tried to walk ended up going back home to Biloxi, Mississippi. Made the trip in a pine box. Between catching rides and hopping a freight in Tennessee, I'd made good time. If my luck had held I'd have been home. But my luck never holds.

Rides had dried up and I'd spent the night before in an abandoned trailer just east of Turpentine. I knew that part of the county some on account of I used to date one of the Bailey girls whose daddy ran the sawmill at the edge of town. If I got the story straight, she was the one who eventually made a schoolteacher. Now that may be true, but when I knew Becky Bailey she surely didn't behave like any schoolteacher I ever had. Just before daylight I'd eaten the last of the apples I'd lifted at the Jellico General Mart the day before and took a chance and drank out of a little spring I'd heard dripping in the night.

Territory down around Turpentine is real lonesome. Especially since the bottom fell out of timber. Not much traffic and what there was didn't slow. I'd just kept walking. About midmorning I'd recognized the old Simpson Fork Elementary School and started cutting across country, sticking to the back roads and jumping in among the withered cornstalks when I saw a car coming. Getting so close to home made me spooky. Every car now sounded to me like the police.

Right before noon the wind shifted and started blowing out of the north, cutting like a cane knife. By mid-afternoon snow was falling and I was so desperately cold I was back to hitching. Problem was, I didn't have a real coat, only a vinyl jacket I'd liberated from the front seat of a Ford pickup at the Tasty Freeze in Corbin.

Some folks might figure I was crazy heading north in February, but I'd given my address to the Georgia authorities as Apalachicola, Florida. Besides, what man in his right mind goes north in the winter? Only Eskimos and crazy men. I planned to be as crazy as a fox.

By the time it started growing dark I was so damn cold I almost didn't care if the law picked me up. But all that passed were a pair of coal trucks running empty and the county salt truck. Then I'd crested a rise and the trees gapped and I'd seen the ramp off the parkway. At the bottom were a few houses and a couple of trailers, an old tobacco barn with a bad case of the bends, and what looked like it might be a gas station or a grocery store.

Inside the store lights were on and only a couple of vehicles were parked outside, a rusted-out Ford station wagon up on cinder blocks and an old pickup with both rear tires flat. As I turned in off the asphalt a security light crackled on by the pumps and I could see tire tracks in the snow. Footprints, too, but they all were leading away from the store and half-filled with snow. For a couple of minutes I stood with my back against the wall of the store, resting in the shadows, listening.

Over the years listening has saved my sorry ass many a time. One of the hardest things for most folks is to just stand still or sit real quiet and listen. Doing time was good for developing listening skills. At first all I could hear was the wind whining up under the eaves. Then I heard a radio playing bluegrass music. Finally, off in the distance—I'd guess a mile or so—I could hear a freight train rolling. For a while it was just a low rumble like distant thunder. Then the engineer leaned on the whistle and that long, low, lonesome sound made the flesh on my arms pucker.

Ever since I was a kid laying awake nights listening to coal trains rolling for Ashland or Corbin, or now and then the Amtrak Cardinal headed for Cincinnati, I'd felt a train whistle late in the night was just about the most lonesome sound on earth. Whenever I heard that moan it made me feel like the whole country had packed up in secret and was leaving without telling me.

A flash of red caught my eye and I swam out of the memories in time to see a cardinal settle onto a cedar branch. Snow showered down like it was snowing in that snow globe Grandma Colby kept in her parlor. A big chill of wind swung around the corner and knifed into my bones. Freezing to death when there was a nice warm store waiting was ignorant. Pulling my jacket up tighter around my neck I headed for the front door.

Before I got there I bumped up against a ledge that jutted out from the rest of the wall. Tools were scattered on the ledge: screwdrivers and a chisel and a monkey-wrench, even a couple of hammers. Snow dusted all the tools. I picked up a claw hammer and tested it in my hand. It had a nice weight and I figured it would swing smooth. My hope was not to have to use it, but holding it gave me comfort. Taking a deep breath, I shoved the door open and stepped inside.

The heat hit me, snatching my breath away, reminding me of the time Lana Powers and I snuck into the Wyandot Hotel in Detroit and pretended to be guests so we could enjoy the sauna. Nobody ever caught us and we had one fine time wandering around and stealing soap and tissues from maids' carts. Lana had the greenest eyes. Behind the counter was a young girl who looked a lot like Lana. Only this girl's eyes were blue and these days Lana had to be fifteen years older than little miss blue-eyes.

She glanced up from a magazine on the counter, gave me the once over, then went back to her magazine. The magazine appeared to be mostly color photographs. The girl was chewing gum with her mouth open.

When the door clicked behind me I jerked. Don't think the girl noticed. She wasn't interested in me. Just in looking at those photos and chewing her gum and drumming her fingers nonstop on the glass countertop.

Off to my right was a rack full of magazines and I pretended to look at one full of pictures of vintage cars and pickups. On page 60 there was a 1963 Plymouth like my daddy drove off to Ohio in. Only this one was white. His had been a faded blue.

Course I wasn't really looking at old cars. Just checking the store out. At first I thought it was just me and the girl, but then I noticed an old man sitting in a rocker up next to a Warm Morning. His eyes were closed. What looked like tobacco juice drooled from one corner of his fishy mouth.

A radio was playing somewhere behind the walls. Figured there was a door in the wall that opened into the family's living quarters. Lots of old country stores were made that way. This one had the door next to a pegboard full of hooks with tools attached. Hoes and rakes, that sort of paraphernalia.

That door got me to worrying. A man never knew who was behind a closed door. My fingers tightened on the hammer handle. I dreaded going back out in that snow, but it seemed like I was going to have to move quicker than I wanted. Probably for the best though. Lingering had got me in trouble more than once.

Just as I turned for the counter the door I'd been studying swung open and a boy in a wheelchair rolled in. His arms looked like pale strands of fettuccini, but he was rolling himself. For a moment his head was down. Then, as though he sensed my presence, his eyes came up and settled on my face. We stared at each other. Time ticked audibly in my head. It was hot in the store and I was starting to sweat.

Something was wrong with the boy's face. Looked like somebody had jammed it into a vice grip and then twisted like hell. His mouth was lopsided and one eye was higher than the other. His head was shaped like an onion, but he had bright eyes, like a squirrel's.

The boy stopped the wheelchair. He didn't say anything, only kept looking at me. I stepped on over to the counter and slapped the old car magazine down. After a couple of seconds the girl looked up. I showed her the hammer.

Her eyes were from another planet. The pupils looked like pin-pricks and they wouldn't hold still. Was something wrong with the whole damn family?

"I need transportation and money. Give me all the cash in the drawer and the keys to your vehicle."

She smiled. Then she laughed. One of those funhouse laughs. Up high in her throat like that part of her body wasn't working right.

I swung the claw hammer a couple of inches and she quit laughing and punched open the cash drawer. All that was in there were a few ones, a couple of fives and a single ten. Even in a place as remote as this I'd figured on a couple of hundred dollars. But that was the way my luck had been running.

"Take it," she said, in a singsong voice. "You won't get far on that. Course that won't matter much, 'cause you'll be walking."

"How do you figure?"

"Nothing around here runs. The old truck out front was the last thing that did and it's got two flat tires and the starter's shot."

"You're lying."

She shrugged and started drumming her fingers again. Under her right eye a nerve was twitching.

"How do you all get anywhere?"

"Walk," she mumbled, "or catch a ride with somebody going the way we're wanting to go." Her fingers drummed harder on the counter.

She had long, fake fingernails and they were painted black. One nostril was pierced and she smelled weird. Took me a minute to figure out what she smelled like. Hadn't smelled weed since before I got sent up the last time.

"Give me the damn money," I said.

"Get it your own damn self."

49

Her hands were shaking now and she kept tightening and loosening her neck muscles. Didn't know what she was using, but it was easy to see the girl was going to need a fix soon. What the hell? We all needed something.

I grabbed the money and started to turn when I heard the door squeak open again and a radio commercial came blasting out. Figured it for the boy getting the hell out of Dodge, but then I heard a growling and a mongrel dog came snarling at me. Big, with an ugly head, and he was coming hard down the bread aisle. A woman I couldn't see shouted, "Sic him, Sam," and the dog jumped for my throat.

I twisted to one side and got an arm up, but the dog sunk his teeth right in. They were big and sharp and came on through the vinyl jacket and my Georgia work shirt.

Because of the jacket he couldn't get a good grip, but his teeth were digging into my skin and his claws were scratching at my hide. I couldn't handle his weight just hanging off my arm. I stumbled back against the counter and swung the hammer like I was driving nails. The woman screamed.

I should have made a carpenter. The claw hammer smacked against the side of the dog's head and he fell on the floor whimpering. Meanwhile the girl had her arms around my throat and I pried them off and gave her a slap that made her funny blues eyes roll around in her head.

Jamming the money down in my pockets, I started for the door. Had my hand on the handle when the woman shouted, "Don't move or I'll shoot."

Guns scare me, period. A woman with a gun flat out terrifies me. I turned around real slow.

"Drop the hammer," she said.

The woman had one of those calm voices that chill a man off real quick and I stopped like a Kentucky State Trooper was standing there. Only I kept on gripping the hammer. Learned a long time ago that the last thing a man does is give up his gun, or in my case a rusty claw hammer.

The woman was standing by the counter. I couldn't see the girl. The barrel of the pistol was pointed right at my stomach. My guts kept contracting. Wasn't a big gun. Just big enough. The woman took a step closer. Then another. She had nice breasts. They poked at her shirt like a boxer's fists.

I shouldn't have even noticed. Losing focus like that can get you killed. But it had been almost two years. A hell of a long two years.

"What are you," she said, "another one of those crackheads?"

I must have given her a funny look 'cause the lines in her face changed.

"You all have been hanging around here for weeks now. You've got Jenny half-hooked on your shit." She paused and nibbled at her lower lip. "And I'll be damned if I let you keep coming around. If the law can't or won't stop you, by God I will."

I kept my mouth shut. Too busy figuring to talk. The woman looked normal. Maybe in her late forties, hair going gray on the sides and getting a roll around the middle, but she held herself real prideful.

Filled out her jeans real nice, too. Didn't have what you'd call a beautiful face. More like pleasant, or attractive. Her brown eyes were her best feature. Them and her fat lower lip. Death and desire sure made an odd couple.

"Not from around here, are you?"

"Nope," I said. "And I ain't planning to stay long. Now if you'll just put that gun down, I'll disappear."

The dog whimpered then and she glanced down at him.

When her eyes dropped I started for the gun, but she was too quick.

"You son-of-a-bitch, drop that hammer or I'll shoot your guts out."

Nothing for it but to do it. Hated like hell to let go of the hammer, but getting gut shot was worse.

Yeah, maybe it wasn't loaded or maybe she would lose her nerve. But those brown eyes were too calm to suit me. Chancing it wasn't worth the risk. I started to lower the hammer.

"What the hell, what the hell?" somebody shouted.

For a minute I thought it might be the woman's husband but she wasn't wearing a ring and anyway the voice was too old.

I let my eyes travel and saw the old man trying to stand up. Tobacco juice had run down his chin and stained the front of his shirt. He took a step toward us and started wobbling. Then everything happened in a big rush.

The boy shouted something from his chair and the woman turned her head and the old man tottered over face first into the Hostess cupcakes. And all the time I was moving.

The woman had started down the aisle and I jumped on her back and rode her down. I could hear the old man hollering and the kid yelling and the guy on the radio talking about Martha White flour. I tapped the woman on the back of her head with the hammer and she went out like a baby.

The woman had been out cold. Hadn't even moaned when I undressed her. I'd turned off all the lights except one lamp on the far side of the bedroom. In that soft light she looked real nice. Brown hair spread across the pillow like dark lace and her body was so full and ripe I could almost taste it. For a time all I did was look.

Well, I was thinking a little, too. Thinking I was a fool for not taking the money and running. But it was colder than hell out there and I had no way to go except walking. The boy had confirmed his sister's tale about the vehicles. I believed him. Just couldn't bring myself to face that snow at night.

He seemed like a good kid. Talked a little while I was lifting him out of his chair and setting him on the floor. Didn't see any need to tie him up. Just leaned him against a couple of bags of Old Roy dog food while he told me that it was just the four of them living out in the middle of nowhere, trying to scratch a living out of the store. He didn't say anything about his daddy and I didn't ask.

I duct-taped the girl and locked grandpa in his bedroom. Then I'd turned out the store lights and tried to lock the front door. However, the lock was shot, so I fixed me a couple of bologna and cheese sandwiches and stood at the window eating them and drinking Coca-Cola straight from the bottle. Best eating I'd had in a week.

In the arc of the security light out by the gas pumps I could see that it was still snowing. Great big flakes now, and lots of them. No headlights out on the road and already three or four inches on the ground. Told myself I'd head out come daylight. Meant it for the truth, too. But at the moment I was buck naked with one arm around the woman. Been so long since I'd held a woman.

Her eyelids fluttered and I bowed my head and kissed her smack on those fat lips. Soft and warm, they were lips just like all the women had in my jailhouse dreams. She opened one eye and then the other. Plain to see she didn't know exactly where she was.

Then she did and she tried to take a swing at me, but I grabbed her wrists and rolled on top of her. She was cussing and trying to bite and I felt myself growing hard against all her sweet softness. Finally she quit struggling and I kissed her again.

She only lay there like a marble statue. Then she spit in my face. I wiped it off with the back of one hand, keeping a good grip on her wrists with the other.

"Bastard," she said. "You might as well go ahead and do it. I can feel you all hard down there and I know what a man like you wants."

A gentle mood had come over me and I nuzzled up against her warm neck. There were days when I wasn't half as tough as I pretended.

"It's snowing like crazy out there and you don't have a vehicle on the place that runs. Is that right?"

"Yeah, the old truck died last week. That was the only one that halfway ran."

"Well then, I can't go anywhere. I'd freeze to death out there tonight. So I thought you and I could just have us a little party. Haven't partied in a long time."

"Piss on you and your party. Where are the kids? And my dad? What have you done with them, you asshole?"

She lifted her head and glared at me. A bruise discolored one cheek. Her face was so close that I could feel the warmth of her breath against my skin.

"If you've hurt any of them I swear I'll kill you. And it won't be quick and easy."

I kissed her dead center between her eyes.

"Relax, they're all okay. I just duct-taped your daughter, put grandpa to bed, and sat Junior on the floor. Never have hurt a kid or an old man."

"Duct tape? You duct-taped my daughter? What are you, a pervert, on top of being a rapist?"

I rolled off her and got up and put on my underwear and pants. The mood had passed. A straight-back chair stood beside the bed and I sat on it and put my shoes back on. First, though, I put on two pair of wool socks I'd filched from the old man's room.

"Nope," I said, "I'm no pervert and I'm not a rapist as you just saw. Just your everyday mad dog killer."

She pulled the sheet up to her chin. "Asshole."

"Oh, give it up. Little duct tape never hurt anybody. Besides, it was what you had handy."

She eased up in the bed, rubbing the back of her head, studying me. "Damn you," she said, "my head hurts."

"Sorry, but you had a gun."

Her mouth opened like she aimed to say something, but then she shut her lips and let her eyes wander around the room.

A Grant Wood print hung above the bed—the one of the farming country. Across the room was an unframed print of Edward Hopper's Sunday Morning. At least we had similar tastes in art.

"What did you do with my gun?"

"It's behind the counter. Only don't get any ideas. The bullets are stored away someplace safe." I'd put them in the boy's hip pocket.

Those brown eyes were clear now and I knew she was seeing me real good. Way she stared at me made me feel funny, like she was memorizing my face. Made me feel good and scared at the same time. Way she looked so hard at me made it feel like she was a type of x-ray machine, only instead of seeing bones she saw all the evil I'd done. Then, like she was one of those mind readers you run across at county fairs, she said, "So you stole a roll of my duct tape?"

"Sure did," I said, bending over to tie my shoe, "and some bread and bologna and cheese." I stood up and started slipping my arms into my shirt sleeve. "Oh, and a Coca-Cola."

"You aim to pay for all that?"

I didn't say anything, only glanced at her face and began buttoning my shirt.

She sat up straighter in the bed, wrapping the sheet around her like a toga. Her breasts bulged against the sheet. She was the nicest thing I'd seen in I couldn't remember when.

Her eyes roamed across my face. I wondered what she was looking for. Women had a way of seeing a lot. Usually more than a man wanted.

"In trouble, aren't you?"

"Don't ask and I won't have to add lying to you to my list of sins."

"Bad trouble?"

"Bad enough."

"Mad dog Killer?" She was grinning a little when she asked that one.

I grinned myself and walked to a narrow window I'd just noticed and pulled the curtain back.

"Not quite that bad."

Things fell quiet between us then. Wasn't an uncomfortable silence. More like a natural one. Outside the snow was still falling. Wind whined in the tops of the cedars and under the eaves of the store. Sounded like a hurt dog. After a while, above that wind, I could hear a train whistle. Wished I was on that train riding off to somewhere. Didn't matter much where as long as it was far away from Georgia.

"That's the CSX," she said. "Coal prices are up and Aberdeen Consolidated is running three shifts, twenty-four-seven. Men are working who haven't had a job in years. That's good for this county.

Last few years it's been welfare or drugs or minimum wage. No way a man can raise a decent family on that."

"No way to run a country," I said.

She nodded. "But now coal is king again and the mines are working and the CSX is running more cars than I ever dreamed they had. Tracks are just across the hill behind the store. Trains sound farther away, but that's because of the cedars and the hill. Loaded cars are headed to Cincinnati and Cleveland. Empties back to the mine."

A faint rumble penetrated the walls. Sounded as if the earth was shifting position. Glass trembled in the windows.

"That one is running empty," she said.

"How can you tell?" I asked, mainly to keep her talking. I liked the sound of her voice.

"By the speed. Empty, they're really rolling. Loaded, they struggle, especially on the other side of our hill. See, they have to climb up Lofton Ridge loaded. First, though, they have to slow for Cox's Bend and then there's no chance to pick up speed before the incline."

She smiled and I watched her lips move, trying to fix the image in my mind.

"In the summertime, when the kids were little, we used to climb the old logging road that starts directly behind the store and put pennies on the tracks. The kids loved the way the pennies looked after the trains ran over them."

Yeah, I thought, smashed. Lots of my days had been smashed like those coins.

"What are you going to do with us?" Her voice was softer now, scarcely stronger than a whisper. She sounded like a little girl.

Without looking around, I shrugged. The snow was falling heavier and the outside world was white and cold and waiting. There were questions I wanted to ask, things I wanted to say. Words failed me at times, though. Too many times I'd said the wrong ones to the wrong people in all the wrong places.

"Don't even know your name," I said.

"It's Amy. What's yours?"

I shook my head. "You're better off not knowing. Just call me Camus."

Funny what a man will read in jail. I felt like showing off for the woman. Done a lot of things in my life because of a woman.

"That's a funny name," she said. "Sounds French. You don't look French."

"I'm not. Just a lost lonely Kentucky boy." I turned around. "It's sort of like we're neighbors."

She stepped out of the bed, the sheet still wrapped around her.

Regret tasted sour in my mouth.

She picked up her clothes and went into a little bathroom and closed the door.

I found a newspaper and read about a drug bust the previous week down around Glennville. Reading always makes me drowsy. I was half-gone when I felt a hand on my shoulder.

"You look tired. Want sleep, or some coffee?"

I needed both, but didn't trust the woman's sudden gentleness. "Coffee."

As she moved away I whispered her name to etch it in my brain and went back to reading the paper. Another shirt factory had shut down. A schoolteacher the next county over had lost it a week ago Thursday and attacked his principal with a butcher knife from the cafeteria. It had taken two bus drivers and an assistant football coach to hold him down until the police arrived. Behind my paper, I could hear the woman rustling pots and pans. I whispered her name again. Couple of minutes later I could smell coffee starting to percolate and bacon frying.

She fried us each an egg and two strips of bacon and put the plates on the table. Then she sat down across from me and smiled.

"Reading that paper you remind me of John. You're about his size. Same color hair, too."

"Your husband?"

"He was."

"Sorry."

"Not your fault," she said and stabbed her egg. It bled yellow all over her plate.

For a minute she was quiet. I sipped on my coffee and waited. She nibbled on that fat lower lip, the one I wanted to kiss.

"Nothing would do him but he had to buy a motorcycle. He was driving a truck for Cumberland Valley Timber. Lumber was going great. Big housing boom. He saved up." She shrugged and turned her face.

I kept my mouth shut.

After a little while she turned back around. Her eyes were wet. "Went for a joyride one Sunday while I was gone to church. Drunk driving a pickup crossed the line."

She didn't say anymore. Just started eating. My egg had gone cold. I ate it anyway. No telling when I'd get another. I drank two cups of coffee and considered a third. Maybe I'd pour one for the road.

When she finished, she fished a pack of Winstons out of a drawer and fired one up. She offered the pack to me. I shook my head.

She shrugged. "One of my vices."

"We've all got them."

She blew smoke out her nostrils.

I wondered if it was still snowing.

"Sorry I pulled a gun on you. I was going to shoot you, you know."

"Thought crossed my mind."

"We've had so much trouble lately." She picked up our plates and carried them over to the sink.

"Drugs?"

"Yeah, the last few years have been awful. According to what I read in the paper, it's as bad as anything in Columbia or Mexico. When John was alive the dealers and dopers knew better than to come around. He'd have shot them on sight."

Something must have shown in my face. Her lips pressed tightly together and she closed her eyes. After a few seconds she opened them. "If you'd seen what they did to innocent kids you'd understand." She made a monkey face.

"They prey on the young, you know. Kids are so weak these days. Weak and desperate. They fall for the first smooth line that comes along. Before they know it they're hooked and don't have a clue how to get clean. Their teeth rot out and they forget to bathe and they'd rob their own blind mother for cash for the next fix, and the lousy dealers stand back and rake in the money, and laugh. Laugh at the kids and the parents, not to mention what passes for the law in these parts.

"No, I wouldn't have blamed John. Not at all. Fact is, if he hadn't been the kind of man to shoot those animals I'd have done it myself. That's why I was going to shoot you. Thought you were one of them. Waving that claw hammer around you sure fit the profile."

She stopped talking and looked down at the floor. Her hair hung down and covered her face.

I thought about the night ahead and what I would have to do in the morning. When you're on the run you are always having to do something. I quit thinking and studied the woman. Late at night a memory can be as good as any picture.

She lifted her eyes and peered through the curtain of her hair. "You notice Jenny?"

"Hard not to. Been around enough to know the signs."

"Figured you had. Every now and then your eyes get that experienced look."

"Seen my share, I guess. Maybe a little more."

"Been going on for a few months now. Couple of older boys she knew from school got her started. I hate the little bastards."

"Guess you've tried counseling?"

"Counseling and tough love and prayer. None of it is worth a shit. Expect I'd better go see about her."

All of a sudden I felt a draft of cold air come sliding under the door. The woman felt it, too. I heard her catch her breath.

Easing out of the chair, I tiptoed to the door with my fingers gripping the claw hammer. Should have known the law never sleeps. Hell, they were worse than the Post Office; neither rain, nor snow, nor dark of night...

I eased the door to the store open. Two men were talking to the girl. They must have untied her.

Jenny's body was shaking; an arm pointed toward the back. The two men didn't look like the law. In their watch caps and saggy pants they looked like bad news. One of them had a ring in his nose like a hog. The other one had a spider's web tattooed across his face. Lovely, I though, freaking lovely. Bad news for sure. Real bad news. I could hear the woman breathing behind me. Her fingers touched my back. They felt good there, but they also seemed to urge me to step into the light.

Thanks to me she didn't have her gun. That was her daughter out there. I had to do something. Like I said, a man on the run always seems to have something he simply has to do. On the run there never is any rest.

I took a deep breath and let it out slowly. If I'd been a believer I'd have said a prayer. The two men sure looked like trouble. Trouble was something I already had in a gracious plenty. The woman whispered something, but I wasn't listening. Learned early on a man had to stay focused if he wanted to keep breathing. My shoes scraped across the floor and the three people on the other side turned as one.

"That's him," the girl screeched. "The one I was telling you about. Watch out, he's dangerous." She stepped back behind the taller of the two men, the one who thought he was Spider Man.

As I took a step closer their faces swung up into the light. They weren't men at all. Boys really. Tattooed and ringed, with long stringy hair and sallow complexions. Both so thin they looked anorexic. Spider Man was taller and the ringed wonder had a face full of pimples.

Pimple Face stuck a hand in his right front jeans pocket. It came back out with a knife. He twisted his wrist and a long blade popped out, glittering as he moved it back and forth like he was warming up to carve the air.

"Nope," Pimple Face said, "he just thinks he's dangerous."

He took a step closer. My fingers tightened on the hammer. I tried to focus on the knife, but just at the outer edges of vision I caught a glimpse of the taller kid sideling off to his right. Something metallic dangled from his hand. I risked a glance. He was holding a heavy chain, the kind you see wrapped around gateposts.

I eased to the middle of the aisle, trying to think. One at a time I could handle them. If they both tried me at once that could be a problem because I had to keep my distance from the knife, but get inside the arc of the swinging chain.

"Better get the hell out here, old man."

I gave Pimple Face a hard look and decided he couldn't be much over eighteen. Still, eighteen was old enough to kill. I'd known younger desperados.

The taller kid was yammering away, really just mouthing. None of the words made sense and I figured he was on a talking jag. He was swinging his chain wildly now, awkwardly, as though it was too heavy for him.

The girl peeked around from behind the boy's back and the chain etched shadows across her face. Then she began tiptoeing away and I saw her hair swinging. Must have kept my eye on the girl a second too long because Pimple Face was slashing at my eyes. I jerked my head to the left, away from the knife.

I was too slow and the blade sliced across my cheek. Didn't go deep but the blood was hot and I cursed myself for losing focus again. Twice in one night. I was getting old.

Pimple Face wasn't a pro. His swing was too long and loose and he was off balance and trying to ready himself for the next slice when I smashed the hammer into his side. The crack of his ribs was audible.

First, he gasped. Then, he started screaming and stumbling around, trying to hold his ribs so they wouldn't hurt. Never heard the knife hit the floor, but I caught a glimpse of its glitter and I kicked it under a pyramid of cereal boxes.

Pimple Face was moaning like he was dying, and maybe he thought he was. He wouldn't bother me again, so I whirled around to face the taller kid with the chain. Only he was already swinging and I only had time to lunge at him, thinking all the time how quick these young kids were. In a single night I'd aged considerable.

I could hear the woman shouting, but there was a roaring in my ears and the chain was snaking across my shoulders and flicking me on the jaw. In all my life I'd never hurt so bad and I staggered under the pain. This time I got lucky and stumbled into the kid with the chain. We danced backwards into the canned goods. All around us cans were crashing onto the floor. One smashed my right foot, but I ignored it and swung the hammer at the kid.

My palm was sweaty and the hammer twisted in my hands and the iron claw raked across his face and he screamed and we both collapsed in a heap. We rolled apart and I came up swinging with the hammer, hoping to crush his skull. What if he was eighteen? He'd tried to kill me.

Only he wasn't there. He was crawling for the door. Crawling like that he reminded me of the dog. Not that I worried much about the hound. The adrenaline was starting to retreat and pain was filling the void. Liquid trickled down my face and I reached out a hand and the fingers come back red.

I started to stand but my legs weren't working quite right and I sat down in the middle of the cans, soup and peas and beans. I tried to read the labels but everything had gone blurry. My head ached and the store was tilting to port. I closed my eyes, but kept a grip on the hammer. That seemed important.

I smelled roses and figured I was dreaming. Then I opened my eyes and the woman was kneeling beside me. Her fingers touched my face and a memory rose like an eager moon.

I'm a kid and one day I find a small brown bird under Mrs. Grissom's mulberry bush and I pick the bird up and hold it to my face. I want to hear if its heart is beating. The bird's feathers are very soft. Just like the woman's hands.

My hair had fallen down and she brushed it off my forehead and started dabbing at the blood with what looks like a dishtowel. I wanted to thank her, but something in the set of her jaw kept me silent.

"Keep still and let me get this bleeding stopped. Those are the two I was telling you about, so don't feel bad about hurting them. They've damn near destroyed Jenny and I only hope they're suffering."

"They're hurting, that's for sure."

"Hush now. I told you to be still. You've got a nasty cut on your cheek. Probably should have stitches."

"Don't have time for that," I said. "Besides, a doctor would have to report me to the law. That can't happen."

"Mom, Mom?"

It was the boy calling. I'd forgotten about him. Time to put him back in his chair. Time for me to be moving on.

"What, baby?"

The woman had shifted her face toward her son. In profile she looked some like a movie star I'd seen in an old black and white film once. Couldn't recall the star's name, but I remember I saw the movie on a Philco in a Motel 6 outside of Lafayette, Louisiana.

My brother Joe and I had gone there looking for work. A housing boom was just taking off and we were going to get rich. All that happened was Joe got himself shot in the mouth by a sawed-off Cajun named Emile Robicheaux. Just because Joe got drunk and made a pass at Robicheaux's wife. A slut if I ever saw one.

I got six months for beating Robicheaux's head in with a tire iron. Wished a hundred times since that I'd killed the bastard.

"Jenny just called the cops," the boy said. "Told them a crazy man was beating us all with a hammer. Said he liked to have killed two customers."

"Damn that girl," Amy said, "all she can think about is where her next fix is coming from. I've got some gauze and tape in the back. Let me doctor you up and then you've got to go."

"Sure," I said, "sounds right," and all the while I was thinking where in the hell am I going to go in this freaking blizzard?

She stood up and hurried toward the back. I still had a death grip on the hammer. I jammed it down between my belt and my pants and worked my way to standing. For a moment I simply stood, feeling my body swaying slightly as though there was a storm blowing. Then I started walking toward the boy.

Took me two tries, but I got him in his chair before the woman came back to do her doctoring. Once I got him positioned, I looked him in the eyes.

"Thanks, kid," I said, "Appreciate the heads up."

He nodded and then let his head roll to one side as he looked up at me. Really, there wasn't anything wrong with his eyes. More like his head was lopsided.

"You'd better get going, mister. I know the cop my sister called and he's hooked up with those two you got in a fight with. Think he uses himself. Worse for you, he just lives a couple of miles down the road."

"What about the snow?"

"He's got a four-wheel drive."

"Damn," I said "and thanks again."

I stuck out my right hand. The kid shook hands like a man.

I heard the woman coming down the aisle. She smiled at me in a way that warmed me all over. Then I heard another sound. Police siren. Too close for my own good.

I jerked my head toward the road. "Give me the stuff. I'll fix my face later."

The siren wailed. It sounded closer.

"I've got to go."

The woman started to say something. Then, instead, she put her lips together and brushed them across mine. One of those kisses that might mean nothing, I thought, or damn near everything.

She jammed the bandages and tape into my hands. Then she tucked a slip of paper into my shirt pocket. The siren was getting real close, mixing now with another sound. Took me a minute to place the second sound. It was a train whistle, off in the distance. Then I heard it again and it sounded closer.

"That's a loaded CSX," the woman said. "Hurry and you can catch it when it starts up the grade. It will be a cold ride, but..." Her voice trailed off. We both knew a cold ride beat the hell out of going back to prison.

She started to say something, but I kissed her lips shut. Just for a second she let her head lie on my shoulder. I could feel her heart thudding against my chest.

"That's my phone number on that piece of paper. Call me when you get somewhere safe. I'd like to know you're alright."

There were words I wanted to say, important words, but over the top of her head I could see headlights in the road and the train whistle was calling my name. My throat had gone all tight, so I kissed her again, turned and started running toward the back of the store. I didn't look back. Didn't trust myself.

On the way out I threw the money I'd stolen on the counter and grabbed what looked like her old man's coat off a peg by the back door. One of those fancy writers I read in stir would make that action beautifully symbolic, but I just slipped the coat on and burst out the back door.

For a minute I was blind. Then my eyes started to adjust and through the falling snow I saw a break in the timber and figured that for the logging road and started running. The cedars smelled like Christmas. I slipped a couple of times and fell once. But I just rolled and came up going low and hard into the darkness beneath the timber.

The train whistle moaned again and it sounded way closer. Figured it was nearing that big bend the woman had talked about. That really got my legs to pumping and I broke out of the timber into open ground and I could see the crest of the hill.

The wind was blowing harder now and snow was swirling like something alive and malevolent in the night. Pellets of it stung my face like tiny needles. Not that I was complaining. That brutal wind was blowing all the beautiful snow around and filling my tracks, and I ran on up the path, smiling and fingering the piece of paper in my pocket while that claw hammer banged against my left leg.

DRINKING BEER IN MORIARTY

AFTER THAT EPISODE AT the bank in Valdosta things fell apart between me and Janet and the week before Christmas I caught the Greyhound to Palm Lake, Florida. My brother was living there with his wife and two kids, bass fishing when he could and managing the local Cineplex to keep the family in groceries. My brother and I had always gotten along, but the day after Christmas he was arrested for kiting checks.

It was Saturday afternoon and we were sitting around drinking beer and watching pro basketball on the tube. I don't give a rat's ass about pro basketball, but Roger liked it and his beer was cold. The first half had just ended when somebody started pounding on the door. Roger got up and looked out the window. Then he looked back at me. His face was flat and his skin looked like an old man's. Only his eyes looked alive. Someone started hammering again and Roger waved his hand toward the door. He waved it like he was very tired.

I got off the couch and opened the door. Two cops were standing there. They asked if I was Roger Krebs and I shook my head and turned and looked at my brother. He didn't protest when the cops cuffed him. Just told his wife to call a lawyer named Simmons who he fished with some. As he went out the door he gave me the old eye roll.

I strolled over to the bay window at the front of their trailer and watched my brother walk to the squad car. His shoulders were slumped and his steps were awkward, like he wasn't sure where to place his feet. For the first time Roger reminded me of our dad.

I stood at the window, watching until the cruiser turned right onto Huego. My brother's wife was talking on the phone in her bedroom. Miranda was talking rapidly and her accent had ramped up and I couldn't understand much. I wandered down the hallway. Just before I reached her bedroom I stopped and leaned against the wall, sorta listening, sorta wondering how Roger was doing, but mainly trying to figure out my next move. Miranda had grown up in the Little Cuba section of Miami and, except for Roger and George W. Bush, she didn't have a lot of use for people whose native language was English, especially if they were unemployed and drank a lot of beer.

I heard her saying goodbye and pushed myself off the wall and hustled down the hall and into the kitchen. Roger had bought a couple of cases of Bud Lite before Christmas and most of one was still left. He wouldn't be needing it. I tugged the fridge open and pulled a can out and carried it out on the wooden deck he'd built with his own hands.

He'd stained the deck to look like redwood, but already the weather and termites were getting at the wood. Maneuvering around a rotten spot, I eased down on one of the beach chairs Roger and Miranda used for porch furniture.

Their trailer lounged at the rear of a trailer court with their yard backing right up to a thicket of palmetto, saw grass, briars, and scrubby pine. Possums lived in that undergrowth, and raccoons, and all sorts of snakes. Snakes give me the creeps.

The day had been sunny and fine, especially for late December, but now the sun was drifting lower and the wind had come up and the clouds were fast moving and tinged with purple. Behind me the door screeched open. Miranda's heels clicked on the rotting wood. Closing my eyes, I lifted the Bud.

Scents of orchids and musk accompanied the rustling of clothes. I kept my eyes closed, hoping she would go away. We didn't like each other. No use in pretending otherwise.

Behind my closed eyes I kept seeing Roger's face swimming up at me out of the dark. His features were distorted, cheekbones flattened and separated, nose growing longer and thinner and lips quivering like butterfly wings. When tiny black and red vipers began to crawl out of his eyes I opened mine.

Miranda was staring at me. The light was going now but enough still shimmered so that in that fading quirky light she looked a little like a Madonna I'd seen in an art history book, when I was still going to class.

Miranda had been crying and the tears had made her eyeliner and mascara run so that she looked like a raccoon. Raccoons made me think of the thicket and snakes. I took another drink.

"What am I going to do, Ray?"

I looked up at the sky as though I might find inspiration in the darkening cloud bank. Surely I could think of something that would help. After all, Roger was my brother—the only family I had left, if you didn't count his kids and my Uncle Charles who lives somewhere in the wilds of Northern California, draws a VA pension, and smokes a lot of weed. For years he'd sent me a Christmas card, always handmade, lovely in a quirky, old-fashioned meets surreal way. Memories stirred like small, dark animals. I chased them back into the underbrush.

"Has Roger called?"

"Not yet, damn it."

"What did the lawyer say?"

"That old fart? Just that he'd make some calls."

Her face was twisted as if she'd swallowed needles. I glanced at the thicket. The pines were only dark silhouettes swaying in a greater darkness, reminding me of drunken Indians—Seminoles, Creeks, lost tribes, lost civilizations, lost lives.

"He hadn't heard from Roger either?"

"No," Miranda said, almost in a whisper. "What do you think is happening to him?" I could hear her throat work as she swallowed. I couldn't answer her question. I didn't want to think about my brother. Nothing good was happening to him.

The wind was still rising and I wished I'd thought to put on my Georgia Tech sweatshirt. It needed washing, but at least it would have knocked the chill off. I took another sip. My beer was getting warm.

Miranda's perfume was making my allergies act up and I sneezed and stood up sniffing and walked over to the edge of the porch where I leaned gingerly against the railing. Hell, I didn't know what was happening to Roger. I'd been in jail only twice—once for a DUI back in my Tulane days, before I flunked out, and then once for vag in some dusty cowtown in west Texas. God, that had been a lonesome three days.

The scent of orchids grew stronger and then I felt Miranda's hand on my shoulder. I glanced down. The security lights in the trailer park had kicked on and I could see that some of her nail polish had chipped off.

"What am I going to do, Ray? What will I tell the kids?"

She was asking good questions, give her that. I was asking myself the same questions. Only I wasn't asking for Miranda. In the four years she and Roger had been married she'd never so much as wished me a happy damn birthday.

Still, she was asking the right questions. What were we going to do? Neither of us worked and, except for my brother and his wife, I didn't know a soul in Palm Lake. Damn Roger anyway, I thought.

Of course I didn't say that. I didn't say anything. Only drank my beer and watched the last light fade away in the west, shivering a little, and feeling sorry for myself now and then. Once I heard Miranda crying.

When it was dark, I said, "I'll think of something." Truth was, I didn't have a clue, but I'd think of something. I always did.

She murmured in the darkness, but the lab next door had started barking and jumping around and pulling on his chain and I couldn't hear her clearly. I didn't care enough to ask her to say it again.

She didn't care about me, see. She was only scared. Scared, I understand. But understanding wasn't enough. Understanding is never enough; it's only a beginning.

When the lab calmed down I could hear the wind in the pines and the owl who lived in an abandoned barn at the edge of the field where some farmer named Rollins had grown sugar cane thirty years before. Wal-Mart had gone in up the road and speculators had bought up all the farmland for five miles on either side. In a way it made you want to laugh. After all that farmland got bought up all that had ever been built was a Dairy Queen and a Shell station.

After a while I heard her clomp back across the porch. I drained my beer and wondered what the hell I was going to do. The clouds were coming apart and I could see a few brave stars. They looked cold and lonely.

After a while I got tired of staring at the stars and went in the house, grabbed another beer and lay down on the couch. Miranda had gone to her room, but she'd left the television on in the living room with the sound down low. An old black and white World War II movie was playing. It was about this squad of American soldiers trying to hold on against the Germans in the Battle of the Bulge. I went to sleep watching James Whitmore marching the squad down a road. "You had a good home, but you left, right, left."

About two o'clock I woke up with my back aching and bladder about to burst. I rolled off the couch, stumbled down the hall to the bathroom where I took a long piss and thought about what I was going to do.

Outside the bathroom were those strange little sounds that you hear only in the night when the rest of the world is sleeping. For a moment I yielded to temptation and stood in the hallway listening. In the near dark the walls seemed close and enveloping. Part of my mind kept thinking that maybe this was the way God spent his nights, listening to all his children in every universe sleeping. I was still hungover enough to be drifting back and forth across that white line that runs down the middle of the mind and leads to the edge of sanity.

Then, somewhere out in the blackness, a dog barked and I came back into myself and walked down the hallway to the little room where I was staying. All that was in there was my duffel bag and a sleeping bag and pillow that I was borrowing from Roger. I stuffed my dirty clothes into the duffel bag and rolled the sleeping bag up and carried them both outside and laid them on the damp grass. Then

I went back inside, easing the door open, and grabbed the rest of the beer. Okay, I'm a thief, but Roger wasn't going to need either the sleeping bag or the beer for a long time.

For a moment I stood there on the lawn staring at the broken string of lights downtown, saying a silent good-bye. I was always saying goodbye to someone. Then I lugged all my crap into the deepest shadows, pulled the beer cans out of the box—there were six or seven left—and stuffed them into my duffel bag, which I slung over my shoulder. Tucking the sleeping bag under my arm, I started walking toward the highway trying to swing along like the soldiers had in that old black and white.

Maybe it was seeing that old movie, but I'd dreamed about Ken Mitchell, an old army buddy of mine who lived in a little town closer to Miami called Moriarty. He'd called me just this past Thanksgiving and we talked about old times, telling lies and shooting the shit. If I remembered right, the town was small and a few miles away from the coast, but there had been a construction boom going on—some South Korean company had come in and was building a plant where they would make axles for GM. Ken was helping build the plant and I figured maybe I could hook on with his outfit. I couldn't remember the name of the motel he'd been living in—some Mom and Pop place—but, since the town was small, I figured to find it without much trouble.

Transportation was my problem. My cash amounted to three dollars and forty-seven cents, and, since all the credit card companies had grown allergic to me, the only way I was going to get to Moriarty was to pull a Kerouac.

Hitchhiking isn't popular these days, so I cut over to the Heart of Dixie Truck Haven and hung around, drinking coffee and chatting with the drivers. Ninety-nine percent of the drivers for the big national firms won't give you a ride. They can't; they'd get fired if they did. But sometimes one of the independents will get bored enough or lonely enough or take pity and give a man a lift. Took me three hours but just before dawn a black guy out of Maryland who was hauling furniture agreed to give me a ride. He had yellowish eyes and a peculiar way of moving his upper lip, but I didn't have a choice.

I followed the man between idling rigs and across broken asphalt, tossed my bags into the cab and hauled my carcass aboard. The black guy climbed in behind the wheel, jotted something down on a sheet of paper attached to a clipboard, and shifted into gear.

I felt very high up, almost detached from the earth, as if I was taking a strange carnival ride. It was still dark and the truck's headlights sent twin shafts of white light shooting across the darkness.

While we were crossing the parking lot and merging onto the highway the driver focused on the road. Once we were rolling he took his right hand off the steering wheel and stretched it toward me.

"Name's Franklin."

I wasn't sure if that was his first or last name, but I just shook his hand and mumbled, "Ray."

The night spread before us, black and amorphous, with only a stray light poking through the darkness now and then like some wandering star. The hum of the tires against the asphalt began to vibrate in my brain. My eyes felt full of grit. I rubbed at them and wished I could drink a beer, but I was uneasy about opening one. The driver could get in big trouble if some cop spotted an open container, so I turned and put my face against the cool window glass and stared out at the darkness. To pass time I imagined I was an astronaut riding through deep space.

"You travel much?"

The driver's voice jerked me back inside the cab. I had to swallow twice to get my throat working. "Some," I said. "Been on the road for a few weeks now."

He nodded, the lights from the dash flickering on his face. His dark skin glistened in the light like polished obsidian. Lights playing across his face made me think of cavemen and campfires.

"I'm on the road all the time," the driver said. "Some trips are only day trips, but usually I'm gone for a couple of nights. Haul all up and down the east coast, but once I drove a load of pianos all the way to Los Angeles, California. Didn't come back empty either. Hauled half a load of washing machines to Phoenix and dropped the other half of the load, which was table lamps, in Little Rock." He nodded his head in time to some inner rhythm I could only guess at and his eyes caught the dash lights and reflected them as though some strange essence burned within him.

"Guess all that time on the road gets to be lonely for a fellow," I said. Then I got to thinking that it was also lonely not being on the road. I read in a book somewhere—I think it was a detective story—that a man is never more alone than when he is in a crowd.

The driver sighed and tapped a jazzy rhythm on the steering wheel. "Yeah, life can get lonely out on the road and a man does have a lot of time for thinking. 'Specially in the nights a man gets to thinking about how lonely he is and then he gets to thinking about his woman at home and starts wondering about how lonely she might be getting."

He turned and looked at me then and I tried to read his face, but it was just a wedge of blackness, glittering where the stray lights splashed against it like lost starlight striking stone. For a few seconds our eyes locked. Then he turned his head back to the road unfurling before us under the unrelenting glare of the truck's headlights.

"I do that a lot you know," he murmured, half to me, half to the night.

"What's that?" I asked.

"Wonder about my woman. What she might be doing when I'm out on the road. She's a real nice looking lady, see. And full of energy." His fingers drummed on the wheel. I could almost recognize the tune.

"Not that I know anything, see. Not for sure. It's just a man's got a lot of thinking time when he's driving down a lonesome highway late at night. Too much time, if you ask me. Oh yeah, way too much time."

I mumbled something that sounded vaguely sympathetic and turned my face to the side window. He was talking again, but I wasn't listening now, only staring out at the land covered in darkness, and maybe there was the faintest rim of light in the sky. Like the gold rim on a dinner plate, only this wasn't gold and maybe it wasn't even quite light—only a denigration of the darkness.

"Things happen you know. Things happen in people's lives."

"Guess they do," I said.

"That's why I'm making this trip tonight."

"What do you mean?"

"Well, like I told you, I'm hauling this load of furniture. Only it's not for some furniture store. No, this load is for a fellow from Baltimore who got a divorce and moved down to Miami. He's friends with a guy I went to high school with. My friend's an accountant. Helps this rich guy with his taxes. When the guy decided to move my friend thought of me right off. We've stayed in touch a little over the years, reunions, ballgames, that sort of thing. Anyway my old buddy thought of me. Hadn't seen me in four, five years, but thought of me right off. Now that's a good friend."

"Sounds like it," I said, wishing I had a few good friends. In a way Franklin was on to something. Janet and I had started out as friends. I used to bowl in the Thursday night league with her brother and she got in the habit of coming down to watch. After a couple of weeks we started drinking a beer together after the last frame and, well, you know how it goes.

We really used to be friends, too, laughing at each other's jokes and remembering what songs the other one liked and how they liked their steaks and did they want gravy with their mashed potatoes and how old they were when they learned to tie their shoes and who they kissed first and where they wanted to be buried and why they cried out in their sleep when the nights grew cool, and, and, and...

I closed my eyes and tried to will the brain waves to smoothness. Only I kept on thinking. I opened my eyes and started to reach in the duffel bag for a beer. Then I remembered that it wouldn't be good for some cop to see me drinking a beer in the cab, so I put my hands together like I was praying and listened to the sounds of the highway night.

"You got a family?" he asked, not taking his eyes off the road.

I kept my eyes focused on the headlights. I could sense that he was wanting to look at me but I kept my eyes focused on those headlights like one of those deer you read about in the hunting and fishing magazines.

Time was ticking in my head. I could hear it. The sound was like the metronome my mother had used when she gave piano lessons. I could sense the driver waiting. Franklin struck me as a patient man.

"I've got a wife," I said, still looking at the headlights and the black asphalt ribbon spreading across the night.

"Hear that," he said. "I sure hear that."

I was afraid he was going to ask me some more questions. You could sense that he wanted to talk. Only tonight I wasn't in the mood. I was short on sleep and hung-over and needing a beer. I should have made the effort. Instead, I turned my head and watched the night roll by me. After a while the hum of the tires got inside my mind and smoothed my brain waves out and my eyes got so heavy they came together on their own. I could hear the driver say something, only it was like he was talking to me from a long way away.

I woke up with sunlight lathering my face and air brakes hissing. The rig was rumbling along the side of the road. Gravel pinged against the metal underbelly of the monster.

Blinking against the light, I sat up and licked my lips. They felt dry as bricks. I had no clue where I was. I could smell my own sweat, mingled with stale beer.

"Where are we?" My voice sounded scratchy—like an old vinyl record.

"Moriarty," he said, showing me his snaggly teeth, nodding at an abandoned Esso station and a Cracker Barrel. Now that it was daylight I could see that he had a mustache. Just a neat little pencil 'stache, the kind one of those British actors wore fifty years ago.

Moriarty didn't look like much, but then, I wasn't such hot shit myself. I began gathering up my possessions. The radio was on and the announcer was reading the news. An alligator had turned up in the kitchen of the Fontainebleau.

I popped the door and started to swing my legs out. Then I remembered my manners and twisted around and stuck out a hand.

"Thanks for the ride."

The driver nodded and shook my hand. In the light I could see that he was older than I'd figured. He had a young voice and a youthful way of moving. The mustache gave him a certain style.

"Good luck," he said.

"You, too. Keep 'em out of the ditches." I patted the dash and swung my legs out again and hopped down, slipping in the loose gravel and dropping my sleeping bag. Scooping it up, I jogged down the shoulder toward the Cracker Barrel. Halfway there I turned to wave, but the big rig was already rolling south. People seemed to be moving in and out of my life before I fully grasped they were there.

I strolled into the Cracker Barrel with a fat man and two chubby boys. Aromas of brewing coffee and frying bacon hit me like a hammer. The store was crowded with people, tourist types, and nobody seemed to even notice me as I worked my way through the wind chimes and Hershey bars and framed pictures of roosters crowing. I washed up in the bathroom, combed my hair, and put on my cleanest shirt. An old man in a bolo tie gave me an evil look, but nobody said anything.

Hauling all my paraphernalia, I eventually got to the front of the line and got my name on the list. Ten minutes later they called it and a lady with lacquered hair and varicose veins led me to a two-top next to the kitchen. I ordered coffee, pancakes, and bacon and eggs.

Cracker Barrel is a great place when you're low on cash. They tend to believe the virtues they espouse, especially the one about honesty, allowing a man to carry his own ticket into a room full of so much merchandise you can hardly walk and then wend his way to the cash register. If the room is crowded it's not much of a challenge to slip out the door unnoticed, with breakfast covered by the management. Not that I mind paying; it's just that I was broke.

Over my second cup of coffee I asked my waitress about motels in Moriarty. Her name was Judy, and she had bad skin but a nice voice, and she told me there used to be three. Then, back in the fall, the

Twin Pines had burned. The other two were The Blue Dolphin and Ramsey's. I was sure Ken wasn't staying at the Blue Dolphin.

Judy seemed like a nice person, the kind you wished you'd met twenty years ago, and I hated like hell to stiff her. Picking up my check, I gathered my bags and trudged out to the lobby like I was the second coming of Billy Graham. A busload of Japanese tourists were coming in the door. Walking out the door without paying was so easy I almost felt ashamed.

Ramsey's was seven concrete block buildings semi-circled in a stand of white pine. Each building was painted a different pastel color. A narrow blacktop road in need of repaving separated the office from the other units. The office was also concrete block, but it had an awning and was fronted by a split rail fence. The office was painted jungle green. I crossed the lane and walked around the fence and under the awning. A bell tinkled as the door swung open.

The small room was hot and empty. The air felt tired, as though it had been used up and trapped in the room for years. Nobody lounged behind the counter and I began to wonder if Ramsey's had given up the ghost. Then I could hear noises coming from behind a closed door. Seconds later it swung open and a middle-aged man in need of a shave stepped into the room.

Wiping his hand on a flowered dish towel the man stared at me with blue fish eyes. He put both hands on the counter and swallowed. I watched his Adam's apple bob up and down. He looked me over like I'd just gotten out of jail.

"How many nights?"

"Actually, I'm looking for someone."

"Who ya looking for?"

"Guy named Ken Mitchell. When I talked with him at Thanksgiving he was staying here, I think."

"We got a guy named Ken staying here. What's your friend look like?"

"About my age, an inch or two shorter. Rusty colored hair. Wore it short last time I saw him. Been working outdoors for years. Skin's all red and blotchy. Used to have a little wispy mustache. That sound like your Ken?"

The man behind the counter nodded. "Our Ken wears his hair long now. Otherwise, close enough. He's in number four; the tangerine." Fish-eyes nodded toward the cabins. "Don't know if he's in today. No phones in the cabin so I can't call. Anyways, he drives a blue Ford pickup. If it's there, he's there."

I crossed the lane and turned down the gravel road that connected the units. Inside the pines the air was cooler and the scent of pine needles was sweet and pungent at the same time. A cardinal flitted between the trees and the gravel crunched satisfyingly beneath my shoes. The long highway night was behind me now and Palm Lake was fading like a bad dream. Sure, I felt guilty for leaving Roger and Miranda in the lurch, but not enough to take the edge off the strange buzz that comes when you're short on sleep, full of bacon, and half hung-over. Also, the guilt level for my brother and his wife was several degrees below that I had for Janet.

The parking spot in front of number 4 was empty and I sat down on a concrete step to wait. I pulled a beer from my duffel bag and drank it while the air grew still and mosquitoes hummed in the weeds beyond the gravel. Sweat began to pool under my armpits. The hum of the highway drifted across the open fields. My eyes felt like they'd been smoked. I closed them.

On the far side of Ramsey's someone was mowing a yard. The hum of the motor reminded me of the hum of the black man's truck motor. I wondered if he'd ever gotten his furniture delivered. Then I wondered a while about his unfaithful wife. That got me to thinking about Janet and Valdosta and what had gone wrong. I pulled out another beer.

I hadn't meant for anything to happen. It was only like a dare. A dare and one too many beers. Oh hell, one way or another it had gone wrong. What the hell could I do about it now? That's what I kept asking myself until the brain waves smoothed out and the world drifted into the pines.

The sound of a motor woke me up. For a minute, while I was still half dreaming, it seemed to me that it was the motor of the guy who'd given me a lift. I couldn't figure out why he was coming back for me.

Then I came all the way awake and sat up and rubbed the back of my neck. A blue pickup was chugging into the parking place. The driver stared at me out the window like I'd dropped in from outer space. His hair was longer, and dark with sweat, but I'd recognize that hook nose and those thick wormy lips anywhere. Ken was a good guy. We'd been friends a long time. But he'd never win a beauty pageant.

I waved and watched the recognition spread across his face. He jammed the Ford into park and killed the engine. The door creaked open and he hopped out. As he hit the ground he made a face as though the bottom of his feet were tender. Sweat stained his shirt and a fine yellow dust powdered his face.

For a minute he just stared. Then he blinked, pulled a dirty rag out of his back pocket and swiped it across his forehead. A grin curled his thick lips, reminding me of a basset hound I'd had as a kid.

"Well, look what the hurricane blew in."

"Kick it, old man."

I stood up and we shook hands like a couple of aging boxers.

"Didn't have a clue you were in Florida, Ray. What brings you down South?"

"I'm sorta on a vacation."

Ken peered at me out of the corners of his eyes, but didn't say anything. After a few seconds he nodded at number 4. I followed him in.

All the windows in the unit were closed and the air was still. "Let me switch the AC on." Ken twisted the knob on a small window unit. "Too poor to run this damn thing all day and have to keep the windows closed on account of the thunderstorms and the bugs. Never have seen a place with so many bugs." He shrugged. "No screens."

I looked around the room. Part of it was a small kitchen with a round table and two chairs. The other section had a single bed shoved against the wall and a television set on a metal stand. The stand leaned toward the Gulf. At the far end of the room was a closed door. I figured the bathroom was on the other side of the door.

Ken looked almost like I remembered. Something around the eyes was different. They looked like polished glass—all light, no heat.

"Not the Taj Mahal."

I shrugged. "Better than what I've got at the moment."

"Thought you had the good life going in Valdosta."

"So did I."

He tugged the refrigerator door open and pulled out a pair of longnecks. He handed me one. Sweat formed on the glass.

"What about Janet?"

I twisted the top off. I was tired of questions about Valdosta and Janet. I'd been asking them myself all day. I took a slug. The beer was cool against the lining of my throat. I felt hot all over, like I had a fever. Maybe I should go and live in a jungle where there were only monkeys and parrots. I didn't like questions anymore. Especially ones involving me. Maybe I was allergic to them. I liked that concept and played with it for a few seconds.

"Things just went sour between us. Nobody's fault."

My tired eyes were jumping around and to focus them I stared at a picture on the wall above the bed. It was a picture of a flower in a pewtery looking vase. It was a reproduction. The flower petals were smeary looking, a weird blue, the blue you see in the eyes of old men of the sea. I'd seen that blue in the alleys of New Orleans in the hot summery dusks.

I drank beer and studied that shade of blue. It was an old timey blue, a spooky blue. Staring at it made me feel old too. Old and blue and smeary.

"Inseparables always tear apart in the end," I said, still staring at that picture. The phrase kept resonating in my hot brain until I said the words again. Then I twisted my face away and looked at Ken.

He was staring at me like I'd been staring at the picture—like he was memorizing my face. He lifted his beer and his head tilted back until he was staring at the water stains on the ceiling. He drank for a long time. Just to be sociable I took another sip. Then I looked out his one window. The glass was dirty and water specked. The pine trees looked cooler and darker than I remembered.

"Ray," he said, setting his bottle on the table and walking toward the back of the unit, "I've got to grab a shower. Help yourself to another beer, okay?"

"Sure."

"Won't be long, but I've got to get some of this sweat and crud off me."

"Hear that."

"After I take my shower I'll drop you off anywhere you like. Downtown, or the bus station. Wherever. We can have a real good talk about old times on the drive."

I felt hot all over and I must have looked at him funny, 'cause he stopped and shrugged and said. "Sorry, to cut out on you, Ray, but I didn't know you were coming. Got a date tonight." He winked. "A hot date. You know how it is. Plus, I've got to work tomorrow. Life is just too full right now, if you know what I mean." He made his eyebrows crawl like drunken red caterpillars. He winked at me again. Dusk had started to fall and the light was changing and now his eyes were exactly the same shade of blue as the flower petals in the painting.

I took another drink of beer, a longer one. Yeah, I thought, his eyes looked smeary now.

"I could just wait for you here, Ken. Don't mind at all. Save you having to drop me somewhere."

I looked up then. He was pulling his dirty shirt over his head.

"It's not like I have anywhere I have to be."

For a minute the shirt covered his head. Then he jerked it off and tossed it on one of the kitchen chairs. "Ray," he said, tilting his head to one side and half smiling, "I'll probably be bringing her here after the movie. For an intimate interlude, if you know what I mean."

I might drink a little too much and am occasionally stubborn, but I could recognize the old brush off. I drained my beer. "Go grab your shower," I said.

"You want another beer?"

"Sure," I said, "hand me another one." I could have gotten it myself but I was hacked. All this way and all I get is a couple of beers in a lousy 1950's tourist cabin.

I sat at the table, listening to the water running, starring at the picture on the wall. I finished the beer. Ken was taking one hell of a long shower. Then the water stopped. I got up and snagged another beer. Standing there in front of that ancient refrigerator I realized I was tired of waiting on somebody to drop me off some place I didn't particularly want to go.

Or maybe I was just tired. What I really wanted right then was to go and lie down on Ken's bed and drink beer and smoke cigarettes and watch television. Anything so I didn't have to think about Roger or Miranda or Janet or Valdosta. Didn't even want to think about that poor sad driver hauling some other man's life to Miami. Just didn't want to think anymore.

Maybe that old war movie would be on again. This time, I told myself, I'd stay awake and see every frame. James Whitmore was a damn fine actor. Always gave you a performance to remember. Maybe he wasn't any kind of leading man, but he was the sort of guy you could see yourself having for a neighbor. Janet had never liked war films. She didn't like guns or tanks or men dying with their guts in their hands.

"You had a good home but you left, right."

Yeah, I sure wanted to go lie on that bed, but I knew Ken would be leaving soon. At least I had experience with leaving. Since I had to go, I figured I might as well head outside. Before I left I helped myself to a couple more beers. I left Ken one beer. He had a sad refrigerator. The only other items in there were some sliced bologna, a tomato with a bad spot, three or four slices of fake cheese, and something shaped like a bar of moldy soap on the back of the bottom shelf.

I opened the door and stepped outside. The air had turned musty purple. Trucks were humming out on the highway. Between the hummings I heard Ken call my name, but I didn't want to talk to him anymore.

As quickly as I could I gathered up all my stuff and hustled off into the pines. Janet and I had picnicked once in some pines out in Oregon. Multnomah Falls.

A cardinal whirled scarlet before me. There had been lots of birds in Oregon. I wondered what Janet was doing now. I wondered if she ever thought about Multnomah Falls.

Pine needles scratched at my face and mosquitoes whined in my ears. It was dark in the pines. I put three large pines between me and Ramsey's and sat down with my back against the biggest pine I'd seen since Oregon. Out there in the enveloping night the big rigs were really whining.

I wondered if my buddy from Maryland had delivered that load of furniture. Would he ever hook back up with his wife? Funny, but sitting there in the deepening dark it seemed real important that the man from Maryland get back together with his wife. I drank to their happiness.

I sat there quietly in that pine thicket, drinking beer and watching the lights come on all along the highway. They were swaying a little, blinking now and then like they were signaling me. Only I couldn't decipher the message. I finished the beer and opened another.

Ken was outside now. I could hear him calling my name. He called it over and over. Then I heard him thrashing around the brush. I sat real still and listened to Ken's thrashing and cursing and the whine of the mosquitoes and all those voices inside my head.

A whippoorwill started up down by the road. Somebody had fired up a grill in back of one of the units. I could smell the burning charcoal. I bet myself they were grilling at the flamingo pink unit.

I couldn't hear Ken anymore. I stood up and peered through the darkness. His truck was backing out of its parking place. I watched it roll away until its image merged with the greater darkness.

The ground seemed to be swaying and I sat back down and stared at the lights along the highway and drank my last beer, thinking about what lay behind me and what lay before me.

When I finished the beer the moon had come out and the whip-poorwill had gone silent. Tossing the bottle into the undergrowth, I picked up my worldly possessions and started walking for the highway, chanting softly, "You had a good home, but you left, right."

Maybe I'd go back to Valdosta, I thought, but first I'd take a side trip to Maryland. Never had seen Chesapeake Bay. Then again, maybe I'd walk all the way to Multnomah Falls.

The big rigs whined in the night and the mosquitoes whined in my ears.

"You had a good home, but you left, right."

MEATLOAF SPECIAL

IT WAS TUESDAY NIGHT and it was raining. You could hear the rain pecking on the glass. We were eating supper. At least my wife and I were still sitting at the table. I was drinking coffee and she was picking at her green beans. She looked tired. After eight hours of running a checkout counter down at the Kroger on Grinstead she was about worn down.

She used to work part-time, a couple of days a week. But after I got laid-off back in March, she aggravated Mr. Baker, the manager, until he put her on full-time. At first I wasn't crazy about the idea. Back then I was still drawing unemployment and hoping the construction business would turn around. The last couple of months she'd been working full-time and I'd been trying to help around the house. Even cooked a little. Meatloaf was my specialty.

"God, I'm tired," she said.

"You look it. Hard day?"

"You wouldn't believe it. Must be that Labor Day is coming up. Bet I rang up fifty bags of charcoal and I couldn't begin to count the hot dogs. Not to mention the buns and the soft drinks."

"What about marshmallows?

"What about them?"

"Sell any?"

My wife gave me a tired look. Tired like she was tired from working and with my questions and of me. "Why do you want to know, Ralph? Why in the hell do you care about people buying marshmallows?"

I set my cup down and got up and walked over to the window. When she was tired she wasn't interested in answering questions. You could see the rain falling in the streetlights. The drops were making dimples in the puddles. It was really raining out there. It would be a terrible night to be out in all that rain.

"I don't really care," I said, still looking out at the rain. "I was just thinking about when I was a kid and my mom and dad used to take us on picnics. We'd drive out to Bernheim Forest and hike and look at the birds and squirrels, and almost every time before we came home we'd roast hot dogs and marshmallows."

"Maybe you ought to think about getting a job."

"I always burnt my marshmallows."

"Did you hear what I said?"

I turned around and looked at my wife. She was stuffing green beans in her mouth. She chewed them up and then she shoveled a load of mashed potatoes in.

"I heard you," I said and walked back to the table and started picking up dirty dishes.

"Did you even check the classifieds today? Or did you just sit around drinking beer and smoking your nasty cigarettes."

"I looked."

"And?"

"Nothing, unless you're a nurse or a music teacher."

"Bill got a job. He got a job and he was laid off the same day you were."

"I know," I said and carried my plate and silverware into the kitchen. I placed them on the counter and hauled out the dishpan. Bill and I had worked together at Snyder Construction. Since he lived just across the breezeway we'd usually ridden to work together.

I squeezed some dishwashing liquid into the pan and turned on the hot water. "Yeah, but I don't have a brother in Arizona who builds highways."

My wife sipped at her iced tea. She wrinkled her nose. Not enough sugar, probably. "He sends Allison at least a hundred dollars a week, sometimes more."

"Good for him. You wanna bring me your dirty dishes?"

"Help yourself, Ralph. I'm gonna go check on Allison. I've haven't talked to her all week. Bet she's really lonely without Bill."

"Probably so," I said, plunging my hands into the water. The water was too damn hot and I bit my lip. My wife said something on her way out the door, but I wasn't listening.

I finished the dishes and wiped off the counters. I thought about sweeping the kitchen floor. Instead, I got a beer out of the fridge and went into the living room and sat down and turned on the radio. There was a Reds game on and I drank my beer and smoked a cigarette and listened to the Reds. It was the fifth inning and the Reds were trailing the Cardinals 7-5. Pitching had been our problem all summer. My wife came back during the seventh inning stretch and I got up and followed her into the bedroom.

I sat on the side of the bed and watched her undress. For the first time I noticed that she was getting a little thick around the middle. Her breasts still looked good though. She sighed a little as she unhooked her bra.

"How was Allison doing?"

My wife rubbed her breasts and made a face. "Damn that bra's a killer." She shook her hair out. "Lonely, like I figured."

"She heard from Bill?"

"Last week, she said."

"He liking the job?"

My wife shrugged. "I don't know. She just said he sent her an envelope with five twenties in it."

"No note?"

"She didn't say. Mostly, we talked about a movie she went to see."

"What movie was that?"

"The one down at the Rialto. The comedy I wanted us to go to. Remember?"

"Aw, Becky, you know I can't stand those silly romantic comedies."

"And I'm supposed to go with you to all those old war movies?"

I lay back on the bed and patted the comforter. "It's not so late," I said, looking at her reflection in the mirror on the back of the bathroom door. "You wanna fool around?"

"Oh, Ralph, It's almost ten and I still have to take a bath."

"I don't mind waiting."

"Ah, honey. You know I've got to work tomorrow."

"Just something quick."

She tossed her bra in the hamper and stepped out of her panties. They were blue, with little white dots. For a minute she stood there naked as the day she was born, just staring at me. I stared right back at her. She eased into the shadows on the far side of the room. I wondered what she was thinking. My wife has one of those inscrutable faces, like you read about in detective stories. I began to think she wasn't going to answer me.

Finally, she sighed and leaned against the wall. "When are you going to get a job, Ralph?"

"I'll start looking hard tomorrow."

She shook her head. "That's what you always say," she said, and started walking toward the bathroom. I watched her butt cheeks wobble as she walked. My wife always has had a nice ass.

She shut the door and I heard the lock click. In a minute I heard water running. I lay there and listened to the water run. Then it stopped and I heard her step into the tub and out of nowhere I remembered when we were first married and she liked to take bubble baths in the evening. Back then I would go on in and sit on the toilet and watch all those bubbles and marvel at how soft and smooth her skin was. Sometimes I would bend over and kiss her. A couple of times I even took off my clothes and got in the tub with her.

I listened for a while, remembering those sweet, first days. Then I got up and went and grabbed another beer and turned out all the lights except for the reading lamp and stretched out on the couch with a detective magazine.

I read about a superintendent of schools in Illinois who murdered his wife because she had been fooling around with the basketball coach. Then I read about a woman who hired a guy to kill her husband for the insurance.

I got to wondering about Bill and how he was doing out in Arizona. Then I got to thinking about Allison. Becky was probably right, Allison was undoubtedly lonely. I finished my beer and turned out the light and smoked a cigarette in the dark, watching the lights of the passing cars reflect off the windows across the street and thought about my wife, and Allison. Without old Bill around, I figured Allison must be pretty lonely. Lonely I understood.

Just before I dozed off I heard the midnight freight rumble by on its way to the coast. Half asleep, I sorta wished I was on that old train, no matter where it was headed.

After my wife left for work in the morning I remembered I was out of cigarettes. If I'd remembered in time I could have had her pick me up a carton at Kroger's. Still, I wanted a smoke to go with my second cup of coffee. I didn't want to walk the six or seven blocks down to the 7-11, but I also didn't feel like going without any smokes all day.

The air was cooler than I'd expected and I went back inside and pulled my old windbreaker out of the closet. I hadn't worn it since early spring and once I got out in the sunlight I could see a big stain on the left sleeve. There was even a rip down at the bottom. I vaguely remembered getting hung up on a corner of a piece of tin Bill and I were using to patch a barn roof. As I started down the stairs, I thought about old Bill and wondered how he liked driving a truck for his brother. Then I thought about my wife's voice nagging at me about getting a job.

The wind was up, blowing dust in the air and yellowing newspapers and empty Styrofoam cups into the street. That morning was full of aromas, diesel fuel, dog shit, and rotting garbage. The air was cooler than the day before and clouds scuttled across the sky like something dangerous was after them. Somehow the day felt different than the ones that had preceded it, as though some essential element had changed.

Halfway down the block I heard someone call my name. Under the whine of the wind and the traffic it was difficult to tell where it was coming from. I leaned against the red brick building and listened. I had an aunt who heard voices. Later, she saw little green and blue people. I had enough trouble without hearing voices.

In a minute somebody called "Ralph" again and I stepped away from the building and looked back towards my apartment building.

Allison was leaning over the balcony railing, her auburn hair blowing in the wind, waving. I hadn't seen her since Bill left for the job in Arizona and something about her seemed different. I waved back. After a few seconds I figured out that she had let her hair grow. That made her look younger, wilder, although maybe part of the wild look was due to wind. Still, something about her at that moment made me think of a wild animal.

"Hey, Ralph, where you going?"

"Down to the 7-11. I'm out of cigs."

"Good deal. That's where I hoped you might be headed. Would you mind to bring me back a pack of menthols? The generic brand."

"Sure."

"Can I pay you when you get back? I'm having trouble finding my purse this morning."

"Okay," I yelled.

She waved and shouted something, but the wind kicked up again and I couldn't catch what she said. So I just smiled and waved. When I rounded the corner I stopped and counted my money. If I bought generic I'd have enough. That thought brought me up short. Like I'd been drifting and banged into a brick wall.

As I walked by Suliman's Dental Clinic I repeated the word drifting, drifting, drifting, changing the inflection each time. Something about the word had struck a chord. Three blocks later I'd figured it out.

When I was a kid, my mom and I lived for a couple of years with her mother. My dad had moved out and jobs were hard to find for a woman who only had a tenth grade education and didn't know typing. Lot of Sunday nights my Grandma Angeluci took me to church. I still remembered the name of the church, Grace Pentecostal. Remembered the preacher, too. He was fat and had greasy black hair.

What I remembered best about Grace Pentecostal was the singing. Folks there sang a lot. Loudly. One of their favorite hymns was something about "drifting too far from the shore."

By the time I got back up the stairs I was slightly out of breath. I knocked on the door. Traffic was picking up and I leaned against the wall and listened to all those people who were in a hurry to go somewhere. Some of the people were in such a hurry that they were blowing their horns. Just a few months ago I'd have been one of the people. Probably I'd have been blowing my horn. Sure, I needed a job, but I had to admit I was sort of glad I was out of the rat race.

I knocked again. In a few seconds I heard footsteps. The door opened and Allison stuck her head out. She was blinking and her eyes had a glassy sheen. She shook her head. Her hair was full of tangles.

"Oh, hey Ralph, come on in."

I stepped inside and closed the door behind me with one foot. I hadn't been inside the apartment since Bill went west and it felt spooky standing there knowing he was a thousand miles away.

I'd bought two cups of coffee to go with the cigarettes and I handed her one. "Got us some coffee. Wasn't sure if you took anything with your coffee?"

"Anything's fine. Did you get the cigs? I'm dying for a smoke."

I dug her pack out of my pocket and handed it to her. Her fingertips were cool.

She nodded at the couch. It was in the middle of the living room, directly in front of the television. The set was on, but the sound was turned down so all that you could hear was a low murmur.

I sat down on one end of the couch and took the lid off my coffee cup. I peered at the TV through the steam. A man with shellacked hair appeared to be selling cookware sets. He held a box up to the camera. The name of the cookware was scripted on the box. Goucher Waterless Cookware, Windsor, Connecticut.

I could hear Allison moving around in the kitchen. The refrigerator door opened and closed. A cabinet door slapped shut. Glass tinkled. Her footsteps were slow, as though she was looking for something or had lost her way. I started to say something, but then I heard her humming to herself. It was a tune that made you think of roses and moon shadows. I was sure I'd heard it before, but I couldn't name it.

I was still trying to remember the name of the tune when she came into the living room. She walked in front of the television and sat down in Bill's recliner. For the first time I noticed that the leather was cracked. I sat back and sipped coffee.

The man selling cookware had given way to a hemorrhoid commercial. Hemorrhoids were not my problem. I watched Allison light a cigarette. She put the lighter down and took a long draw, then pursed her lips and exhaled smoke.

"Thanks for going, hon. You don't know how bad I needed a smoke."

"No problem. I was going anyway."

She nodded. I took another sip of coffee.

"Bill used to buy our cigarettes. I always forget until I get home." She shook her head and turned her eyes to the TV. The commercial was over and now a woman with the longest neck I'd ever seen was holding up a necklace. Something in the necklace sparkled.

"He used to buy them by the cartons."

"Heard from him lately?"

"Got a letter yesterday."

"He doing okay?"

"Has a cold."

"Sorry to hear that."

"Yeah."

Another woman walked on stage. She had six or seven bracelets on each arm. She stood beside the other woman and shook her bracelets at the camera. I wondered if wearing that many bracelets was bad for her arms.

"Hey, Ralph," Allison said.

I tore myself away from the bracelet queen and looked at Bill's wife.

"I added a little something extra to my coffee. You maybe want some, too?"

She made her eyebrows do jumping jacks. She had green eyes, more emerald than jade. I couldn't remember ever noticing that before. They reminded me of a certain cove on Dale Hollow Lake.

"Really perks the coffee up."

The coffee was pretty lousy. A Hindu family ran the 7-11, and whatever their specialty was, it wasn't coffee. A shot couldn't hurt.

"Sure," I said and she smiled and set her coffee on an end table and pushed out of the recliner. She was still in her bathrobe and the robe sort of came apart, revealing a lot of thigh. I watched her stroll to the kitchen. Under the robe her bottom wobbled and she was careful about placing her feet. I started wondering a little then.

In a couple of minutes she was back with a pint of Old Granddad. She splashed a little in my cup. I stirred it around with a finger.

She walked over to her chair and sat down. Then she poured more whiskey into her coffee and fired up another cigarette. She smiled at me through the smoke and I nodded back.

We sat quietly for a while, drinking coffee, watching a game show. Then we watched the news and then one of the last of the soap operas came on.

"Gets a little lonely now and then, you know?"

I looked at her then. Her eyes were open, but I didn't think she was seeing anything in the room.

"Life gets that way sometimes," I said.

She nodded, but kept staring at whatever world she was seeing.

"Ralph?"

"Yeah."

"You think things ever turn out the way you want them to? I mean exactly. The way you might dream them?"

"Suppose they could," I said.

"Have you ever known them to? I mean personally?"

"No, not personally, but I'm only one guy and it's a big old world out there."

"Yeah," she said, "guess it is."

She went quiet and the rumble of the traffic floated through the room like a displaced spirit. I stood up and walked over and looked out the window. A garbage truck was rolling by, headed west. Coming east was a line of cars with headlights burning. At the front of the line was a hearse.

Directly below her window an old man walked a decrepit looking basset hound. As I watched them work their way down the block, I noticed a dead pigeon in the gutter. Dead flies littered the windowsill. Nothing but the dead and the dying, I said to myself.

Looking out the window depressed me so I headed back for the couch. On the way I stopped off and poured Allison a shot. Her cup was empty. So was mine. I poured us both a stiff shot. Seemed like one of those days where a man just needed a little something extra to help him survive. I sat and sipped and thought about Becky working and how I should probably be out looking for a job. Tomorrow, I promised myself, tomorrow.

The soap opera was over and I counted seven commercials before a rerun of some comedy my wife used to like came on. One of the characters talked through his nose. His voice grated on my nerves. I could feel a headache coming on and I figured Allison might be getting one, too, so I poured us both another drink. Only a half-inch or so of liquid swirled around the bottom of the bottle.

During the next show, which was some kind of home repair number with a guy who looked like he had never carried a two-by-four in his life, she dozed off. The man was dressed in designer jeans. Even wore an earring. Never worked with a guy who wore an earring, although I'd heard some of the younger dudes were starting to sport them.

Earring man and his crew were renovating a kitchen. Halfway through ripping a wall down to the studs, Allison started snoring. I eased off the couch as quietly as I could and tiptoed to the door. It squeaked as I swung it open, but she only stirred in her sleep and let her head fall back against the back of the recliner.

For a few minutes I stood at the railing, watching the cars and the clouds and the crazy man on the corner who was wearing three or four coats and a Santa hat and shouting at cars as they rolled by. I couldn't catch all of what he was saying, but the gist of it was that he was the Prophet Alphonso and he was delivering a message straight from somebody he called the Holy Anointed One. The message was that change was coming and every man, woman, and child needed to be purifying their soul.

I looked at my watch. My wife would be home in an hour. I was supposed to cook meatloaf tonight. It was one of her favorites. My secret ingredients were eggs, olive oil, bread crumbs, and steel-cut oats.

The crazy guy on the corner looked up and saw me. He started pointing and jumping up and down. I waved. He waved back. Then he saluted, a crisp military salute. I'd served a tour in Uncle Sam's armed forces, so I snapped one off and turned and headed for my apartment. Becky would have had a long day. Probably would have grabbed a Coke and some Nabs for lunch. She would be starved. Meatloaf was the least I could do.

I guess the meatloaf was alright. It looked okay. I thought it tasted fine. My wife didn't say whether she liked it or not. She did eat some along with a couple of slices of bread and some corn I'd warmed up from a can.

She didn't say much, though. Even when I asked her about her day she didn't do more than mumble a few words and sip on her iced tea. After supper, she pushed back and went into the living room and turned on the TV.

I gathered up the dishes and carried them into the kitchen. I put away the leftovers and washed the dishes. While I was getting that done I drank a beer.

I stood in front of the sink for a long time. Maybe it was that beer, but inside my mind everything was real calm and peaceful. I could hear the murmur of the television and my belly was full and faint traces of my wife's scent lingered in the room like lost butterflies. The dishwater was warm and it was pleasant to rub the dishrag across the smooth surfaces. It seemed like nothing bad had ever happened to me, or ever would.

As I was finishing up on the meatloaf pan I got to wondering what Allison was doing. Part of me wanted to go over and knock on her door, but I could hear the canned laughter on the television and I knew what I was thinking was only trouble. I wedged the meatloaf pan on top and draped a towel over the pyramid. On the way to the living room I grabbed another beer.

Becky was sprawled out on the couch. Her bare feet dangled. I sat down in my chair. A show about some silly people in a restaurant was on the tube. I sipped on my beer and watched two waitresses throw spaghetti at a cranky old man sitting in front of the counter.

When the commercial came on, I asked, "Hard day?"

"Busy," my wife said, "busy and long." She twisted over onto her side and looked at me. She wasn't wearing her glasses. Her whole face looked like it was sagging. I felt sorry for her.

"And what did you do all day?"

I shrugged. "Oh, I did a little housework and watched some TV. Took a long walk. Cooked supper."

"Put in any applications?"

I took a hit off my beer. "Didn't see any Help Wanted signs."

"You have to ask sometimes, Ralph. What do you think? They're going to come out on the sidewalk and beg you to come work for them?"

"You never know, Bec, you just never know."

"Maybe not Ralph, but I sure as hell know one thing."

"And what's that?" I asked, easing back in my chair and putting my feet up on the footstool her mother gave us last Christmas.

"You're lazy, that's what. I work myself to death and you sit around and watch TV and take long walks. There's something bad wrong with that picture, Ralph."

"Now, hon..."

"Don't now hon me." She sat up and swung her feet on the floor. "I've had enough. Every other man I know has a job. Even all those guys that got laid-off with you. Even Bill."

"You want me to go to Arizona, Becky?"

She stood up and stared down at me. I couldn't be for sure, but it sorta looked like her eyes were tearing up. "I don't care where you go, Ralph. I'm going to bed."

I sat there and watched her walk to the bedroom. When the door had clicked shut, I got up and crossed the room and stretched out on the couch. The cushions were still warm and I could smell remnants of her perfume.

I turned the volume down and for a long time I simply lay still, smelling her passing, listening to the faint, intermittent throb of the late traffic, staring at the ceiling, trying to make sense of everything. Never did reach any conclusion. When the news came on I got up and went and corralled another beer. Only had two left.

I carried my beer over to the window and drank it standing up. Outside the moon was up and pouring down out of the sky like wayward cream. Moonlight splashed through the Bradford pears and painted pale mosaics on the grass. At the same time I could see the silent, flickering reflection of the television screen in the window glass. The dual images made me feel like I was a man seeing two different universes at the same time, and trying to live a little in each one.

I finished my beer. An old Gary Cooper movie came on. I grabbed the next-to-last beer and sauntered back to the couch. The bedroom door was still closed.

Coop was a sheriff in a town called Hadleyville. I'd seen the movie before. When the bad guys ride into town, the rest of the town deserts old Gary. He has to fight his battle all alone. Being alone was no fun. For sure, I knew that.

Halfway through the movie I finished the beer and got up and went to the bathroom. On the way back to the couch, I grabbed the final beer. Last thing I remember was Gary Cooper standing in the middle of the street, slinging sweat and looking worn out and scared at the same time.

Metal clanging against metal jarred me awake. My head felt like an overripe cantaloupe, beginning to come apart at the seams. Moving as gently as possible, I raised my head.

My wife was in the kitchen, scrambling eggs. My stomach turned over and I got up in a hurry and hustled to the bathroom.

Even after mouthwash, I could still taste vomit. I filled a glass from the tap and sipped. Becky was finishing up her eggs and toast when I poured myself a cup of coffee and sat down.

"Morning," I mumbled.

She snorted and chuckled artificially. "Aren't you a pretty sight this morning?"

Her voice sounded shrill. My brain throbbed. "Give me a break, Becky," I said.

She shook her head. "God, Ralph, if you could see yourself. You'd better get a grip, and quick, 'cause you look like you're on a long, downhill slide."

I swallowed a little coffee. "It's not that bad."

"Ever since you got laid-off you've been going the wrong way, sitting around all day, smoking and drinking and watching television. For pity sake, Ralph, get out and hunt a job. Be a man for a change. I'm tired of carrying the whole load."

"Hey," I said, "don't I cook and clean and get in groceries?" I lifted my head and looked across the table. Her face might have been marble.

"Alright, I'm only carrying ninety-five percent."

"Okay, Becky, I'll look for a job today."

She pushed back and stood up and carried her plate over to the sink. When she had finished running water, she turned. "All I can say, Ralph, is I hope you do. At least look. Surely you can do that much."

I drank more coffee. "You'll see, I'll make something happen."

Her lips smiled then, but her eyes didn't bother. "I hope so, Ralph. I'm not going to put up with your lazy butt ways much longer. I'm tired of coming home night after night, with my legs aching and my back breaking, too tired to do anything fun. Hell, Ralph, most nights I'm almost too damn tired to eat."

"Ah, baby, I'm sorry. I'll find something."

Her eyes stared at me until I felt like my skin was staring to burn. "Don't you care? Don't you care about us?"

"Becky, I love you. Surely, you know that."

She shrugged. "Talk is cheap, Ralph, real cheap."

I tried to think of something clever to say. Only after so many beers and dead men face down in the dust I couldn't think of a single thing to say that would make any real difference. Anyway, she was right. Talk is cheap. Gary Cooper had proved that. I sat there and watched her face change.

She rearranged her mouth and turned on her heel and went and brushed her teeth and fixed her face. I drank my coffee and was pouring another cup when she headed for the door.

As she walked by I reached out a hand and tugged her closer. I wanted to give her a kiss, but she turned her head and my awkward mouth only brushed the side of her face.

"Have a good day," I said to her back.

The door swung open and she stepped into the hall. She twisted her neck and peered over her shoulder.

"Try to find a job, Ralph."

"You can count on me."

She nodded and sighed and went down the hall. I stood leaning against the counter and listened to her going down the stairs. Then I carried my cup back over to the table and tried to think what I should do and how I could make my mind quit quivering.

In the end I walked back down to the 7-11. The owner, an older guy, was behind the counter. When my wife and I talked about him, I always referred to him as the Hindu. Actually, I think his real name was Habib.

Anyway, when I put my twelve-pack of Bud on the counter he quit straightening up the cigs and came over. He nodded and I nodded back. He nodded again and I said "Good morning."

He smiled and said something that might have been good morning. I'm not sure. I was too busy staring at his teeth. Old Habib had very bad teeth. Several of them were broken off short, while some of the others had dark spots. Worse, some sort of red juice was floating around in his mouth. For a second I thought it might be blood. Then he spit some into a Styrofoam coffee cup. I was about to ask him what it was when I remembered I'd promised to look for a job.

"Need any help around here?" I asked.

"What?" he said, "what are you asking?"

99

His black eyes were open wide and flickering like a broken movie projector. He had wild eyes, like one of those fakirs I'd heard about on a National Geographic special. Those eyes sort of chilled me off some. They made me wonder if he had a machete or a bolo knife under the counter.

"I was asking if you needed any help around the store. You know, like a clerk to work the night shift. I'm sorta between jobs at the moment, you see."

"A job? You want a job?"

I nodded. "That's the idea."

He looked down his nose at me for a minute. He had a very long nose. It was thin, like giant fingers had pinched it almost closed. I wondered how he breathed. Maybe, I thought, that was why he spoke in such a high-pitched voice.

"No," he said, "I have no jobs. My sons work for me, all three of them, and my wife and my daughter. That is enough. I do not need any more help." He grinned and leaned closer. His breath was bad, like he'd been gnawing on decaying meat. "Sometimes, I think I already have too much help." He tittered like a damn girl. "My wife, you know."

His eyes glowed like a lion's that I'd seen once at the zoo. His tittering made my skin pucker. I paid for the beer and got the hell out. It felt good to breathe fresh air, even if was sort of smoggy. It also felt good to know that I could honestly tell my wife that I been looking for work.

I honestly meant to just haul my beer up to my apartment and sit around watching television. I planned on doing some light housework during the commercials. If there wasn't anything good on, I might walk down to the corner and get a paper and go through the classifieds, marking a few want ads with a pencil, just to show how serious I was. But, somehow, when I got to the top of the stairs, instead of turning left, I turned right and marched down the breezeway and knocked on Allison's door.

I wasn't sure what to expect. I could hear her moving around inside her apartment.

"Who is it?"

"Ralph."

"Oh, hey, great. Hang on just a sec." She rattled the chain and then the door swung open. She was brushing her hair and had on a negligee the color of ripe peaches.

"Oh, goody, you brought us something to drink. Don't just stand there."

I stepped inside and handed her the twelve pack. It felt like I was giving her a present, for her birthday or Christmas or something.

She looked at the twelve pack for a minute and then she sat it down on a table by the door and stood up and gave me a kiss. She had to stand on her tiptoes. She wasn't very tall and she was barefoot.

"You're a sweetie."

"How's that?"

"For coming by to visit and bringing along all this good beer." She kissed me again. She had soft lips. Her breath smelled like Colgate.

"I'll just go and put them all in the fridge." She picked up the beers and started for the fridge. "Unless you want one now?" she said, over her shoulder.

I could tell by the way she asked the question that she was ready for a beer now. I glanced at my watch. A quarter to eleven. What the hell.

"Don't guess one could hurt," I said.

She pulled her head out of the refrigerator and smiled. I could see the tops of her breasts. They looked smooth and pale.

After we drank the first beer, she said she was hungry and got up and fixed us tuna salad. While she worked on lunch she drank another beer. I kept her company. We drank another beer with the tuna.

The same old shows were on TV. I didn't understand how anybody could watch that crap day after day. Even the news at noon seemed the same. Only the fires and the burglaries were taking place in different houses from the day before.

As near as I could tell, she didn't care much for the programming either. Or maybe she was just a little nervous. She kept getting up to change the channel, or rejigger the blinds, or go to the bathroom. Sometime during the course of the morning she had squirted on some perfume. We drank another beer apiece and talked a little. Not about any big world events. Just everyday things like the weather and the price of hamburger and how it got kind of lonely with your spouse at work or out of town.

Just before two o'clock she stood up and looked at me. A big old smile was spreading across her face. After four beers and a bellyful of tuna salad I wasn't feeling too bad, myself.

"I feel like dancing," she said, and twirled like a top. She spun all the way around twice. When she was twirling herself she put me in mind of a young girl I'd known growing up in Butchertown.

She stopped twirling and when she quit laughing she leaned her face toward me like she was going to kiss me again, only this time she just said, "Let's dance. You feel like dancing, Ralph?"

Now I'm one of the top ten worst dancers in the world, but it was only the two of us and I'd had four beers. So I nodded and she went into the kitchen and turned the radio on and fiddled with the stations until she found one playing dance music that might have been new in the 40's.

She came back carrying two beers. She was still in her negligee and her little breasts bounced up and down as she walked.

We both took a good swig and then a real pretty slow dance tune came on and we looked right into each other's eyes and sat our beers down on the coffee table and wrapped our arms around each other and wobbled around the room. When the song was over we drank more beer. Later we danced another slow one. Somehow the melody to this song made you sad.

She laid her head on my shoulder. Her hair tickled my face. "Bill's been gone for over three months," she whispered.

"Sounds about right," I said, thinking of my wife and the way Allison's breasts were mashing against my chest at the same time. I felt a little lightheaded, too. But that was probably all the beer and tuna fish and slow dancing. We kept waltzing around the living room and she kept whispering.

"I haven't danced in forever."

"Me either."

She pressed tighter against me. She smelled like lemons and flowers and one minute past midnight. "Lots of things I haven't done in a long time, if you know what I mean?"

I slid my hand lower on her back. "Guess maybe I might."

She rubbed her lips along my neck. They were soft and moist. "You interested?"

I started rubbing the small of her back. Now and then my fingers drifted south. She didn't seem to mind. "In what?"

"Oh," she murmured, "in another beer? Or maybe something else?"

I twisted my arm and glanced at my watch over the top of her head. It was getting on for three. Still, my wife was working until five.

"Maybe, just maybe I am."

She quit dancing and pulled her head back and looked straight into my eyes. Her eyes seemed bright and sleepy at the same time. "In a beer or something else?"

I grinned at her. "Any reason a man can't have both?"

She smiled real wide and I could see where she was missing a tooth, way back on the left.

"Not a reason in the world," she said and lifted her face to me.

I kissed her then. Soft at first and then hard. When we broke the kiss off, she took my hand in hers and started walking toward the bedroom.

We took to fooling around a couple of days a week when we knew my wife would be at work. Allison was really good in bed. She had a nice little body and she could work it like a snake on a hot rock.

In between times, though, those get-togethers bothered me. I mean the fooling around and all. Never had been much of a church-goer or a Bible reader, but my mom had hauled me to Sunday school often enough when I was kid so that I understand right from wrong. But the Biblical right from wrong was treated by parents and preach-ers as an unbreakable law, one that couldn't be bent. Life wasn't that way, though. Black could be gray, or even white and it was hard to see things real clearly, especially while they are happening.

Between times next door I tried to be extra good at home. Seemed to me that I just might be able to offset some of my sinning by being extra nice to my wife. I'd try to have supper ready whenever she got home and I kept the place clean. Ran the vacuum cleaner just about every day. Even got to be a pretty good hand at dusting.

What pleased her most though was that just about every day I'd tell her where I'd been looking for work, or where I was going to go next and drop off an application. If it was a place across town, lots of times she'd give me cab fare.

Of course, I didn't really go to all those places. Lots of times I took the cab fare and bought beer and cigarettes. But I did go to some. Once I even got a job. The work was building a loading platform on the back of a warehouse down in the west end.

Anyway the work lasted for a couple of days and it made my wife real happy when I gave her two tens and a five out of my pay. She smiled real big and hugged and kissed me right on the mouth. That night after we turned the lights off, she scooted over to my side of the bed and snuggled up real tight. Then she went to rubbing and kissing on me. We hadn't made love in a long time and I'd been with Allison the day before, so I wasn't sure what to expect.

It turned out to be nice. I mean I got off and she acted like she did, too. Although with Becky I could never be sure. Funny thing was that the whole time we were doing it a part of my mind was wondering about Allison. Of course, sometimes I thought about my wife when I was screwing Allison. Guess I was messed up.

Fact was my whole life was a big mess. I wasn't working and I was drinking too much and starting to grow a beer gut. Plus, I was screwing my buddy's wife. Part of the time I wanted to keep on doing every single last thing and the rest of the time I just wanted to walk away and forget all about everyone. Sometimes, late at night, when I lay on my back staring into the dark, I felt like I was actually starting to split in half. The first time that happened I gave up drinking for three days.

If my wife suspected anything she never let on. Maybe she was more quiet than usual, but then she was working long hours. She got to working so many that after a while she started to complain. The manager at her Kroger's kept promising to hire more cashiers, but after a month neither of us believed him.

Allison and I weren't doing it every day. My wife had at least one and usually two days a week off. Then once in a while Allison had to go see her aunt in Hardin Memorial Hospital down in Elizabethtown and one time I fell down and broke off a tooth and had to go to the dentist. But most days we got together for what we called extracurricular activity.

This particular Tuesday my wife got up extra early. Mr. Baker, who was the manager at her Kroger's, had called a staff meeting for all employees. She figured it was a rahrah meeting to get the employees pumped for the upcoming holidays. I hadn't slept well the night before and was still shaving when she came in to say she was off.

For a minute she stood at the edge of the bathroom. I could see her face in the mirror and I studied it without turning around. Emotion was working beneath her makeup and I wondered what was on her mind. For the past couple of weeks she'd been giving me looks I hadn't seen before and I was afraid she was getting suspicious.

"You look nice," I said, although she didn't particularly. What she looked was tired.

"Thanks. Big meeting, you know."

"Hope it goes well."

"They might be hiring extra for the holidays, Ralph. They did last year. You ought to go down and put in an application."

"Ah, I wouldn't be any good with those new machines and all that money." I grinned at her in the mirror. "Never was good at making change."

"You wouldn't have to be a cashier. I know one of the stock boys quit last week and Ben Peterson in produce is going to retire right after Thanksgiving. He's been working there for over thirty years. You could be a stock boy, Ralph. It's not a bad place to work. We could maybe work together, huh?"

I twisted my neck and wrinkled up my face and ran the razor along my upper lip. "Yeah, guess I could swing by and drop off an application. Might do that this afternoon," I said.

I thought I said the words okay, but maybe not. Or maybe she read something in my face. Anyway, she sighed real deep like she was truly disappointed in me. That hurt, but it should have hurt more.

"I gotta go now, Ralph."

"Give me a kiss," I said, turning around.

She sighed again and paused long enough to turn up one smooth check. I kissed it lightly and she turned and walked across the bedroom like she was in a hurry. I could hear the front door slam over the buzz of the razor.

I finished shaving and studied the face in the mirror. It was my same old face yet there was something different about it, as though something elemental was in the process of changing. I studied it for some time. Finally, I decided that I didn't particularly like it. A certain hardness about the eyes bothered me. I told myself I was playing mind games with myself. Maybe my wife was right. Maybe I was spending too much time alone. Maybe I did need a job.

I combed my hair and got dressed. Then I went out to the kitchen. She hadn't even made any coffee. She always made coffee. For a minute I just stood there and looked at the empty pot. Something about the day felt out of synch. Like the world had shifted on its axis without warning.

After a while I started a pot of coffee. While it was brewing I went through my wife's dresser. When we first got married she kept a diary, but I hadn't seen her writing anything in it for years.

I didn't find anything I didn't expect, except a yellowing clipping of our wedding announcement and a small picture of us. It took me a couple of minutes to place it. We were in swimwear, standing on a raft in the middle of a vast expanse of blue water. The shoreline was behind us and boulders dotted the beach. Beyond the boulders the land was dark with pine trees.

After a couple of minutes I remembered that one day on our honeymoon we had driven over from Duluth and spent a pair of days and nights at a lake where one of my wife's aunts had owned a cabin on this lake. She let us borrow it for a weekend. Suddenly I could feel how cold the water was swimming out to this raft and how hot the sunlight had been on my back as we lay on the raft.

I could vaguely recall this guy coming by in a motor boat and taking our pictures. That part of the country was a popular vacation spot twenty years ago and I guess the fellow made a living taking photos of couples on their honeymoon and families on vacation. If I was remembering right he had reddish hair and a funny way of swallowing his vowels. I wondered if he was still alive. For no good reason that seemed important.

Why in the world had we gone to Duluth for our honeymoon? Why not Florida? Then I recalled that all her life my wife had wanted to stay in this fancy hotel in downtown Duluth. I'd forgotten the name, but remembered that they had big glass windows in the front and the lobby was full of sunlight and big chairs and lots of well-dressed people sitting in those chairs reading magazines with slick covers and smoking. Funny what a man will remember, and what he forgets.

I put the clipping and the photograph back where I'd found them and double checked to make sure I'd closed all the drawers. Then I went back to the kitchen and poured myself a cup of coffee. After looking at the photograph and the clipping I was feeling lonely, so I carried my cup on over to Allison's. She might be lonely, too, I thought. Halfway down the corridor I noticed I was still wearing my house shoes.

Two steps from Allison's apartment I stepped in a pile of dog shit. Had to be Mrs. Blaney's Boston terrier. She lived one floor below and was always letting that four-legged monster out. Without question, that dog was a shit manufacturer par excellence. I'd seen him in action.

I tried to wipe the crap off on the welcome mat, but I was afraid to wear the house shoes into Allison's. At the very least the odor would linger. I slipped them off and tapped on the door.

It took her longer than usual to come to the door, and when she did she had on a big old fuzzy green bathrobe at least two sizes too large. I figured it for Bill's.

I stepped inside and bent to give her a kiss. Instead of her lips, she turned up one side of her face. A sense of déjà vu washed over me. If I'd been smart I'd have retreated. Instead, being lonely, or horny—they're often the same—I just kept going.

She closed the door behind us and I walked over and sat down on the couch. I sipped my coffee and watched her walk around the room. Usually she came over and sat down beside me. Snuggled up, my mother would have said.

Today she walked back and forth in front of the window, pausing only to finger open the Venetian blinds now and then and peer out. Her pacing made me think of the big cats at the zoo. My wife and I used to go to the zoo each summer. We used to do a lot of things.

I finished my coffee. The last swallow was cold and afterwards a few grounds clung to my tongue. I picked them off and wiped them on the rim of the cup. Allison was standing at the window. I studied her back.

I put the empty cup down on the table. "Something bothering you?"

For a moment, she didn't even acknowledge that she had heard me. I was beginning to wonder what I had done wrong when she turned and walked across the room to a small desk tucked into one corner. A stack of papers leaned precariously on one edge of the desk. Surely, they weren't all bills. Allison wasn't one for paying attention to detail, but...

She plucked an envelope from the top of the pile and carried it back across the room and handed it to me.

"What's this?"

"A letter from Bill."

I glanced at the envelope. The postmark was Bisbee, Arizona.

"And?"

"And he's coming home."

I sat up straighter. My throat had gone kinda dry and I swallowed a couple of times to lubricate the old vocal chords. "When's he starting back?"

"Yesterday. At least that's what he said he was doing in his letter. He mailed it on Friday."

I looked more closely at the postmark.

"I only got the letter yesterday afternoon." Her voice broke on the last word and she turned and walked over to the window. Her shoulders were shaking. I got off the couch and walked over and held her. I rubbed her back real slow and whispered in her ear. All I could think to say was "It'll be alright," although I wasn't at all sure anything was going to be alright. For sure it wouldn't be the same again.

Her robe had gaped open and I could feel her breasts rubbing against my chest and in spite of the letter I started to get hard. I moved my hand lower on her back.

"Don't Ralph."

"But, baby, you feel so good."

She pulled her face back and the movement thrust her middle forward. I pressed against her.

"Quit, please."

"But why? You haven't minded before."

"Bill is on his way back now. He's driving here this very minute."

"You said he left yesterday. He couldn't possibly be within five hundred miles."

"It just doesn't seem right."

I bent my head and ran the tip of my tongue around one of her nipples. I could feel it hardening.

"And this doesn't feel right?" I said and began working us over to the couch.

"Don't Ralph," she said, but she wasn't hitting me or anything so I exerted a little more force and pressed her down on the couch. I knew it wasn't right, but I was in the mood and this might be my last chance. I promised myself I'd be a good and faithful husband after this.

Her legs had come apart and I wedged my body between them. "Just once more for old time's sake," I whispered as I unzipped.

"But, Ralph, I don't feel right about it."

"What makes today any different than yesterday?"

"I don't know," she said, "it just feels different."

"Well, see how this feels," I said and stuck it in.

For a minute I thought everything was going to be alright. She was starting to respond. I could feel her getting all wet down there and I started thrusting a little harder.

Then she started to cry, just a few sobs at first, then steady, but low. There was rhythm to her crying, like the sea.

I felt myself going limp and quit moving and just lay there on top of her, listening to her crying, thinking about what I had done, and become. All that thinking made me half sick to my stomach and I lay my head on her chest and listened to her cry.

It was surprisingly warm and comfortable and I closed my eyes. Gradually Allison's sobbing grew softer. A fragile peace seemed to have settled over the apartment. I tried to make my mind as calm and clear as a high mountain lake I'd seen once in Wyoming.

Allison grew very soft and still. I wondered if she was changing her mind. I eased my head to one side and studied her face. Her eyes were open, but they had that look that meant that she wasn't seeing me or anything else in the apartment. My guess was she was trying to see at least as far as Arizona.

There wasn't any use looking anymore. I could hear her breath and smell the coffee on her breath and the remnants of her perfume. Another essence seemed to linger. Whether it was regret or loneliness, or maybe nothing more, or less, than sadness I couldn't say. I lowered my head to her chest and listened to her heartbeat. Just hearing the rhythmic thumping made me feel better.

To tell the truth, I guess I dozed off. At least I drifted into that zone that is partly sleep and partly dream and yet allows your mind to retain some semblance of reality. The world felt warm and pleasant and I could sense my brain smoothing out.

Just at the edge of sleep I felt Allison stiffen beneath me. I heard her gasp and then she went as stiff as a corpse. I opened my eyes and looked at Allison's face. Her lower lip was trembling and her eyes were open wide.

"Goddamn you, Ralph. You son-of-a-bitch."

I gagged on the bile in my throat and rolled off Allison onto the floor, tugging on my pants and trying to think what in the hell I was going to say to my wife.

She was standing in the doorway and the light was behind her, framing her hair, half blinding me. "Now, hold on," I said.

"No," my wife screamed, "I'm not holding on, you lying bastard. I guess everything you have ever said to me has been a lie. Here I am working my ass off being nice to every old fart and bitch that has to have a loaf of bread or a half gallon of milk while your lazy ass is over here fucking somebody I thought was my friend."

Allison wriggled upright, pulling her robe around her. "Oh, Becky, I'm so sorry. I never meant to hurt you."

"Shut up, Allison, just shut the fuck up. I don't ever want to hear your voice again or see your face. And the same goes for you, mister."

For a moment my wife simply stood there trembling. I had my pants on now and I pushed off the floor and walked around behind a high-backed chair. From this angle, I could see that my wife had something in her hand. She had been known to throw things. This time I couldn't blame her.

"I came home to tell you the good news that I'm being made a manager at the store and I don't have to work until Thursday. I thought we might do something special." She shook her head. Her hair swung like a dark sail in shifting winds. "I just didn't know how special it was going to be, you asshole."

I could see now she had one of my house shoes in her hand. Damn that dog to hell. I swore I was going to kill that four-legged bastard if I never did another thing.

I glanced at Allison. She had turned and buried her face against the back of the couch. Her shoulders were shaking and her muffled sobs were harsh in the sudden quiet. My eyes shifted back to my wife. She was in the doorway, trembling the way a flower will in a thunderstorm.

"What's the matter, Ralph? Don't you have another lie for me?"

"Now, hon, it's not what you think."

"It's not?" She cocked her head. "You know, for once you might be right, it's probably worse."

"Now, baby..."

"Don't you now baby me, you son-of-a-bitch. Too goddamn sorry to work, but you can sure as hell fuck my friend. Alright you asshole, fuck her for all I care. Just get out of my life and stay out. Both of you."

I tried to tell her I was sorry then, but it was too late. Maybe it wouldn't have mattered anyway. She had started throwing things by then: my house shoes, the lamp on the table by the door, a vase full of flowers, books, figurines. Allison was sobbing and my wife was screaming and I was ducking and cussing when I could catch my breath. When my wife grabbed one of Allison's brass candlesticks I hustled into the bedroom and locked the door.

For a long time I could hear my wife smashing china and breaking glass. Several items shattered against the bedroom door. I sat with my back against it waiting for the storm to subside, planning how I could work my way out of the mess.

When the word work popped into my mind, I started to laugh this crazy laugh. If I'd only looked for a job none of this would have happened. The whole thing was funny as hell.

After what seemed like a long time I became conscious of a quiet. Moving cautiously, I stood up and cracked the door.

The front door was wide open and the living room was empty. I eased out into the living room, one arm protecting my face. I shouldn't have bothered. I started looking for Allison. We needed to talk. I glanced at my watch. By now, Bill must be in Oklahoma, maybe even Missouri. Yes indeed, Allison and I needed to have a long talk.

I found her locked in the bathroom. She wasn't talking. Not even a yes or a no. After ten minutes I gave up trying. Short of breaking down the door there was nothing I could do. And I'd fucked up plenty for one morning.

I wandered back into the living room and hunted around for my house shoes. The wind was whining in the breezeway. I figured the door to my apartment would be dead bolted. For once I was right.

I bruised my knuckles and wasted another ten minutes of my life pounding on the door. Finally I began to get worried that somebody would hear and call the police. There were plenty of nosy neighbors around.

I walked back over to Allison's. Maybe she would loan me a couple of dollars and one of Bill's old coats. There was a chill in the wind that was worrying its way into my bones.

Naturally her door was locked, too. I could see quite clearly that the day was only going to go downhill from there.

To keep warm I started walking. It was difficult to walk in my house shoes, but after a few minutes I fell into a sort of shuffle that, while I'm sure it looked awkward, actually propelled me right along. Before noon I'd walked all the way down to the Belvedere. I sat on an iron bench and watched the lunch crowd meander by, talking and kissing and eating sub sandwiches. By the time the crowd thinned out my ass was cold from sitting on that metal bench, so I got up and wandered along the river, staring at the dark, moving waters, trying to think.

In the end I walked all the way to old Habib's 7-11 and borrowed his cell phone. I tried to call Allison, but she wasn't answering. Then I tried my wife, but she hung up in my ear. I even tried to call my old boss, but all I got was his answering machine. I didn't bother with a message.

Instead, I gave Habib his phone back, turned and walked out into the dying afternoon. Habib probably would have given me a couple of bucks if I'd asked, but something wouldn't let me. Guess after a man gets so far down something in him refuses to go lower.

Back when I was working I'd driven by the Wayside Mission on East Market just about every day. I started hoofing it to the mission. Didn't see where I had much of a choice. By the time I made it the sky had gone hard dark and there were holes in the bottom of my house shoes.

People of mercy served at the Mission. Supper was long gone, but they rousted me up a cold meatloaf sandwich, a bag of greasy potato chips, and an apple that was only slightly bruised. As I ate I tried to remember when anything had tasted even half as good. In a way it seemed to me that the universe was playing a dirty trick on me with that meatloaf sandwich. Maybe I'd have to atone for my sins by eating meatloaf for the rest of my life.

My cot was in a corner next to the men's room. It didn't smell so good over there, but I had a warm blanket and my belly was reasonably full. Most of the night I just lay there, listening to men snore and fart and mumble in their tortured sleepings.

I didn't sleep much. Mostly I lay on my back thinking about my wife. She would never forgive me. I knew her. Before she did I'd be just another doddering old man with nasty pants sniveling in his lonely room at the old folk's home. By morning Bill would be deep into Illinois. Louisville was about out of possibilities for old Ralph. Even a fuck-up like me could see that.

In the morning they found me an old pair of sneakers that were only a half size too big and a purple and gold sweatshirt that at least was warm. After runny eggs and hard toast I wandered outside. The sun was out and the wind was down. The air was still cool though and I shivered as I hustled across Market.

I knew I was going somewhere. I just didn't know where. All my folks were dead and Bill had been my one friend. About the only thing I had going for me I figured was that I surely must have used up most of my bad luck.

As I bummed along I started singing the old Chuck Berry song, "No Particular Place to Go." I wished I had a car. Even a bus ticket to Akron would be nice. I used to know an old boy from Akron. He sold shoes for a while at the Oxmoor Mall. We got to talking about football one day. We both wished we'd played it in high school. He hadn't because he had a club foot. I hadn't because I was too lazy.

What I needed was a job, a fresh start, a vision. I meandered around downtown, trying to stay in the sunshine. By ten o'clock my guts were starting to growl. By eleven the wind had started to kick up again and I wished I'd thought to ask the mission for a cap and some gloves.

Around noon I found myself on Fourth Street walking toward the Lutheran Church with the wind at my back. The afternoon loomed before me like an endless, empty ocean. I felt like crying.

A TARC bus rolled by and then a Metro Police car. Everybody was going somewhere. Everybody but me. I was wandering straight to nowhere. As I walked by Ermin's Bakery I could smell bread baking and soup on the stove and my eyes started watering a tear or two. The wind was like a stiletto in my back.

Then I heard a funny barking, honking sound. At first I thought it was coming from the Cadillac lot on Fourth. Then I heard it again and looked up. A lopsided V of Canada geese were winging their way south. I stood on the corner and watched them until they were just a speck on the southern horizon.

Then I hitched up my shoulders and started jogging south following the geese. I was out of shape and wobbly on my feet. I got a stitch in my side and my breath rasped in my throat. But I kept jogging. One last lost bird, seeking shelter from the cold.

A Hell of a Lot of Years

THE CARDINAL WAS CRIMSON against the snow. Hurley Embry squinted from his bed across the room. Nowadays he watched the birds. What the hell else did he have to do? Read the Bible? He'd tried that; Exodus gave him indigestion.

Eighty-two years old and stuck in the damn Hickory Hills Nursing Home. Just because he had a fainting spell last month his daughter had stuck him in a nursing home. Claimed Doc Biddle said that he'd had a stroke. Well, so what if he had? A few days in bed and he felt damn near good as new. 'Cept for the headaches and the shortness of breath and a game leg. But that leg wasn't bad all the time, he told himself, only at the most embarrassing moment possible. In some ways his leg reminded him of Edna.

Never should have married that woman, Hurley thought. If he hadn't married her, he'd never had Lucinda as a daughter and wouldn't be in this hellhole. Lucinda had no intentions of taking care of an old man, even if he was her father, and stuck him in a home first chance she got.

Hickory Hills was one of those homes that looked good in the color brochures, but once you got in them, look out. In the six weeks he'd been there Hurley hadn't had a decent meal. Forget about a good meal, he'd settle for a cup of hot strong coffee.

Under the covers he squeezed a tennis ball he'd talked his son-in-law into smuggling in. Hickory Hills wanted patients to use stuff the home owned, then charge sky high fees. Damn place also had more rules than the army and that, Hurley knew from personal experience, was saying a lot.

About the only good thing Hurley could say about his daughter was that she had married Quentin Grigsby. Not that Quentin was any great shakes, but at least the boy minded. If it hadn't been for him coming by every day scattering sunflower seeds on the window sill, Hurley wouldn't have been able to watch the birds.

Not that he could see them good. Sorry staff never cleaned the windows. Course it was foolish to expect that since they didn't do much more than run a damp mop over the floor a couple of times a week, spray air freshener around until the room smelled like a whore-house, and hang one of those blue cakes over the side of the toilet. Three days ago he'd thrown a snotty Kleenex over in the corner just to see how long it would lay there. It was still there, big as day.

Getting old was hell. Never been so glad of anything in his life as when they pulled the catheter out. The Bible had those passages about weeping and wailing and gnashing of teeth. Whoever wrote that must have had to have a catheter. Talk about pain and suffering. He ought to sue.

Ever since the catheter had disappeared Hurley had felt his strength coming back. That was why he'd asked Quentin to bring him the tennis ball and why he did leg lifts under the sheets. Had worked his way up to one hundred a day. Late at night, when the aides were snoozing or playing cards in the break room, he'd begun walking around the room, making laps. Up to twelve now and no relapses.

Not that getting stronger was going to do him any good in here, and Lucinda wasn't about to let him out. Hurley balled up his fist and struck himself a good lick on his thigh. Most stupid thing he'd ever done, and that was saying something, was to sign those papers. Now he could hardly take a crap without her permission. And how she hated him. Okay, he'd been a bit rough on her when she was younger. But she was a headstrong young girl and needed discipline.

Hurley felt pressure in his bowels and raised one hindquarter off the air mattress and farted loudly. Damn, he thought, I'm rotten inside. Greasy meatloaf and prunes. Bastards were killing him. Maybe that was the plan. Well, he had a plan for them.

A slash of red caught his eye and he whipped around in time to see the cardinal winging it for a line of pines. A pair of sparrows were on the ledge now, and a dove. Sparrows were okay, nice ordinary birds, but he wasn't crazy about those doves, always cooing around. Hurley wished a blue jay would swoop in. Blue jays reminded him of himself when he was younger.

The door squeaked open and Sondra Johnson swished into the room. She was the day nurse and, from the expression on her face, not overly fond of him. Looked like she'd just bit down on a hunk of lemon rind.

That was all right, 'cause he wasn't particularly fond of her. Hurley had known her since she was a kid stopping by his Conoco Station to buy gum and candy, and later cigarettes. Always had a holier-than-thou air about her, he thought, and passed gas silently under the sheets.

"Here you go, Mr. Embry," she said, wrinkling her nose. "Time for your afternoon medicine." She sniffed. "Phew, what a stink. Have you messed yourself, Mr. Embry?"

"Don't think so," Hurley said, "but you're welcome to stick your finger down there and find out."

"Really don't think that will be necessary. I'll have one of the aides check you this evening. Now, take your pills like a good boy."

Good boy, my ass, Hurley thought as he palmed the pills. Three pills in the afternoon, every afternoon. The blue one was to calm him down, help him sleep. The green one was to help his bowels move. As far as he could find out the orange one was just a sugar pill.

He slid the orange one in his mouth and, when Sondra had her back turned fooling with the blood pressure monitor, he let the other two drop beneath the sheet. He was damn tired of calm and his bowels would move when they were good and ready. Had for over eighty years.

The nurse fussed around with a couple of machines he didn't understand and scratched on his chart. Hurley pretended to take the other two pills. A female cardinal fluttered down to the window sill and he watched her through the dirty glass. The sky was iron gray and smoothing over.

"Bet you it'll snow before dark," he said.

118

The nurse sniffed and glanced out the window. "You may be right. Got your pills all down?"

Hurley nodded.

"Good. Time for your breathing treatment." The nurse had been fooling with a plastic tube stuck on a handle. Vapors came out of one end of the tube. They looked like smoke. "Here you go now, breathe good and deep for me."

"How 'bout a Camel or a Winston, instead of this peace pipe?" Hurley asked as she thrust the apparatus in his hand. "Hell, Sondra, I'll even take one of those sissified Virginia Slims you used to buy."

"Now, Mr. Embry, you know you are supposed to call me Nurse Johnson. Doesn't do for the patients to be too familiar with the staff. Nothing but problems there. Now, take your treatment."

Hurley puffed unenthusiastically.

"Anyway, I'll have you know I haven't smoked a cigarette in ten years."

"Good for you," Hurley said. "Give me one and I'll smoke it for both of us. While you're at it, pour me a shot of Jack Daniels. On the rocks."

The nurse pursed her lips and Hurley studied her, grinning. "Packed on a few since you quit smoking, ain't you Sondra?"

"My weight is none of your business, Mr. Embry. Now, I have other patients to see. Patients who appreciate my interest in their health. So take your breathing treatment and I'll be back to check on you."

"I'd appreciate a shot of whiskey."

"Your breathing treatment, Mr. Embry."

Hurley snorted. "Still got a mouth on you, ain't you? Should have busted your butt forty years ago."

The nurse leaned down until her face was only inches from Hurley's. He could smell garlic on her breath, and lemony lotion.

"You touched me enough back then, and in some mighty private places, you old reprobate," she whispered. "Should have reported you to Child Welfare. Keep messing with me and I'll do it yet. Now, you old fart, get to puffing."

She showed him her teeth. He maneuvered the pipe back to his lips and puffed on it lackadaisically until Sondra Johnson's shoes disappeared.

"Ass as broad as an axe handle is long," he mumbled and laid the breathing apparatus on the bed. For a few minutes he watched some sparrows at the feeder. The cardinal didn't come back and Hurley felt his mind growing restless.

He'd never been a reader, just a newspaper on Sunday and the Bible when he was sick of trying to live right. He purely despised television. Invention of the devil, his old man had called it, and Hurley guessed he'd been right. Nothing worth watching since Gunsmoke bit the dust. Never understood how Edna sat in front of the set for hours, watching what she called soap operas. Soap operas, his hairy ass. If she was so damn interested in soap, she could have hustled on down to the station and washed windshields for the customers. And Lucinda had been as bad, all those game shows with the squealing and the so-called comedies with their canned laughter.

Neither one knew a durn thing about real life. Living in fantasy worlds, that's what they had been doing for thirty years. Well, if it was fantasy they wanted let them move into Hickory Hills with him. Actually, that was more like a nightmare, but so were they.

If he'd only had a son, Hurley thought, but he stopped himself short. No future in that sort of thinking. Never had been.

He turned over on his side, farted, belched, and shut his eyes, trying to remember every detail of the Big Bend in the Cumberland.

For better than seventy years he'd fished that river. All the way from Harlan down to Croley Bend below Williamsburg. The Big Bend at the south end of Knox County was the stretch he liked best. Just below the bridge at Dozier, with that old burnt out Freewill Baptist Church on the far side. Willows and beeches had grown almost in the water by the deep hole where the really big catfish were. That hole was close to the white rock where he and Gladys Pursiful had sunbathed when Edna had gone off to see her mother in Knoxville. Hurley had always felt at home along the river.

He hadn't been to Big Bend in a long time and he lay on his side watching the sky darken and lower and a squirrel run along the window sill, trying to remember exactly the way sunlight sparkled on the surface.

Snowflakes stared drifting down from the sullen clouds and Hurley shivered under his sheet. He needed to make one last visit to Big Bend before his time was up. He had something that needed doing and before the supper tray came around he studied on the plan that had been crinkling the edges of his mind for a week.

Quentin came while Hurley was trying to gag down mushy cardboard disguised as mashed potatoes. The boy reminded Hurley of some dogs he'd owned over the years, not too bright and lacking any real ambition, but anxious to please and good to mind.

"Bring it?" Hurley mumbled around a mouthful of doughy potatoes.

Quentin closed the door and looked at Hurley. "What?"

Hurley grimaced and swallowed.

"God damn slop they serve in here is awful. Bet them boys on the wrong side of the bars up at Eddyville eat better than this. Know my damn hogs did." He scratched at his nose. "You bring what I told you to?"

Quentin peered at the old man, squinting.

"Boy, you ought to buy you a pair of spectacles."

"Got taters on the end of your nose, Hurley."

"Fuck them taters, Quentin, you bring the juice?"

Quentin nodded and patted his jacket. "Got her right here."

"Good boy. Now go and put it in that little skinny closest over there. Just stick it down in one of my boots."

"Don't you want a sip first?"

Dang, Hurley thought, if the boy don't look like his feelings is hurt. What a pussy.

"Sure," he said, "that's a good idea, Q. Uncap her and let's have a snort."

Quentin pulled the bottle out of his coat. His thin mustache quivered while he fiddled with the top of the bottle. Hurley shook his head. Quentin's mustache put him in mind of a fishin' worm set down on a hot rock.

The boy got the bottle open and handed it to Hurley. Out of habit, the old man wiped off the lip with the sleeve of his pajamas. Then he took a good stiff drink and handed the bottle back to his son-in-law.

"Damn if that didn't go good. Get yourself a hit and then stick it in a boot afore that witch of a nurse takes a notion to stick her head back in. Then go feed them birds for it gets plum dark."

"You're out of sunflower seeds, Hurley."

Hurley swallowed what he wanted to say and nodded. Unless the entire free world conspired to fuck him over tonight he aimed to be out of this hellhole before daybreak.

"Alright," he said, "just be sure and get another bag afore you come back. Get a forty pounder this time. They're a better deal, plus the seeds last longer. Tell that uncaring daughter of mine to give you the money out of my next government check. Ought to be here on the third and I'm damn sure she's aiming to cash it."

Hurley watched the boy amble over to the closet that was about the size of a cheap gun case. That didn't matter. All that was in there were the pants and the shirt that Hurley had worn in, and his boots. His wallet and keys were missing-in-action. He'd checked already.

The boy came back over and sat down in the visiting chair. For a few minutes they chatted about how much it was going to snow, why the price of gasoline was so high, and why liberals wanted to take away a man's guns.

Hurley didn't really give a rat's ass about any of that, but the boy had brought the whiskey, which was more than anybody else would have done, and he was married to Lucinda, which entitled Quentin to Hurley's deepest sympathies.

After what he judged to be a decent time, Hurley began to pretend to be sleepy. In a few minutes the old man felt himself grow drowsy. Quentin was rambling on about the basketball Wildcats, but Hurley didn't even bother to nod anymore.

Hurley woke up not knowing where he was. Then he did, and he sat up and glanced at the alarm clock on his bedside table. The luminous hands both pointed to eleven. He started breathing easier.

The Bennett boy came on at midnight. Hurley eased back down on the pillow and stared into the darkness, remembering when he was younger and had laid awake worrying over sins he committed and burdens he'd left unlifted. When a man was alone at night there was no need to lie. God, if there was one, already knew everything and there was nobody else around to pretend for. For a moment the memories were so sharp that they cut him and his eyes bled. Biting his lower lip, the old man lay in the darkness, sobbing.

After a bit he got a grip on himself and sniffed and wiped the back of his hand across his eyes. Alright, he'd drunk too much and maybe he had smacked Edna a time or two. But, hell, every man did something like that, if he was any kind of a man. Those acts he could handle.

No, what weighed on him like iron bars was one lousy sunny Sunday afternoon down at Big Bend. Shouldn't have even thought about what he did that day. He knew how that tormented him. Memories just slipped up on a man sometimes, though. Caught him unawares.

Still, it had only been one time. And he'd been drunker than hell. Why should a man have to suffer the rest of his life for ten minutes worth of drunken foolishness? That was the question, that was the damn question. Even the good book said something along the lines of judge not lest ye be judged.

Damn, Hurley thought, he lived a hell of a lot of years and it all came down to having his ass stuck in a lousy old folks home because his own daughter wouldn't lift a hand. Just a little help and I could make it, he murmured. Just a lousy ounce of forgiveness. Jesus, or somebody like that, had said to forgive seventy times seven, or some such number. All Hurley asked for was for just one person to forgive him one time. That didn't seem like much.

From what the old man could tell forgiveness must be just about the most rare thing in the world. For sure there was a hell of a lot less of it lying around than gold.

At night Hickory Hills filled with sounds. Old women sobbed and old men hollered out and the aides squeaked up and down the halls in hospital shoes. If he lay real still Hurley could hear the shush of the oxygen machines and the beeping of the telemetry at the front desk. Even the whispered conversations between the nurses. Some nights he wondered if they were talking about him.

Tonight he didn't give a damn. Tonight was his great escape. Steve McQueen he wasn't. Never had been worth a damn on a motorcycle. But that didn't matter diddly tonight. Hurley rolled over on his side and stared out the window, trying to focus on what lay ahead.

Just before midnight one bright eye swam out of the darkness, crested the rise and turned in to the parking lot. In the yellow glow of the security lights Hurley could see the caved in side of the Bennett boy's Ford pickup. He smiled and let out breath he hadn't been aware he was holding.

Twenty minutes later the door to Hurley's room inched open. A thick shadow slipped inside and the door snicked behind it. Hurley snapped on the lamp standing on his bedside table.

"Cold enough out there for you, boy?"

"Freeze your balls off if you stand around long. Wind's cuttin' like a knife. Be glad you're in here, Hurley."

Not for long, the old man thought. Aloud he said, "Yeah, room's nice and warm."

The boy came over and peered at a pair of monitors, then he sacked up the trash in the can and swiped Hurley's nightstand with a white rag. As the boy bent over, Hurley caught a faint whiff of pot.

"Thirsty, Ricky?"

The Bennett boy turned and eyed Hurley. In the poor light his face was a shadow inside deeper shadows.

"Depends. What you got?"

"Whiskey, good stuff, too. Not some old rotgut."

"Whiskey? Now where in the hell did you get whiskey, Hurley?"

"I've got friends."

"I bet. Well, maybe a quick shot, if it really is the good stuff."

Before Hurley could reply a disembodied voice crackled over the loudspeaker. Hurley strained to make out the words. All he could understand was Room 26.

"Got to go," the boy said, "Howard Henson's done shit his Depends again. Unless something else comes up I'll swing back by in about twenty."

Hurley nodded. "See you then."

As soon as the door clicked shut the old man swung his legs out of the bed and placed his feet on the floor. For a minute it was all he could do to stand. He could feel his legs trembling beneath him and his body swayed like a willow in a high wind.

"Better this way," he mumbled as he slowly worked his way across the room. His legs were still wobbling like a young colt's, but now that he was actually moving Hurley felt better.

He tugged the bottle out of his boot and hauled it back to the bed. He'd been saving some of his water cups and he pulled a couple off the top of the stack.

One of them he filled halfway with whiskey and sat on his meal tray. Before he poured anything into the other cup, he dug way in the back of the shallow single drawer of his bedside table. Hurley smiled when his fingers closed on a balled up Kleenex. He pulled it out and opened it. Four little blue pills lay in the palm of his hand. They put Hurley in mind of hummingbird eggs.

Hurley dropped the four pills in the cup and drowned them with whiskey. Smiling, he sat the cup on the far end of his meal tray and crawled into bed. When the door squeaked open again he was sipping calmly from one of the cups.

Two twenty-two. Two had always been his lucky number. Time to roll.

Hurley eased out of his bed. Tiles were cool against his bare feet. With the whiskey in him he felt stronger.

By now the pills should have worked, if they were going to. He slipped his arms through his shirt. His fingers trembled as he buttoned his shirt, but he got his pants on without trouble. His socks seemed to have disappeared, but Hurley didn't bother to search. Just wedged his feet into his boots and headed for the door.

Hurley eased the door open and stuck his head out in the hall. As empty as Jesus' tomb. Both ways. From the times Quentin had wheeled him up and down the hall Hurley knew that the break room was in the back. He stepped out in the hall.

His legs weren't worth a shit, Hurley thought as he ran a hand along the concrete block wall for support. Back in his heyday he'd wandered hills from first light to way past dark, hunting squirrels, cutting timber, just roving. Now it was all he could do to make it down the hallway at the old folks home. Getting old was pure hell, Hurley thought, wondering how many of the golden years a man could stand.

The door to the break room was closed. After midnight there were only a couple of aides and a nurse. Joyce Gravitt was the night nurse and Hurley had overheard she stayed in her small office behind the reception area, watching old movies until somebody buzzed.

The other aide was a worry, but Hurley was counting on finally getting some good luck. By God, he was overdue. Hurley opened the door to the break room, going slowly, listening for squeaks.

A television was playing in the break room, but the volume was muted. The only sounds Hurley could hear were his own raggedy breathing and the Bennett boy's snores.

The kid lay on an old couch on his back. Stuffing was coming out of the cushions. One of the kid's arms dangled over the side. Leaning against the wall, Hurley let his eyes wander.

Nobody else was in the room. Pizza remains lined a cardboard box. Three coats hung on pegs.

Now we're getting there, Hurley thought, as he pushed off the wall and wobbled towards the coats.

He figured the one with the fake fur collar belonged to the nurse. That left a denim jacket and a vinyl car coat with a rip in one sleeve. Halfway there, Hurley recognized the car coat. The old man grinned.

By the time he made the back door the world was starting to tilt south and sweat dampened his forehead. He sure wanted to sit down just for a minute, but Hurley was afraid that if he did that he'd never get back up. Taking a deep breath, he leaned a shoulder against the door.

Cold air smashed against his face and ripped breath from his lungs. Hurley stumbled and went down to one knee. Gravel dug into his hide. If a bench the smokers sat on in good weather hadn't been within reach he wasn't sure if he could have got his ass up. Have to be more careful, he mumbled as he started for the pickup. All his life he'd been a Chevy man, but tonight he figured a Ford would do. The fool Ricky had left the truck unlocked and, grinning and grunting, Harley hauled his carcass into the cab.

A touch of heat lingered in the cab and Hurley hesitated, relishing the warmth, grateful to be out of the driving wind. Then he pulled the key out of the coat pocket, jammed it in the ignition and twisted. The engine growled, caught, then roared to life. Hurley shifted into reverse and spun the wheel. Clear of the other vehicles, he braked and jammed the gear shift into drive.

Headlights were likely to attract more attention than he wanted, so he coasted half-blind across the parking lot and drifted down the winding drive. Sycamores lined the drive, ghostly white in the middle of the night, and ghosts he'd forgotten about swirled up in his mind. Old men saw lots of ghosts.

Near the bottom of the drive Hurley pulled on the headlights and glanced at the dashboard. Three quarters of a tank. Shit, I could drive to Louisville on that, he told himself. The highway loomed before him and he braked to a halt. For a minute, maybe two, the truck idled while the old man made up his mind.

Turn right and he could make Louisville by daylight. Left and Big Bend was only an hour away. Hurley licked his lips. Deciding got harder to do with every passing year and he'd lived a hell of a lot of years.

Hurley shook his head. Only playing mind games, that was all he was doing. Very day Lucinda stuck his ass in the home he'd made up his mind. Wasn't changing it now. Anything else would be an excuse. Excuses, he'd had a lifetime of them, giving and receiving.

Waves of weakness washed through him then and he coughed and shivered and spat on the floorboard. When the waves had passed, Hurley sat up straighter, took his foot off the brake, and twisted the steering wheel hard left.

Snowflakes fluttered in the arc of the headlights and wind whined at the windows. That other trip, the one time he'd taken Lucinda, it hadn't been cold like this. Fact was it had been so hot their clothes were soaked with sweat long before they got to the river. In those days he'd been a heavy drinker. Beer, mostly, although he sucked down whiskey and vodka when he could afford it.

That hot day it had been beer. Old Milwaukee, if memory served, and, as he rounded a curve with Lusher's Grocery deep in shadows on the right, the taste of that beer filled his mouth. Hurley bent to the wheel and pressed the accelerator toward the floorboards.

He'd been big dog drunk when they got to the river that hot Sunday. Hadn't been feeling any pain. Well, he was feeling plenty of it now. His game leg ached and there was that arthritis in his back and these days an anvil seemed to be sitting on his chest. Maybe he was suffering penance, or whatever that old television preacher had yammered about on Sundays. Maybe he shouldn't have watched so many religious programs, Hurley thought, or read the Bible so much after he got old. Religion, least too much of it, might not be good for a man. Hurley wasn't sure. Lately, he got a little confused now and then.

By the time he hit the Bell County line he was sweating bullets. Sweat beads dotted his forehead, just like they had all those years ago, but this time it was a cold sweat. Blood sang in his ears and his arms trembled.

Driving to Big Bend was harder than he'd figured. For a couple of miles Hurley wasn't sure he was going to make it. Once the road whirled and he felt the pickup swerving, but he jerked the wheel and by the time he crested Logan Hill and shot through Flat Gap and down the long curl to Reynolds Valley the white line was running straight and knew he'd make it.

Made it that other time, too, and maybe he shouldn't have. If he hadn't then he might just be in his own place, or at least with his daughter instead of Hickory Hills. Everything might have been alright if he just hadn't made that one trip to Big Bend.

But he knew he was only kidding himself, which was why he'd had to make this one last drive. He was close. There was the old Howley place and the gravel road that led to Anderson's lumber mill.

The river ran beside the road now. When the light was right he could see the surface shimmer. Snowflakes drifted down and kissed the moving water. Eyes glittered at him from the side of the road, but he was by them before he could tell whether they belonged to a deer or a dog.

Half a mile down the road was the pullout and Hurley eased the Ford off the asphalt and onto the gravel. Snow was flying. The wind was whipping it against trees and rocks and the old truck.

Keeping his foot on the brake, Hurley dug a stained envelope out of a back pocket. Wasn't much in the envelope, a five dollar bill and two ones, his Medicare card, and his draft card, although why in the hell he had kept that he had no idea. Those few things and one picture, colors faded, a corner torn, stained slightly.

She had been a cute kid. Beautiful little girl. Everybody had told him so. Hurley didn't have a clue how she'd inherited her looks. He was all angles and planes, and Edna, while pleasant enough to look at, 'specially after a couple of beers, was no Homecoming Queen.

But Lucinda had been a real charmer. At least before she turned mean. Staring at the aged photograph, Hurley wiped cold sweat off his forehead with the back of his free hand.

He knew what had turned Lucinda mean, turned his own daughter against him. That knowledge made his heart hurt. Or maybe it was his heart acting up. Doc Biddle had warned him about doing too much. Over exertion, the bastard had called it. Well, just a little more exertion and it would really be over. In spite of the pain in his chest and the pulse pounding like a pneumatic jackhammer in his temple, he had to smile.

His eyes were starting to glaze over and his throat felt tight. Hurley wished he had a beer to open things up. But then he remembered the other drive and the beer and the way Lucinda had cried and pounded his back with her little fists. Oh, he'd stopped, but the damage had been done. One of those sins of commission the Bible and that old preacher talked about. One of those unforgiveable sins. When Hurley felt like being honest, he had to admit he couldn't quite forgive himself for that one. For the last time he glanced at her picture, closed his eyes, and pressed his lips to hers.

When he opened his eyes they were dry and his forehead was cool. He took a deep breath and whispered a few prayer words he'd learned. The he gritted his teeth, took his foot off the brake and tapped the gas feed.

For an instant the wheels spun in the snowcaked gravel. Then they caught and Hurley jammed the accelerator to the floor. He could feel the motor throbbing beneath his feet. The old pickup seemed to be shaking apart.

He hit the brush line doing thirty and then the pickup was airborne, soaring between two willows, through the falling snow, dropping into the greater darkness, toward the rushing, waiting water.

For the last time Hurley whispered his daughter's name.

THE LUCKIEST GUY IN THE WORLD

I WOKE FROM A DREAMLESS SLEEP, not knowing who I was or where I was. For the first seconds I felt like a young boy again and I almost called out for my mom and dad. Slowly, as though they had to travel a great distance, sounds began to filter into my consciousness. Birds were chirping beyond the room and I could hear the sounds of cars passing in the street and, faintly, the lilt of music filtering through the floor from the apartment below. The sheet was a cool shroud against my naked body. By now, I was awake enough to know who I was and I eased the sheet back and swung my legs off the bed.

As I slid into running shorts and shoes I studied my wife's face. She was still asleep. Her lips were parted and a strand of hair hung down across her face. The hair was the color of warm butter, but that wasn't exactly real. She colored her hair.

In high school she'd been a cheerleader. College hadn't quite worked out and for a couple of years she'd been a model. Later she'd been a dancer. North of thirty, she was still beautiful and took great pains with her looks.

As for me, I'm nothing special. Just your average looking guy with a GED and thinning hair. Since the accident I can't even carry on a conversation. Grunt a little, or squeal, that's about it. To get a woman like Tammy to marry me must make me about the luckiest guy in the world. At least that's the way I figured it.

Seeing her face haloed in the first pale blush of daylight, I wanted to kiss her. But she was snoring, very gently, very ladylike, so I tied my running shoes and tiptoed out of the bedroom.

It was still quite early and the courtyard was deep in shadow. On the roof of the building across the alley the pigeons looked asleep. I put a pot of coffee on and while it was brewing I performed my morning ritual. Then I stood at the sink and drank a cup while I watched the morning come alive. When I heard the first TARC bus round the corner I rinsed out my cup and went down the stairs. The stairwell was dark and the apartment house was so quiet it seemed asleep. Without consciously thinking I found myself tiptoeing again. The stairs were prone to squeak.

In the courtyard the air was cooler than I expected and a breeze ruffled the birch leaves. I could smell bacon frying and the aroma of fresh coffee was strong. Stretching as I walked, I headed toward the street. At the sidewalk I turned and jogged down Fourth, heading toward the Ohio River.

Daylight was still struggling and traffic was light and the sidewalks, except for one stray dog and a drunk passed out on the corner of Fourth and York, were empty. A light breeze was coming in off the Ohio and I ran with the smell of dead fish and diesel oil in my face.

This morning I felt extra good, so I didn't turn back at Fourth Street Live. Instead I went all the way to the end of Fourth and pounded down the stairs beyond the Galt House and trotted down the Belvedere, past the Belle Of Louisville and Joe's Crab Shack.

I had to turn and come back then. I was already late, but Lester wouldn't mind. Anyway, most of the time, we set our own schedules. Metro Government wouldn't mind either. That's who we work for. Scraping roadkill off the asphalt and shoveling it off the sidewalks and the shoulders of the road.

We're contract employees. They pay us by the job—not the hour. We don't work—we don't get paid. But they don't care when we work. As long as we keep the streets of Louisville reasonably clean and dispose of the remains properly they leave us alone. And pay us. Not much, but they pay.

Five years ago the Metro road crew did this job. Then, Metro council got all excited about privatization. Lester knew the mayor's brother. I knew Lester from high school.

By the time I pounded past the library I was sweating bullets. Damn stuff even ran down the crack of my ass, but I just bowed my neck and pumped harder. Try to keep in shape. The older a man gets the harder that becomes. For sure my glory days were behind. Not that I really had any.

I ran past the complex and slowed to a walk. I strolled around the block to cool off and work the lactic acid out of my leg muscles. School buses were rolling when I walked up the sidewalk. One of our neighbors, a black dude named Leon, was standing on the stoop, smoking a cigarette. Bird droppings dotted the wrought-iron railing. Lot of birds nest around here, pigeons mostly, and starlings.

Rumor was Leon had played college football. Somewhere down south. Louisiana, maybe. Mr. Detwiller, who lived above us, told me Leon had been a linebacker. I'd never played sports much. When I was younger I fished some and hunted now and then. But that was before my dad died.

Though he had a bit of a pot gut, Leon's biceps were still huge and defined. The top of my head came to the bottom of his chin and he had to outweigh me by sixty pounds. Part of me was glad I'd never put on a football helmet.

I nodded at Leon and he blew smoke out his nostrils and said "Morning." His voice sounded like damp sandpaper. He was leaning against the railing and his legs sprawled in front of the door. I had to step over them. As I passed I could smell his sweat and smoke. I took the steps two at a time. They creaked in protest.

Tammy was up now and banging pots and pans in the kitchen. Usually she wasn't up so early and her unwashed face floated like a dirty moon above her Girls Who Read Are Sexy t-shirt. It tickled me when Tammy wore that shirt to sleep in. I'd never seen her read anything more challenging than People.

She rubbed her eyes. Below her left eye mascara was smeared.

"Hi, honey, you want some eggs?"

I smiled and nodded.

"Scrambled or fried?"

I held up two fingers.

"'Kay, baby. Go grab a shower and I'll have your eggs on the table when you get back. Sunny side up, right?"

I nodded and nuzzled her neck. Stale perfume filled my nostrils and I jerked my head to the side and sneezed.

Tammy nudged me with an elbow. "Go on now, you old sweathog, and grab a shower. Hustle, you don't want to keep Lester waiting."

I turned and walked to the bathroom, stripping my damp t-shirt off as I went. I took a quick shower, shaved and brushed my teeth. I could smell bacon frying and coffee brewing. When I finished shaving I stared into the mirror, wondering once again how I could be so lucky. I wasn't good looking, or extra smart. Ordinary about summed me up. Ordinary that is until the day of my accident.

As accidents go it wasn't anything monumental. At the time I was working the warehouse for Derby City Pipe and Culvert. Joe Vanderhorst and I were loading a shipment of sixteen inchers to go to a chemical plant in Saint Louis. Even after an OSHA investigation, nobody's sure what happened. One minute I was bent over tying my boot laces and the next Joe was shouting and I looked up just in time to get hit square in the throat by a section of pipe that had broken loose from the bindings.

For a while they thought I was dead, and I vaguely remember wishing I was. Spent two weeks in Jewish where they fixed me up as best they could. The back end of the pipe had swung around and knocked a few teeth out and given me a nasty gash along one cheekbone. The worst though was my throat. Damn pipe crushed my voice box and didn't do my breathing any good.

The docs at Jewish operated three times on my throat to improve my breathing and got me a set of teeth and stitched me up so that my scar wasn't so bad. Now I breathe as good as anybody and I've got no complaints, until the blues hit me. Then I wish they had let me die.

Still, I got a nice settlement from Derby City and while I was in the hospital I met Tammy. She was a nurse's aide. At first I figured she was just feeling sorry for me, but after she kissed me one evening when she brought me my tray I figured my luck had finally turned. That was the same day I got the formal settlement offer. Luck runs in streaks.

We'd been together now for almost two years. I put on a clean shirt and my cleanest jeans, combed my hair, and went out to breakfast.

Tammy already had the eggs and bacon on the table. She was sitting in her chair, staring into her steaming coffee. I grabbed one of my pads and pencils and wrote, What's the occasion?

That's the only thing the docs at Jewish couldn't really fix—my voice. Sometimes, I can sort of squeak. Usually that's when I'm scared.

Tammy studied my question for a minute. She looked like she was ready to go back to bed. I wasn't surprised. She almost never got up this early. I tried to remember if it was her birthday.

"Just wanted to give you a treat, baby. You've been working so hard lately."

I smiled and for once was glad I couldn't talk. I didn't have a clue. Sure, I'd been working, but nothing worse than usual. I started in on my eggs and bacon. Tammy sipped at her coffee. Then she smoked a cigarette. For the first time I noticed that she smoked the same brand as Leon. Since the accident I notice odors more.

"You working the usual, baby?"

I looked up from my eggs and nodded.

"When you think you'll be home?"

I held up four fingers and a thumb.

Must have had a question written across my face because she said, "I've got to run out and do a couple of things, but I wanted to be sure and be here when you got home. Promised Mrs. McIntyre we'd come over when you got in. She wants some furniture moved."

I smiled and nodded and jammed a forkful of eggs between my lips. She smiled back and sipped at her black coffee. Tammy was one for watching her weight.

She didn't have much more to say, though it looked like she had something on her mind. I finished my breakfast and sat for minute, listening to the traffic on the street and the pigeons cooing around on the window sill. Then I got up and kissed her cheek and ran water over my plate. She walked across the kitchen and into the bathroom. In a minute I heard the shower running.

I bent to retie my shoes and caught a glimpse of yesterday's mail on the counter under last Sunday's Courier-Journal. Just the corner of one envelope was sticking out. Guess I'd missed it somehow.

I thumbed through the stack. There was a bill from LG&E and a letter from Derby City. The letter had been opened. It was brief and to the point. My disability payments would run out next month. Five hundred a month wasn't big money, but it beat the hell out of a stick in the eye. I'd have to figure something out quick.

On the way out the door I grabbed my cap. I pounded down the stairs and out into the sunlight. Mrs. McIntyre, a widow who lived on the third floor, was walking her cat on a leash, and she smiled and nodded at me. I waved and kept moving. Some days I took the bus, but today I walked, taking my time and staying in the shade when possible. Lester lived over on Baxter and I usually met him at his house. If it was snowing or raining or below zero he came and picked me up.

Lester was a couple of years older than I was and at least forty pounds overweight. He mostly drove and I did most of the shoveling. Of course, he had a pickup and I had a girl's bike I'd found behind some trees in Cherokee Park. Lester only helped if the carcass was too big, or too far gone for me to handle alone. I didn't really mind. He paid me in cash and never seemed to mind that I couldn't talk. Course the fact that he talked enough for both of us might have figured in.

Lester was already in the truck, lounged behind the steering wheel, eating a Hostess cupcake and smoking one of those cheap cigars he claimed came from Cuba. Both doors were standing wide open. A squeaky-voiced woman was talking on the radio.

I slid in and pulled my door to. The frame was bent where a former Miss Shively had T-boned us one evening just before dusk. Fortunately, she'd been drinking all afternoon at the Seelbach and had only been going about twenty-five, in reverse. Her husband, who was a hedge fund manager over in New Albany, offered Lester a grand to forget it. Cash. Lester smiled all the way to the bank.

Lester made a point of looking at his watch. Like it mattered. Then he rolled his eyes, farted, and blew smoke out one corner of his mouth. I grinned and he cranked the engine. As usual, it growled before it caught. We fastened our seatbelts—Lester obeyed the law when it suited him—and rolled down the driveway.

I glanced in the rearview mirror. Lester's wife was standing in the doorway, waving. Or maybe she was shading her eyes. Sometimes Mary looked at me in a way that chilled me some. Like she was going to take a bite out of me.

At the first stoplight, Lester turned the radio down. "Aggravating conservative talk show hosts. They're ruining radio. Every damn one is a wingnut."

I nodded. I didn't listen to the radio much. TV neither. Lots of evenings I was so tired after a day of shoveling roadkill off asphalt that I fell asleep right after supper. Usually slept straight through till the alarm went off. Not as young as I used to be. Nights when I was feeling energetic Tammy wanted to go out. She liked to dance. I've got two left feet.

"Can't stand to hear those women that talk through their noses. So damn whiney it makes my balls ache." He cleared his throat and spat through the open window. "Anyway, we've got to shovel a bulldog off Algonquin Parkway and deer parts are supposed to be all over the west end of River Road."

He coughed and turned and looked at me. "I feel like a couple of glazed doughnuts, Champ. How about you?"

Smiling, I shook my head, looking at Lester's stomach as I did. Ever since high school he'd been heavy. But the last year he'd really packed on the pounds. His stomach brushed against the steering wheel now. But it wasn't my business. He drove straight to a bakery he liked down on Mellwood Avenue and chomped doughnuts as we headed over to Algonquin to find what was left of a bulldog. Bulldog guts wouldn't bother me. I never liked bulldogs. See what I mean about how lucky I am.

Long before noon we'd scraped up the bulldog, two cats, a possum, and what might, at one time, have been a squirrel. Never did find the deer parts. I was still full of eggs and bacon, but Lester was hungry. You might think a man working the Scavenger Patrol wouldn't get hungry, but I guess a fellow can get used to almost anything. I've seen old Lester grab a smashed up deer by the antlers and fling it in the bed of the truck then climb back in the cab and start munching Dixie loaf on white bread. Then again, Lester is almost always hungry, which is why he must weigh close to three hundred pounds.

We were rolling down Bardstown Road when Lester licked his lips and swiveled his eyes toward me. "What about it, Killer, you interested in some lunch?"

I shrugged.

Lester glanced back at the traffic and swung out around a rusty Chevy. "Don't know about you, but I'm nearly famished. Overslept this morning and didn't get a real breakfast. Pop-Tarts and a banana don't do it for this old boy."

I grinned and looked out the window. No use writing him a note about the two Snickers bars he'd chomped down about ten o'clock.

"Want Chinese, Champ? Me, I could go for a big plate of moo goo gai pan. You like Chinese, don't ya, kid?"

Lester kept on rambling. I just looked out the window. I'd heard all of Lester's palaver before. You never knew when you might see something real interesting outside the pickup. I remember once, we were down in Portland, I saw an iron coming sailing out an open window. Never did find out why. Figured maybe some lady got tired of ironing, or was trying to brain her husband and threw high and outside.

Today all I saw was a woman pushing a kid in a stroller and a tom-cat with one ear. Seeing that cat reminded me how lucky I was. After all, I'm just an ordinary looking guy—on a good day—and I didn't go back for seconds when the smarts were passed out. Somehow, and I maintain that it has to be luck, I'd ended up with Tammy.

If it hadn't have been for the accident I probably never would have met her. Why she fell for me I can't say. Maybe she's sort of like those women who are always taking in stray dogs and cats. Something inside just won't let them turn away from a suffering creature.

Nights when my back ached and I couldn't doze off I'd lay there after she went to sleep and listen to her breathing and watch the bands of moonlight play games across her face and wonder why in the world she had ever married me. She was still a fine looking woman.

Granted, between the disability payments and what was left of the settlement after two weeks in Vegas and the cash I made with Lester, plus picking up the odd job now and then, she didn't have to work. But that was alright with me. I liked coming home to her all perfumed and powdered and every so often a good, hot meal on the table. Sometimes it was only Kentucky Fried Chicken or takeout from the Jubilee Dragon, but that was okay, too; she wasn't that great a cook. But what a body, and the best kisses I'd ever had.

She had her moody spells, sure, but they never lasted. Guess everybody has those. Every few weeks she'd grow real quiet for a day or two, and then she'd be out some at night, maybe drinking a little, partying some. But what the hell? How could I blame her? Mr. Excitement I've never been. So I just let things slide and after a few days life would be back to normal. Sure I wondered, but...

"You know, kid, you've got to be one of the luckiest men in the world."

I twisted in my seat, stared at Lester's moon pie face, and turned my palms up.

"Yes indeed, my boy, one day all this will be yours." He waved a hand vaguely around the cab of the pickup. "Decided last night, when I couldn't sleep and got up to do some thinking, that when I go I'll leave my empire to you. No kids, see, and Mary she likes staying at home. I'd leave her to you too, but I like you too much for that."

He laughed then and punched me in the arm. "Speechless with gratitude, ain't you, kid? Don't blame you boy, you're one lucky son-of-a-buck." Then he laughed again, punched me harder and started telling some tale about a bobcat and a preacher.

I just listened and thought about what he'd said about his wife. Some days she gave me looks.

An ambulance went by going the other way with its lights flashing and siren whining and Lester made his usual joke about the meat wagon. I thought about my ambulance ride and wished the poor sucker well.

We got behind an old lady in a rusty Buick and Lester rode her bumper all the way out past the Watterson Expressway. Sunlight glittered off bumpers and glass until it was nearly blinding. I kept an eye on the side of the road for business.

Lester wheeled the truck into a shopping center I'd never been to before. There was the usual smattering of small, retail businesses arranged in a concrete and plate glass U: a coin laundry, a computer repair store, one of those check cashing places that ripped you a new one—that sort of complex. Sure enough, there was a Chinese restaurant with one of those ubiquitous names. Better still, in the far corner of the U was a used bookstore.

Reading is one of the things I do. Nobody expects you to talk if you're reading. I'd stumbled across an allusion to a book called The Stranger written by some guy with a strange enough name. Couldn't remember it for sure; something like Camus, which I figured was foreign—maybe Dutch or French.

Out of sympathy for his fellow man Lester parked the pickup around back. That, and the fact that somebody had planted a few honey locusts along the perimeter and they were throwing a thin, splotchy shade. He powered the windows down and we got out and strolled across the parking lot. Lester was in front of me; he moved quick for a big man when he wanted to. A dark streak as wide as a sheet of paper colored the back of his shirt.

The place was one of those all you can eat buffets. Steam trays of rice and fried pork and gallons of egg drop soup. You paid up front. Lester paid and we headed for the plates.

Lester went back at least twice. One trip finished me and after a couple of minutes of watching him eat I wrote a note on the back of a napkin and got up and went outside.

The heat was building, carrying the humidity along with it. A light breeze was coming in out of Indiana and I could smell the pickup. I tugged my Reds cap lower and walked through the sunlight across the parking lot. It was so hot I thought of Hemingway's line from The Sun Also Rises, "It was baking hot in the square." Halfway across, for no particular reason, I wondered what Tammy was doing.

The bookstore was cool and dark and I lingered. They didn't have The Stranger, but I picked up a Richard Ford and a Bukowski I'd been looking for. My luck was still coming in.

Since we didn't have any scrapings lined up, I paid for the books and sat down on a cracked leather sofa somebody had jammed in a corner in the back next to a coffee pot and framed photo of Mahatma Gandhi. An old electric clock hung on the wall. I figured ten minutes wouldn't hurt.

I got lost in the Bukowski and when I looked up over half an hour had gone by. Not even Lester would eat for that long. I struggled off the couch, jammed the books under an arm and hustled out the door.

Squinting against the sun, I stared across the parking lot. Heat waves shimmered above the asphalt, but I could see the Chinese place clear enough. Outside, there was a bench under the awning and I figured Lester might be sitting there waiting on me. Maybe napping. He was prone to napping after a big meal, especially on hot days.

The bench was empty and I guessed he'd gone on to the truck. Sometimes he worked the crossword puzzles. He liked the ones that came in special crossword books, the kind that were all about sports, or movie stars, or politicians. I can't stand crossword puzzles. The clues are way too cutesy for me. Still, like my Grandma Elliott always said, it wouldn't do for us all to be alike.

Lester probably was asleep, I told myself as I marched across the parking lot. The asphalt was soft beneath my feet. When Tammy and I first got married we used to take long walks. I tried to remember the last one.

I could see the pickup now and, sure enough, Lester was asleep behind the wheel. I slowed and stopped for a minute in a deeper patch of shade. I pulled my sweat rag out and wiped my face. Then I walked around the pickup and pulled the door open. The hinges squeaked like they were in pain. I wedged my boots on the floor-board between a jug of transmission fluid and a cardboard box full of candy wrappers, used Styrofoam cups, and old *Courier-Journals* that had been accumulating since Easter.

Old Lester must really be gone, I thought. His head hung down on his chest and he was as still as the carcasses we scraped off the road. What the hell, I decided, and let my head ease back against the seat and closed my eyes.

Damn truck smelled worse than usual. I swear it smelled a little like piss and shit, but it was hard to tell. I was grateful for the breeze.

Maybe it was the heat, or maybe it was my hard run that morning, but I'll be damned if I didn't doze off. Naps aren't really my thing. Hardly ever take one unless I'm coming down with the flu.

Don't think I was out long, but I woke with a start, my breath foul in my mouth, sweat running down my cheeks, and feeling the afternoon had started growing old without me.

I glanced at my watch. It wasn't late. Just after one o'clock. Lester's cell phone was buzzing. He was always forgetting and leaving it on vibrate. Probably a call about something dead on the road of life. I leaned over and put a hand on his shoulder.

He didn't move. The old fart must really be sleep deprived, I thought. He was always complaining about not sleeping well. According to his self-diagnosis he had sleep apnea.

I reached over again. This time I shook him.

I shook him again, harder. His head lolled and his mouth hung open. His tongue was twisted and taut.

I could feel my pulse throbbing in my temples.

In spite of the heat, I shivered.

He was as still as the dashboard. I jumped out of the cab and started running for help.

The EMT's got there first, took one look at Lester and loaded him up in the ambulance. They tried to ask me questions, but I just pointed at my throat and flashed them a little sign language. I wasn't great at it and they were worse, but the message got across. They weren't interested in me anyway. They just shook their head and said something about a massive coronary. My brain wasn't tracking too good right then, so I walked over under one of the scrawny locust trees and stayed the hell out of the way.

Stretched out on the gurney, Lester's inert body looked like a statue. Maybe one of those on Easter Island that had finally toppled. I stood in the sparse shade and watched the ambulance wind its way out of the parking lot. For a long time after the lights disappeared I could still hear the wailing of the siren.

Two Louisville-Metro cops rolled up just as the ambulance hit Bardstown Road. Once I got them to understand I couldn't speak, things went alright. I wrote them a couple of notes and showed them my driver's license. They had me write out a short statement and sign a couple of forms. They asked about the truck and I wrote that I'd go by in the morning and give the keys to Mary. They promised they'd let her know about Lester and the truck. Also said they'd be in touch. They made that sound like a threat, but I just smiled and nodded. What was I supposed to do?

I waited until their vehicle was out of sight, then I retrieved my books and walked a block and a half to a TARC stop I'd noticed before lunch. I just couldn't face getting behind the wheel of a dead man's truck. Not so soon, anyway. A bus going my way was due in seven minutes.

Mrs. McIntyre was sitting out front on a wrought iron bench that had been there for as long as I'd lived there. Bird droppings dotted the seat and the whole thing needed painting. Sunlight coated the old lady's face, but she was sleeping like a newborn, mouth open, snoring gently.

From under the bench her cat gave me the evil eye. I gave him the finger, cut across the narrow strip of grass and started up the stairs, wondering what I was going to write to Tammy about Lester. First the disability payments were stopping and now it looked like my job was gone. I didn't own a truck and Lester hadn't had time to make a will. Maybe I could work a deal with Mary. Looked to me like my luck was suddenly running south.

The scent hit me right away. I stopped on the second step and sniffed. Smoke, but strange smoke laced with perfume and incense. For a second I wondered if the building was on fire. Then I heard voices coming from my apartment. Staying close to the wall, where the steps didn't squeak as bad, I began tiptoeing up the stairs.

As I climbed the voices grew louder. One I recognized right away. Tammy's. The other took a minute. Seemed like I'd heard it, and recently, but fact is I hadn't figured it out until she said his name.

"I'm telling you, Leon, it won't be any trouble. He sleeps like a rock every night. Poor dumbass works like a damn Trojan all day. Plus, I've got some sleeping pills that would knock an elephant out. I'll slip two or three in his iced tea and the man will never know what hit him."

"But why snuff the dude? Why not just leave him. I've got a cousin in Memphis who owes me big time."

"Because, you igno, I had him take out a $500,000 policy a couple of years ago. Stupid agent didn't want to make it for that much at first, but, after I went by his office and told him that thanks to the disability check there was no reason to worry about the premium payments, and gave him a blow job, he saw things my way."

"But, baby, why not just keep making the premium payments. Death is kinda like a final thing, you know."

"Leon, you've a big dick and a tiny mind. Remember, I told you that I'd been paying the premiums out of the fool's disability check and then last week he got a letter from Derby City telling him the disability payments were ending."

She sighed then and something squeaked. Somebody leaned on a car horn out in the street and the ex-priest who lived on the other side of the landing turned on his radio. Holding my breath, I eased across the landing and squatted in front of my door. I recognized the strange odor now—weed. And spent sex. Or that might have been my imagination.

"Wish I knew what I'd done with that letter. Should have torn it to bits first thing. Oh, well, the dummy never worries about bills or anything like that. Sad, ain't it, how that man trusts me and him not even able to speak? Just looks at me with those big brown eyes. Makes me think of a damn dog. Well, when a dog gets old you put it down, right? Right?"

"Guess so."

"Sure that's right. Just think, this time tomorrow the dummy will be as dead as that nasty roadkill he scrapes off the streets. Now bring that big black dick over here. I'm hotter than hell."

She laughed then and Leon mumbled something, but I was already turning and heading for the stairs.

Made myself take them real slow. Damn things were bad to squeak. You had to be lucky not to step on a bad spot. I didn't want any part of Leon, or Tammy, not even with a head start. Long gone was the only answer for me.

Guess old Lester was right after all. I was the luckiest guy in the world. Louisville at least. Not a single squeak and the bus at the corner was just pulling in as I jogged up. The old pickup started on the first crank.

By five o'clock, just when she'd be expecting me home, I was driving between the cornfields of flat Illinois staring into a sun so bright it made my eyes water.

HAPPY NEW YEAR

FOR THREE DAYS THE wind had been howling like a lost dog, driving me crazy, well crazier. Being cooped up inside that apartment above the bakery wasn't helping. Not that the weather was solely to blame.

The light was going and I pushed off the sagging couch and hobbled over to the window, leaning on the cane when the pain ramped up. The weatherman who lived inside the radio had been calling for snow all week, but the heavy stuff had slipped north. All we'd gotten were flurries that drifted in the wind. The sky had that gray, sullen look, like the clouds could open up any minute and dump a foot—a cold, nasty ending to a cold, nasty year.

I got my back against the plaster and tugged one end of the curtain. The street was empty except for a bum in a raincoat that hung down to his ankles. I watched him wobble around the corner, let the curtain fall back, and began to work my way to the kitchenette, staying out of the pale ingot of light that pressed through the window.

I could have closed the curtains, but I needed to be able to check the street without attracting attention. They were out there waiting. Even if I couldn't see them. My grace period ran out at midnight.

Just to hear the sound of another human voice I'd kept the radio on all day, the honey-voiced announcer recalling the events of a year dying on the vine. A cheap calendar hung on the wall. December's photo was of a cardinal sitting on untracked snow. His feathers were as red as blood. A truck rumbled by on Mill and I ripped the calendar off the wall. Then I killed the radio. Enough of this lousy year.

Staying close to the wall I eased back to the window. Streetlights had popped on and the wind whined at the window. In the office building across the street the lights started going out one by one.

Finally there was just a single light burning. I stood there watching it, knowing they were watching the apartment. Maybe the old bum was watching them. Perhaps every person in the world was watching another. It seemed terribly important that the last light stay on, as though it was the last light in the world.

A police car rolled by, headed east. In its headlights I could see snow falling. When I looked back at the building the last light had gone out. I felt defrauded, like when I was a kid and my old man got off from the lumberyard one Saturday and took me downtown to watch the big Christmas parade. Only my mom had written the wrong day on the calendar. When the crippled guy who ran the newsstand on the corner of Dewhurst and Maxwell told us we'd missed the parade by a week, my dad cursed until his face was red and the veins in his neck stood out like taut strands of telephone wire.

A white film covered the sidewalks and rooftops. Cars and cabs worked their way through the falling snow. I need to be moving, too. How to do it was the problem. I hobbled to the bedroom and lay face down on the bed, willing myself to sleep.

My eyes were heavy. Lately, I'd slept only poorly, wrestling with nightmares and nocturnal visions. As I lay there trying to sleep the night came alive with sounds, as though it had been saving them up all year and couldn't stand to let the old year pass without voicing them.

Horns blew down in the streets and the wind chattered at the window and I could hear the hiss of the radiator in the living room and the clatter of pans from the bakery below and the scratchings behind the walls and the gurgling deep in my gut. I lay there in the dark knowing I needed to be going, afraid to move. I rolled out of bed and found my cane and worked my way to the kitchen and drank from the tap. As I turned off the water I heard the back stairs creaking.

The apartment was a place where time seemed to have been held captive. Word was the apartment had been modified forty years ago by the old guy who owned and ran the bakery downstairs. Last year, one month after burying his wife of sixty-two years, he'd moved to an

147

old folks home. Now his son ran the bakery. I'd lucked into this place when Jimmy Keough, who held the lease, got picked up for passing bad paper in Detroit. Jimmy's brother knew I was looking and I had fifty bucks. That bought me two weeks. Now I was out of time and money.

Two sets of stairs lead up to the apartment. You entered the front ones from the street and visitors used them. The back ones rose straight from the kitchen. The old guy must have used them to travel to and from the bakery. In the fourteen days I'd been here nobody had used them. Now they were creaking. I lugged the pistol out of my belt and sat on a wooden chair behind the kitchen table in the gathering darkness.

I laid the pistol on the table and stared at its dull gleam as I listened to someone climb the back steps. The gun was just for show. I was fresh out of bullets. In the poor lighting it might buy me a minute, or two.

Footsteps sounded on the landing. The back door opened into the kitchen. It didn't have a lock. I picked up the gun, leaned deeper into the shadows, and fixed my eyes on the door. Seconds later somebody knocked. I didn't move. Another knock. My fingers tightened on the butt of the pistol.

"Hello. Anybody in there?"

I leaned forward. The voice was a woman's, not young, not old.

"I know you're in there. I heard you clomping around last night and nobody has come down either set of stairs all day." The voice paused and I could hear her breathing, not hard, just a little fast. Was the woman a Trojan horse?

"Come on, now. I just want to know that you're okay." She pounded on the door again. "Tell me you're okay and I'll go away."

"I'm alright," I said. "Now, go away."

"How do I know you're telling the truth? Open the door and let me see. What's the matter, big guy, you afraid of a woman?" The door swayed open half an inch, then fell back. "Come on, just let me make sure you aren't bleeding to death and I'll go away."

Cursing under my breath, I pushed the chair back and hobbled to the door, twisting my right hand behind my back, wondering why she hadn't just pushed the door open. The barrel of the gun felt comforting against my back.

Standing out of the swing of the door, I listened. All I could hear was one person breathing. I sniffed for perfume, but the odors were flour and grease and, more faintly, cigarette smoke. "Go away, I'm not bleeding or starving. I don't have measles, mumps, or chicken pox. Don't even have a cold. Your concern is appreciated, lady, but go away."

"Let me see you first."

I let the silence build.

"How do I know you're not a movie?" She laughed then, a nice laugh. The sort of laugh you used to hear on front porches on hot July nights in towns like West Plains, Missouri and Bardstown, Kentucky and Jellico, Tennessee. I'd heard that laugh all across the south and the Midwest. My mother had laughed that laugh, and my sisters, and Susan Carmichael whose dad had owned the drugstore in Digby. Hadn't thought of her in years. Pulling the door open I wondered if her hair was still the color of ripe wheat.

The woman stepped into the kitchen and pushed her face forward as though she were going to study my features through a microscope.

"So you are real," she said. There was something strange about her eyes, but her face was twisted so that shadows fell across it like an early night. The only light in the room was what passed through the windows and slipped in from the hall. Out on Mill the streetlights were faint stars. A single, naked bulb hung in the hallway.

"I'm real, alright. Now you've had your sighting, so turn around and go back down the stairs like a good girl."

"But, I'm not a good girl, see." She took another step into the kitchen.

"Okay, so you're wicked. You still need to go back downstairs."

"Why's your hand behind your back?"

"You don't want to know."

149

Somebody making a late run down Mill tooted and she turned toward the sound and I could see what was wrong with her eyes. They were what my Uncle George used to call catawampus. One looked slightly left and the other peered right, so that neither one seemed to be looking directly at you. I shrugged. "Since you're here you might as well check around. You're probably hoping to find a band of gypsies camped out in the living room or a tribe of bushmen hiding in the closet."

"Thanks. Think I will." She sashayed past me.

"Who are you," I said to her back, "the landlord?"

"His granddaughter," she said without turning around, and laughed again. Had to admit I liked that laugh.

She crossed the kitchen and walked over to the living room window and stood with her back to me. I drug a kitchen chair over to the far corner of the living room.

"What's wrong with your leg?"

"Sprained my ankle," I said, although it felt like I'd torn a muscle. Funny what a single misstep can do to a man. I rubbed the toe of my shoe with the tip of the cane. The gun pressed against my lower back like a guilty conscience.

"Why are you sitting in the dark?"

"I like it that way."

"Ah, a man of mystery. So was your friend."

"Who are you talking about?"

"Jimmy, the guy who was here before you. He and I used to talk." She turned then and her profile was sharp in the streetlight. It was snowing out on Mill Street, flakes falling like cold, fat feathers. If I squinted it was almost a homey scene. Then the wind howled like a gut shot dog.

"Heard you talking to my dad about the apartment, so I know you know Jimmy."

For just a flicker in time I'd forgotten she was there and her voice startled me. I was grateful for the shadows.

"Where is he now?"

Just to feel something real I rubbed my hands together. The darkness was getting into my mind, filling my body, eating away at my bones until I felt like I was nothing more than a mind floating in the shadows.

"Jimmy took a little vacation."

"The bum. He promised to take me dancing."

"Don't think he'll be doing that soon."

"Why not? Is he taking a long vacation?

"Two to five. At Joliet."

"Oh."

I wanted to get up and take another peek out the window. I wished the woman wouldn't stand in front of the glass that way. Might make the men across the street think more than was good for me.

For a time the woman and I simply inhabited one small room in a universe so big it was beyond even a vivid imagination like mine. There was something in that concept, but I wasn't thinking straight enough to make the pieces fit. Now and then a truck rumbled by and once a couple of kids shouted something at each other. But their words were muffled by distance and snow and it was like listening to the clutter on a telephone when the connection doesn't quite go through or the skip on a radio late at night.

I could hear the woman's faint breathing, smell her essence, even see her silhouette. But I couldn't see her face, only the snow behind her falling in the glow of the streetlights. It was like she was a ghost, or a mirage, or a half-formed angel. She started walking towards me.

"I could use a smoke. You want one?"

"Sure."

She handed me the pack and her fingers brushed against mine. I shook a cig out. "I don't have a light."

"Here's a box of matches. Keep it. Keep the pack, too. I've got another one downstairs. Speaking of which, I'd better be going. Next batch of dough should be ready. People will want their bread tomorrow, when they sober up."

151

I flicked the match head against the side of the box. In the sulfuric flare her face made me think of the Middle Ages. Probably I'd been reading too much. "You bake bread?"

"Yeah, Schiller and Sons Bakery. Only, it should be Schiller and Granddaughter. I do most of the work. Me and my brother. Spend twice as much time here as my dad and uncle put together. That's how I got to know your friend. And notice those two men hanging around the old Kingman Deli across the street."

"So that's where they are."

"Yeah, I've seen them on and off all afternoon. Figure they were the same two that were standing on the corner yesterday. Guess the weather drove them inside." She exhaled smoke and touched my shoulder with one hand. "You know those guys?"

"By reputation only."

"They looking for you?"

I took a drag off my cigarette. I held the smoke for a long time, savoring the harshness. Finally I expelled it, slowly. "You don't want to know."

"Like that, huh?"

"Like that."

"Knew Jimmy was full of it. Was too nervous to be an insurance salesman."

"Oh, he's a salesman, all right."

She laughed then and I was glad I'd made her laugh.

"Well, I've got to go," she said. "Rising dough waits for no man, but come on down after a while and I'll buy you a cup of coffee and all the glazed you can eat."

"Thanks," I said. "Might do that later. Thanks for the smokes, too."

My eyes followed her dark bulk across the kitchen. She pushed the door open and the light from the single bulb haloed her head. "By the way, my name is Louise. Don't believe I caught yours."

"Just call me Ray."

"Well, Ray, don't forget it's New Year's Eve and I get the distinct impression that neither one of us is going out celebrating. So come down and we'll have our own celebration, even if it's just coffee and crullers."

I didn't say anything. I didn't know what to say. She just stood there, smoking and staring back at a strange man half in shadows. I wondered what she thought she saw. Women can see wonderful, terrible things when they stare at men.

In the end she blew smoke out her nostrils and let the door swing shut. I sat in the dark, smoking and listening to the echo of her footsteps. When they had faded away I ground the cigarette out in a dirty coffee cup and hopped on one foot over to the window. Snow was falling like it planned to bury the earth.

By seven the aromas of baking dough and fresh cinnamon and brewing coffee were drifting up the back stairs and sliding under the door. Those scents reminded me I hadn't eaten in a while. I sat on the floor in the dark, my ankle throbbing. Now and then I glanced at my watch. The hands seemed be flying.

At fourteen minutes past eight I scooted over to the couch and hauled myself to my feet. I stood swaying while I fumbled for my cane. Then I started hobbling toward the back stairs. On the way I grabbed my jacket off the back of the kitchen table and jammed the revolver down in one of the pockets. The only cap I had was an old Cubs baseball cap and I tugged it down tight. Midnight was coming and Tony Sarduchi never forgot a promise. Worse, he always delivered on his. Guys in the business called him the Postman.

It was hell getting down the stairs, but in the end I made it, upright and in one piece. Off to the left was one of those old swinging doors with a porthole window. Through the glass I could see the kitchen. A dark hall curved to the right. Chilled air swirled up out of the darkness. I looked right, and turned left.

As the door swung open she turned. Her hair was stuffed up under a paper cap. In the light I could see her eyes were the smoky purple certain grapes achieve when they stay too long on the vine.

"So the doughnuts got to you."

I leaned against the counter and we both straightened our caps at the same instant. That made her grin and a smile played around with the corners of my lips.

"Thought I'd let you know I was leaving. Jimmy's lease is up at midnight, you know."

A strand of tawny hair had come loose and fallen down one side of her face. She swiped it behind an ear with one hand, leaving a cheek smeared with flour. She caught me staring at her and her smile broadened. She had full lips.

"You don't have to go," those lips said. "We don't have another tenant lined up. I could speak to Dad. Get him to let you stay till we line someone up."

"Time for me to be moving on."

"Suit yourself." She wiped her hands on a red and white striped towel hanging from a hook on the edge of the counter. "First though, have a hot doughnut. What kind do you like best? Glazed? Chocolate? Cream-filled? I'll bet you're a cream-filled guy."

"I've got to be going."

"Oh, come on. You've got till midnight. Go on now, get around the counter and grab a stool. I'll serve you like a real customer."

I glanced at the clock on the wall. Not quite eight-thirty. As I watched the second hand sweep my stomach growled at me. Fingering the revolver inside the coat pocket, I tried to remember when I'd eaten last.

"Just hand me whatever you've got. Maybe one that didn't come out quite right and I'll get out of your hair."

"No way. I need some company. It's not right for a girl to be alone on New Year's Eve. Go ahead, Ray, and have a seat at the counter and I'll pour you a cup of coffee. You like coffee, don't you? Black, I bet."

"Yeah, I like coffee alright, and black is my style. But I'm kinda superstitious. Never like sitting with my back to an open window."

She stuck a white mug under a big silver urn and lifted the handle. The coffee was as black as the earth of the Mississippi Delta. Steam vapors rose from the mug. The aroma made my guts gurgle.

"Shades are all pulled down, 'fraidy cat. We're closed, remember? Those two couldn't see you if you were a zebra."

"Well..."

"Go on, Ray. I'm not going to bite you."

I took a deep breath, then let it out as I picked up my cane. The floor was damp and I slipped once before my free hand could grab the counter. I cursed and hobbled faster. Stoicism was something to read about in college philosophy books.

It was a relief to sink down on the stool. Between the stairs and the slick floor I now had a damn fine idea how this night was going to unfold.

She slid the mug in front of me. "Well, final customer of the year, what sort of doughnut will you have? On the house, of course, to celebrate surviving another year."

"I'll take a cream-filled. You must be part gypsy."

She laughed, that tinkling, wind-chiming, starlight in the treetops laugh. "I've been called worse, mister."

She turned and walked down the counter toward a glass case. For the first time I noticed that there was a hitch to her stride. The left leg wasn't quite right. Using a slip of waxed paper she pulled a long john off the top shelf and put it on a paper plate.

"Bon appetite."

I knew it was rude, but I grabbed the doughnut with my fingers and jammed half of it in my mouth. Fear and hunger make a man do strange things. The doughnut was still warm and the cream oozed out between my lips and after I swallowed I flicked out my tongue and licked it off.

"You're a hungry boy."

"Sorry."

"Don't be. Eat all you want. I've got a case full. Nice to have the company."

I nodded and picked up the mug and sipped. Her coffee was still hot enough to burn my tongue. Making a face, I thought about Tony Sarduchi.

A shadow fell across the counter. I looked up into her face.

"Another one?"

"One more, then I've got to go."

"What about a caramel this time?"

"What are you," I struggled for her name, "Louise, a mind reader?"

"Not really, and I don't do magic balls or tarot cards, although I have been known to play strip poker."

I nodded. The clock on the wall said it would be nine o'clock in seven minutes.

"What's the matter, Ray? Don't you think I'm clever?"

"Yeah, you're clever alright. Just got a lot on my mind tonight."

"Those goons across the street?"

"Yup," I said and sipped at my coffee.

She slid another doughnut onto my plate. The smell of warm caramel took me back to my Grandmother Glotzback's kitchen.

"Why do they want you, Ray?"

"You're better off not knowing any more. I've already mouthed too much."

"I'll be twenty-seven tomorrow. Plenty old enough to know what's good for me."

I put the mug down. "Look, Louise, you're a good kid, but those guys across the street aren't the sort either one of us wants for pals. Ever hear of a guy named Tony Sarduchi?"

"Sure, who hasn't?"

"Figured you or your dad might have heard from him or one of his boys. He sells a lot of protection and those two across the street work for Tony. Understand now?"

She put both elbows on the counter. I could smell cigarette smoke and coffee and the fear trickling down my spine.

"What's Tony Sarduchi got on you, Ray? You kiss his wife at the office Christmas party?"

I washed the caramel out of my mouth with coffee. I had to give the woman one thing; she made a strong, hot cup of coffee.

For her own health I really shouldn't tell her a damn thing. Yet I did owe her. Coffee and cigarettes and caramel long johns were debts I didn't want to leave unpaid. The mug thumped against the counter. I licked my lips and cleared my throat.

"See, Louise, it's like this. Most of the time I'm a quiet guy. I sell my line, men's shoes and hats, and go home after work and curl up with a good book. Only every now and then, maybe it's the full moon, I get a fever."

"A fever?"

"Yeah, a fever for cards. Stud poker, to be precise. I used to play a lot before I got into sales and I'm pretty good. Generally I'm lucky when it comes to cards."

"More coffee?"

"Sure."

I watched her fill my mug and one for herself. She lit a cigarette and scratched the tip of her nose. She had a good strong nose—the kind made for sticking into other people's business.

"So let me guess," she said, adjusting her cap, "your luck ran out."

"Down the drain," I said. "November 30, over at the old Franklin Hotel on Clark Street. Got off to a bad start and never recovered. Worst fever I've ever had. Kept losing and plunging deeper. Most of the night I couldn't draw a decent hand and then around midnight I finally got three kings and a pair of jacks. A full house. Nobody else was showing much and I bet the house. On borrowed money. I'd been flat broke since ten.

"And Tony S was holding five little spades. Nothing higher than a nine, but all spades, and all right in a row. Damn straight flush and suddenly I'm ten thousand dollars upside down to a man who eats rabid dogs for breakfast. He gave me till midnight tonight to pay up. Might as well have given me until next Christmas. I don't have the cash and can't raise it. None of my friends have that sort of money."

I shook out a cigarette and fired it up. The woman and I peered at each other through the smoke. The hands on the clock kept ticking the night away, ticking my life away. Tiredness settled in my bones. I'd been living on my nerves.

"Why didn't you run, or get lost?"

"They, or their buddies, have been on me ever since that night. Besides, I don't even have the price of a bus ticket to Tulsa. And, on top of everything else, the one night I saw a chance and made a break for it, I slipped running down an alley and tore hell out of this leg." I swung it under the counter. "Grandma in her wheelchair could catch me now."

My head ached at the seams and my eyes felt full of sand. I rubbed at them.

"There's got to be a way," she said, more to herself than me. "Let me think."

It was my turn to laugh. My laugh sounded like a hyena's I'd heard on a Saturday jungle movie back when I was a kid and still believed in the Tarzan the Ape Man and Zorro.

"Go ahead, think all you want to. Believe me, I've been doing a lot the past few weeks. Came up with zilch. But go ahead and think. You strike me as a sharp lady."

She nodded. "That's the most intelligent thing you've said all night."

I grinned and shook my head. "Yeah, Lou, go ahead and think. I'm just going to rest my head on the counter. Do me a favor, will you, and don't let me go to sleep. Just going to rest my eyes. It's been a long night already, and it's only going to get longer." I eased my head down beside my coffee cup.

"Sure, Ray" she said. "You rest and I'll think."

My eyes were so heavy. I closed them. She was talking again, but her voice was fading.

I could hear my mother's voice calling my name, but I was running down a dirt road that curled between rows of dark trees. I called to her, but the wind captured my words and carried them beyond the great blue mountains that rose like the backs of dinosaurs all the way to the far horizon. And I could hear only the wind. Then she said my name again, as loud and clear as a church bell at Easter, and laid a cool soft hand against my cheek.

Then I blinked and came back to the last day of the year and I wasn't running and it wasn't my mother stroking my cheek. It was the woman with the broken doll eyes, saying my name and stroking my cheek and my mind cleared and I came awake and alert. Tense and hollow and hard inside, like cold iron.

"Ray, you'd better wake up. It's eleven thirty."

I jerked my head and looked at the clock on the wall. I started to chew her out, but what good would that do. I was almost out of time. Tony Sarduchi never forgot a debt and never failed to deliver on a promise. I had to get the hell out of this town in a hurry if I wanted to see much of the new year.

In the knowing place deep in your guts where fear gnaws at your courage like a long-tailed rat, I knew that they were honorable men, as such men go, and I would have my allotted time. My allotted time, but not one minute more. So I swung off the stool and started running for the door.

Only I'd forgotten one small detail. My damn leg. As I went down I tried to choke off a scream and rolled over and got my back against the wall and sat there blinking at the pain, breathing fast with my eyes closed. When the pain eased I opened my eyes and Louise was staring at me with a face full of pity, and for a minute I hated her.

The room had gone so quiet I could hear the clock on the wall ticking. I stared at it as though I could make time stop. But that was only the latest foolish delusion in a lifetime of them. For the first time I noticed the name of the clock, half-hidden by the hands. Regulator. Somehow it seemed symbolic.

But I didn't have time for symbolism or watching the clock or staring at a woman with flour on her arms and her hair stuffed up under a silly paper hat. Reaching up, I gripped the window ledge and pulled myself up.

When the room quit swaying I wiped cold sweat off my face and said, "Hand me my cane."

She walked over and picked it up, studying my face like she was memorizing every freckle and line.

"You don't have to go, you know."

"Yeah, sure, I can stay here and pray Sarduchi makes a New Year's resolution to give me a break."

"You could go to the police."

"He owns half the cops in this town. An hour after I hit the station he'll be giving me a break all right. Both legs if I'm lucky. My neck if he's in a bad mood."

"Can't you pay him something?"

"Lady, what you see is what you get." I turned my pockets inside out. There wasn't even any lint to blow in the wind. "Now give me my cane."

She crossed the floor, the cane before her like a medieval lance. I grabbed one end. She kept hold of the other.

"I've got almost four hundred dollars saved up and I know I can borrow some from my grandfather. Since he went to the home he doesn't spend hardly any money."

For a second I thought about it, but even if she could borrow a few hundred from her grandfather that wasn't going to make Tony happy. I'd only be buying a slice of time, and time was just another illusion.

I glanced at the clock. Fourteen minutes to go.

"Give me the cane, Louise." I jerked and she let go and I stumbled back against the wall, twisting the bad leg again. I cursed and blinked the tears away. Sweat dotted my forehead. I turned and lifted a corner of the blinds. Snow was falling like every cloud in the sky had been ripped open. Letting the blinds drop back I glanced at the clock again.

Regulator.

Twelve minutes.

Using my coat sleeve, I wiped the sweat off my forehead and made myself face her.

"Hate to leave good company, but this old year and my luck are both about up. Besides, running is what I know. Been running all my life, so don't take it personal. Up in that old apartment I kept thinking about how I ran away from home and school and the army and every job and friend I've ever had."

I hobbled over and lightly kissed her cheek. Her skin was soft and smooth and warm. "I'm a runner, Louise. Thanks for everything, you been real sweet, but just let me run."

For a second her hands were tight on my arms. Then she let me go. I started hobbling toward the back door. They were probably waiting, but I'd be damned if I'd make it easy for them. Maybe they were so wet and cold they'd gone home. Nah. Not Sarduchi's boys. As I rounded the counter I turned and lifted a hand. Louise just stared at me.

I turned and bent to it, going as hard as I could for the dark hallway.

"Wait a minute, Ray. I've got an idea."

I stopped, leaned against the wall. "What idea?"

She started walking toward me, talking and making fluttery motions with her hands, like a butterfly I saw once out in Missouri trying to fly over a stone wall. He'd waited late in the season to migrate south and the cold had gotten into his wings. Last I'd seen of him had been a flutter of orange and black still struggling for altitude.

Louise was shaking her head. "Why didn't I think of it before?"

I leaned left and looked at the clock. Eleven fifty-one. "Think of what?"

"The bakery truck. We make deliveries every day to at least two dozen stores on the south side. There's even a uniform and a cap. Says Schiller and Sons in script right across the front of the coat. Cap's one of those old peaked ones. Been out of style for twenty years, but Grandpa got a deal on them years ago. Must be two dozen in the back." She made more fluttering motions.

"Hold on and I'll grab you Ted's coat and cap. Ted's our regular driver. He's about your size." Her face was close to mine. Her breath was warm against my skin.

"Can you drive a truck?"

"If it's got wheels and a gearshift and a steering wheel I can make her go." Just for the hell of it I kissed her on the lips.

"Hurry," I said.

She kissed me back and it was like the night had decided to hold its breath. Then she whirled like a flamenco dancer and went hurrying down the hall.

I stood there, breathing shallowly, watching the hands on the clock race toward the top. Three minutes left and I was praying now.

Then she came scurrying back, carrying the coat and cap. That stupid paper cap was still on her head.

"Here, Ray, let me help you slip this coat on. Lift your right arm. Now the cap. Give me yours. There you go. No, wait, here's the key, and twenty dollars. That will get you a ticket to Toronto. I know because I had to go and take care of my aunt last summer when she broke her arm. Just leave the truck at the bus station. In the morning I'll report it stolen."

She reached up and touched my check again. It felt like her fingers were writing on my face.

"Now hurry."

Buttoning the coat around me, I glanced at the clock.

Midnight.

Time waits for no man.

I stared at her eyes. They glittered like polished glass. Shattered glass.

I kissed them shut. "I won't forget this, Louise. I won't ever forget you."

She said something, only all the syllables were wet. Her fingers touched my lips and I gave her a wink and started hobbling for the darkness, wishing I had a five minute head start and even a couple of bullets.

A chance. That was all I needed. Just one more chance.

Once I was in the hallway the cold slid right inside that coat and I shivered. But all that mattered was that I was running again. Running for the truck. Running for the comforting darkness. Running for the border. Running for one more tomorrow.

I eased the back door open and there was the truck. Old and ugly and a faded yellow under the security lamp, but to me the most beautiful sight in the world. I stepped out the best I could, but carefully on account of the snow, acting like I owned the world, trying not to think about a bullet with my name on it.

The door handle on the truck was like ice and the hinges squeaked as I tugged the door open. I peered out into the darkness, but if they were out there they were keeping it mighty quiet. I tossed the cane in the cab and swung aboard. The seat was cold. I jammed the key in the ignition and twisted. The motor groaned.

I cursed and bit my lip and pumped the accelerator and twisted and the old lady ground to life. For a minute I sat there, letting the motor warm, turning on the wipers, thinking about where I was going. Then I jammed her into first and we started rolling.

"Rolling and running, running and rolling," I chanted to myself as the old truck slid sideways going down the alley. But I twisted her tail and we straightened out and I gave her the gas. My side window was still covered with snow and I cranked it down and let the snow blow back in the cab. I didn't give a damn. I was rolling. On the run. A running man always has a chance.

As I made the corner I asked myself what sort of chance I was really taking. Sure, I knew what I was running from, but what was I running to? That was the question that had been plaguing me all my life.

I could hear bells now. Somewhere happy people were ringing in the New Year. "Happy New Year," I shouted to the night. "Happy New Year, Ray Glotzback, you lucky bastard," I yelled.

Then, more quietly, I whispered. "Happy New Year, Louise Schiller."

Gunning the motor, I pulled out in the street, ducking my head and looking across the street. Two men were walking across Mill. Despite the snow they were walking with a purpose toward the bakery.

Shifting into second, I rolled west down Mill, laughing and crying at the same time. Snow was falling thick and white, covering my tracks and my sins.

In the side mirror the two men were little marionettes, growing smaller by the second. I hoped they wouldn't give Louise too hard a time. She'd been good to me. Undoubtedly the girl was lonely. Otherwise she wouldn't have bothered.

But what the hell. Bullets killed you, not loneliness. Swinging the wheel, I turned north onto Dexter. Now the bus station was only blocks away. I fingered the twenty dollars in my pocket and said a short prayer for Louise.

I couldn't hear the bells anymore and the snow was starting to ease. I could see inside the stores that had security lights and they looked snug and warm and safe. I hoped Louise would be all right. Surely they would only rough her up a bit. One of the stores still had a Christmas tree in the showcase window. All the lights were blue. Even the angel on top glowed blue.

I pushed Louise to a dark corner of my brain, trying not to remember those spooky eyes. They haunted a man, you see. Canada was only a bus ride away. Piss on Tony Sarduchi. Ray Glotzback was rolling. Safe in the snowy night, a lonely man running toward a lonely tomorrow.

The wind was cold on my neck and I cranked the window up. Damn, but I was getting to be maudlin in my old age. My old age, the words sounded good. And to think an hour ago I'd never dreamed I'd live to see it. Sitting there in that cold cab rolling down Dexter, watching the windshield wipers swipe back and forth, I grinned to myself and tipped my cap to Louise, vowing to send her something nice from Canada. Maybe a new dress, purple to match her eyes. Or a coat and scarf and maybe a new alligator purse. Only I knew I was fooling myself. I owed her too damn much and she wasn't the kind of woman who gave a damn about a coat or a scarf, or even an alligator purse filled with five-dollar bills. She was one of those people who are too damn nice for anybody's good.

Just for the hell of it I laid on the horn for a block. Oh well, I'd think of something nice for her up in Canada. Lots of time for thinking up in Canada. All the time in the world. Through the diminishing snow I could see the glow of the bus station sign and I started gearing down.

The bus was pulling up front and people were strolling out of the station, looking up at the snow and pointing and smiling. They were going to Canada. I was going to Canada. We were all going to Canada where there was plenty of snow.

Plenty of snow, and no smoky purple eyes that looked everywhere but at a man and yet saw right through him. Without signaling, I wheeled into the bus station parking lot and cut the engine. The motor pinged as I opened the door. "Happy Damn New Year," I whispered to the night.

It was the first really warm day of April and all the birds in the world seemed to be singing. The back door was wide open and I followed the sunshine in and walked down the hallway. It was quitting time for the working class and traffic was slugging down Mill with brakes squeaking and horns blowing and cabbies cursing in half a dozen languages. Her head was bent over the cinnamon buns and she didn't look up. I leaned against the wall and wondered what she'd say.

The same old Regulator hung on the wall. The hands were still moving. In one minute it would be five o'clock. When the hands marked the hour I started working my way toward her, only now I wasn't limping.

She heard me then and her head came up, with those strange eyes opening wide and her lips coming apart. Suddenly she was shaking, like she'd seen a ghost. I sat down on my old stool and put my elbows on the counter, grinning like I had good sense. She closed her mouth and swallowed. I watched her throat work. She had a nice throat. She opened her mouth again like she was going to say something, only nothing came out. She just kept staring at me.

"Can't a man get a little service around here," I asked. "How about a cup of coffee, lady, and one of those hot cinnamon buns."

"Ray? How? Why?" Tears were forming. "What about, what about..."

I just couldn't stand those tears. I leaned forward and pulled her to me and kissed her hard on the mouth. She tasted like salt. I started licking her tears.

"Ray, why did you come back? You'd gotten away. Those men came and I told them you slipped out when the snow hit. Told them you had gone to Florida." She smacked at my head. "Quit that silly licking and talk to me. What are you doing here?"

"What did those guys say when you told them I was headed to Florida?"

"They just grinned and said they could extradite you from there as easy as taking candy from a baby and that Florida in January sounded like a fine plan. Ray, you quit kissing me and tell me what is going on. Right now."

I quit kissing her then and pulled her to me, her head against my chest and that stupid paper cap tickling my chin.

"I'm not sure, Louise. Guess I just got tired of running. Besides, I never was crazy about Canada. Too damn many moose up there to suit me."

"You're a crazy man, Ray. Pure crazy. Now, damn it," she mumbled into my chest, "quit being silly and tell me why you came back."

I didn't say anything about the run of good luck I'd had at poker north of the border. There are times when words don't signify. Instead, I slipped a finger under her chin then and tilted her head back and kissed her real soft and long.

Finally, I came up for air.

"Well, baby, it's like this. Up there in Canada the only job I could get was clerking in a used bookstore and business was slow and I had time for thinking. Thought about a lot of things, even made a few decisions. But what I really kept thinking about was what I'd forgotten to say to you. Something so important that it got to weighing on me like bricks.

She looked up at me then, with strange lights going off in those eyes I hadn't been able to forget.

"And what did you forget, mister?"

I rubbed flour off the tip of her nose with my finger. "Well, missy, it's like this. In all the excitement last time I was here I forgot to wish you Happy New Year."

"I was right," she said. "You are crazy."

"Happy New Year, Louise, Happy Belated New Year."

I bent down then and kissed her right on those fat, salty lips and she was laughing and crying and trying to say something all at the same time. Only I couldn't hear her because I was holding her so tight that it was like we were the same person, and I pulled that silly cap off and tossed it across the room and kissed the top of her head.

"Happy New Year, you crazy man," she said against my chest. "You know you are crazy, don't you? Crazy for coming back here. Coming back to me, me with a withered leg and these awful eyes. I know what men think of these eyes. They don't have to tell me. I can see the truth in their eyes."

"Way I see it I'd have been crazy for not coming back."

She lifted her face then and looked up at me. Her chin was quivering.

"Don't you realize what those men will do to you if they catch you? Why don't you go while there's still time? You never know when they might come back. Do you want to die, Ray? Is that it? Do you have some weird death wish?"

I looked down at her and smiled. Her fingers were tight on my arms. I could feel her trembling. I bent and kissed her again, nibbling on her lower lip for luck.

"Up there in Canada I figured it all out about your eyes."

"And just what did you figure out, mister?"

"It was really more like a revelation. Came to me one day when I selling an old man a dog-eared copy of Faulkner's Sanctuary. See, Louise, there's nothing wrong with your eyes. It's just they're really stars that have fallen to earth and are looking for a way to get back home."

She started tearing up again and I bent to kiss her, but she whirled away. "Oh, no," she said and started running.

For a second I thought I'd hurt her, but then I could smell oatmeal cookies burning and I started running after her, laughing like a demented bum. There I was, Crazy Ray Glotzback, still running. Only this time I wasn't running away from a damn thing.

THE GREATEST COUNTRY ON EARTH

THURSDAY NIGHT AFTER BOWLING we were drinking beer in Lou's. Lou's is a working man's bar, just like a hundred others in this town, except it's a subterranean dive. You really can't even see it from the street. You have to know that it's there, where it's been for forty years, under the San Remo Hotel at the bottom of a flight of concrete stairs. Dark and damp and the barmaids are real bitches, but it's only a block from the bowling alley.

See, Kemper Auto Parts, where I work, sponsors a bowling team. Five or six of the line guys show up every Thursday night to compete in the City League. After the final frame, we usually stop off for a beer or two. Not many, as we have to crank it in the morning. I was on my second. My last. It had been a long week already.

The other guys were at least one ahead of me, particularly Herb Henley and Johnny Turner. Herb was already getting mouthy and Johnny's neck was flushed. Just finish this one and head home I told myself. Trouble, you don't need.

Herb pounded a fist on the table. "You guys just don't appreciate this country. America is the greatest land on the face of the earth. In the history of the world. Why don't you guys just quit your bitching?"

"No raises for the chain gang for three years and now they're talking about cutting our hours. And all the while the big shots get raises and secretaries and free coffee. Hell, Herb, even supervisors like you got a raise last year." Johnny Turner tapped the rim of his beer can with a middle finger.

"Not much of one," Herb said.

"Bullshit." Johnny said and set his beer down so hard that you could hear the thump above the chatter. "Bullshit. I know for a fact that you started getting an extra three dollars on the hour back in July."

"Fucking snoop."

"Truth hurts, don't it, Herb?

"No way, Turner. Ain't you heard that old saying 'and the truth shall set you free'? And the truth is that America is the greatest country on earth. And you know why? No, you don't have a clue. Instead of bitchin' you need to be listening 'cause I'm fixing to tell you why America is such a great country. That is if you're interested."

"I'm not."

Herb scratched his nose. He had a long one. The tip wiggled like a rabbit's when he got excited. "Well, I'm going to tell you anyway. 'Cause you need to know. All you guys need to hear this, but especially you, Turner. After all, as your supervisor, which is really just another way of saying superior, it's my responsibility to make sure you guys are in the know. See," he tapped his forehead with a finger, "I've got it all up here. Go to meetings all the time and get the real scoop. Not that socialist propaganda you guys on the line put out."

Staring into the mirror behind the bar, I drained my beer, studying the faces that lined the bar, the open and the closed, the young and the old, the vacant and the vanquished. Faces, I like. It's the people I have trouble putting up with.

Angry voices swept over me like a sudden wind and I came back to the table. Johnny's eyes were bulging and Herb's nose was quivering.

"Herb, you're an imbecile. Guys like Owens spoon-feed you a line of crap and you swallow every drop and beg for more."

"Turner, you're jealous. Only the strong survive in the jungle and you're a pussy. All you line guys are pussies, but you're the only one that mouths. Why don't you be like your friend Glotzback here and be strong and silent?" Herb elbowed me in the ribs like we were a couple of high school kids.

"Leave me out of it." I was tired and my nerves were whining. Besides, Herb grew more obnoxious with every beer. Sober, Herb was a pain; drunk, he was an asshole. But I needed my job. I had bills and a hungry wife.

"See, Herb, nobody is buying your line."

"I'm only telling the truth. Just 'cause you don't like to hear it doesn't make it wrong. The fact that you'd rather bitch than take charge of your own destiny only makes you a loser, Turner."

"Shut your face."

"No, you shut up and listen to me. All you've got to do to make it in America is work hard and keep your nose clean. Look at me, I'm the perfect example of what's great about this country." Herb kept talking, but I wasn't there anymore. At least my mind wasn't. I was thinking about Donna waiting at home, Donna and her hungry mouth. What the hell was I doing sitting around Lou's drinking beer with a bunch of sweaty guys and listening to Herb Henley proselytizing about the sure path to success and salvation? I gazed over the heads of the men along the bar and stared into the mirror. A dark-haired man with a sour expression and a hawk's nose was staring back at me. I didn't like the sullen, self-satisfied face.

Herb and Johnny were shouting now and the noise of their voices pierced my skull like roofing nails. Somebody cranked the television above the bar up higher and my back teeth began to ache.

I tried to think about Donna again, except Herb was whining on about trickle-down economics. I didn't really have anything against Herb. After all, he'd put in a good word for me with Hemphill down in Personnel when I applied. And back in high school I'd played basketball with his cousin. Still, that whiney voice grated on my nerves like a dentist's drill. I peered across the table. In the poor light Herb even looked like a dentist. A dentist is one thing I could never be. Looking inside people's mouths is disgusting.

I pushed my chair back and stood up, glancing at the television. A football game flickered on the tube. The quarterback scrambled out of the way of a defensive lineman and flung the ball. It must have gone forty yards. Just beyond the outstretched fingers of the receiver. A loud moan rose up from the crowd and I turned back to the table.

"See you birds tomorrow."

"Ah, don't leave yet, Glotzback."

"Gotta go, Herb. Duty calls."

Johnny Turner laughed. "Yeah, you got a fine looking woman waiting, don't blame you."

Herb waved both arms like he was flagging a cab. "Don't go yet. Don't leave me with these jerks. They don't appreciate me or this country."

"Sorry, Herb. Gotta go."

He said something else, but the television crowd roared just then and I could only watch his lips move. It was like watching a movie with the sound off.

I turned and walked toward the door. Somebody, I think it was Mike Andrews, shouted, but I just waved a hand and kept going. Outside the air was cold and sweet. It tasted like Christmas. Staring up into the streetlight I thought about home. Then I ducked my head and started walking.

Johnny Turner called in sick on Friday and Herb Henley spent the day in a supervisor's meeting. I had a headache. Five hours of sleep will do that to a man on the far side of thirty. All day I was popping aspirin, but I made it till quitting time. A family man can't afford to be sick. Not with the crappy health insurance the bosses slipped in our last benefits package. Donna and I had talked about having a kid. I was for it. She said she was too, only not just yet.

By the time the city bus dropped me off at Cranston it was raining and my brain felt like a midget had crawled inside and was jack hammering to beat hell. I slogged down the sidewalk with the water running down the back of my neck, let myself in with the key, and headed straight for the medicine chest.

Donna was lounging on the couch watching television. Normally I'd have gone and sat down and watched a program or two with her, maybe snuggled a bit. Not this evening, though. My skull felt like an overripe cantaloupe cracking open.

"What honey, no kiss?"

"Sorry baby, headache."

"Come over here and I'll rub your head for you."

I tried to smile. My face felt like it was being carved up like a lopsided pumpkin at Halloween. "Maybe later."

She nodded and turned back to the television. I stepped into the bathroom and took two aspirin. Then I took a long piss, washed my hands and went and lay down on the bed with my clothes on. The shades were pulled and the room was dark. Like a sad, sweet memory, a trace of Donna's perfume lingered in the still air. Traffic rumbled dully down on the street. Closing my eyes, I tried to focus on the perfume. A horn blew down in the street and a pigeon cooed on the window ledge outside the bedroom window. Rain beat against the glass. Then it sounded like it was inside my head.

Hinges squeaked and the door swung open. A bar of light fell across the floor. I raised up onto my elbows and stared at it. The still, silent bar of light had the look of something suddenly dead.

Donna stuck her head through the opening. Light and shadows crosshatched her face. A shaft of light caught one of her cheekbones. From the living room a male voice ranted about liberals and the overthrow of America.

"You okay, Ray?"

"Just got a headache."

"Take anything?"

"Two extra strengths. I'll just grab a nap and I'll be fine."

"You sure, baby?"

"I'm sure. You just wore me out last night. I should have known better than to get mixed up with a younger woman."

Donna laughed. She had a high-pitched laugh that hurt my head even when I didn't have a headache, but I made myself smile.

"Not that much younger. Only five years."

"Yeah, but I've had a hard life."

My head was pounding and I eased it back onto the pillow. The guy was still ranting about liberals and the deficit and the need to reduce the federal government to the size of an anthill. He talked and talked and talked. About every third sentence he said something about America being the greatest country in the world. Or, according to the voice, it used to be until liberals came along with welfare and birth control and green initiatives. And now they had reached a new, perfidious low with their attempts to regulate the free market economy.

I wasn't sure what perfidious was, but it was clear it wasn't anything a decent person wanted to be. My eyelids felt as heavy as small stones. I shut them. I could hear Donna walking across the room. She sat down on the bed, trailing perfume. I wished she would turn the damn television off.

Donna started talking. Something about her mother cooking a turkey. My head ached and I didn't give a damn about her mother or the turkey. All I wanted to do was get some sleep. No, that wasn't quite true; I wanted to smash the television into oblivion.

I lay listening to Donna and the rain and the disembodied voice of the man who loved to hate. The night before was catching up with me. The smell of Donna's perfume grew stronger. Then it faded away and that ranting man went silent. Rolling over onto my side, I tried to think about deserts or mountains or old dogs I'd known. Anything but my headache.

I woke up clear headed and drenched in sweat. Donna was in the bed beside me, breathing softly through her mouth. I could feel her heat. The phone was ringing. Glancing at my watch, I picked up the receiver. Who in the world was calling me at two o'clock in the morning? Probably a wrong number.

My voice didn't want to work. Chatter and a metallic clatter drifted down the line. I swallowed and tried again.

"Hello."

"That you, Glotzback?" The voice sounded far away, distorted by distance and time, yet vaguely familiar.

"Who is this?"

A female voice, shot through with static, mumbled something about a code. It sounded like she was talking on a loud speaker.

"Glotzback," said a male voice. The voice was weak, with another element filtering through it. Pain, perhaps?

"Glotzback, is that you? Are you there? Glotzback?"

"Herb? Is that you?"

"Yeah, it's me. Now, listen. Hold on a second." A scratchy sound came down the line.

Then I could hear muffled voices. I reached for my cigarettes on the nightstand before I remembered that I'd given up smoking over two years ago.

"Glotzback?"

"Yeah."

"Listen, I need your help."

"Now? It's two o'clock in the morning."

"Sorry, but I need you to come to Good Samaritan over on Parkside. Not the new hospital. That's the one that looks like a spacecraft from Mars. I'm in the old yellow brick one. Know the one I'm talking about?"

"Sure, but why?"

"Don't worry about why. Just get out here as quick as you can."

"What about your wife?" As I asked, it occurred to me that I didn't know her name.

Herb moaned low. Then he coughed. I could voices behind him, snatches of strange, fleeting conversations. I heard a woman say blood. It was like eavesdropping on a parallel universe.

"Don't worry about her, Glotzback." He paused then and I listened to the line hum. Donna murmured in her sleep. Rain still scratched at the window. Herb cleared his throat. "My wife's not in the picture anymore, get it? But that's just between us. Okay? Now just get out here as fast as you can. Oh, and bring some money, too."

"Money? Why?"

"Never mind. Just bring it. Please."

For a minute I didn't say anything. I couldn't. I'd known Herb for almost my entire life and I couldn't remember him ever saying please. Instead of a smoke I needed a drink. I sat up and got my back against the headboard. The rain was still trying to get in.

"How much?"

"Two hundred."

"Damn, Herb. Don't think I've got that much. Even if I dip into my horse money."

"Damn, Glotzback. Only two hundred lousy dollars. You can do it. Now hurry."

The line went dead and I sat there listening to the dial tone, trying to think. When a woman with a hateful British accent started telling me to hang up and dial the operator I dropped the receiver back on the cradle, rubbed my eyes, and rolled out of the bed. Donna turned over and the light fell on her face like a vision from an unknown god.

Thirty-five minutes later I was trudging across the rain slickened parking lot at the hospital with Johnny Turner. The rain had slackened until it was just enough to dampen the pavement and keep your windshield wipers swiping.

My head was clear, but my eyes were heavy and my tongue felt like it was coated in fur. I wished we'd stopped somewhere for a cup of coffee, but Herb had sounded rather desperate and I didn't have a clue what awaited us. You know how it is, especially in the middle of the night when you've been asleep—every rotten possibility seems all too likely.

The parking lot was quiet, as was the street beyond. Novelists say that a city never sleeps, but at three o'clock in the morning this one sure was drowsy.

Forty years ago Parkside had been one of the premier streets. Now the glitz had moved on down the line and potholes and burnt out buildings made the street look like a war zone. Every other street-light was burnt out, or shot out, and men moved in the shadows like dark, lonely ghosts. Johnny and I hustled inside the emergency room.

A uniformed guard lounged behind a desk. He had a gun in a holster on his hip. Tilting his cap back, he eyed us suspiciously through thick glasses. He looked at me so long I began to feel guilty. Finally he asked what we wanted. I told him. He told us to wait and motioned to a row of red plastic chairs lined along a concrete block wall that had been painted lime green within recent memory.

I sat down and thumbed through a Sports Illustrated that featured last year's pennant race.

Johnny cleared his throat. "Tell me again, Ray, why I'm here."

"Like I told you, Herb needed someone to pay his ER bill and I'm sixty-five dollars short. Plus, I might need help getting him inside his place."

"Yeah, I know all that. But why am I doing it for that jerk, especially in the middle of the night?"

"Let's just say that you're a good guy."

"Not that good. Not for Herb Henley. Not even in his dreams." Johnny rubbed his eyes with the back of his hands. "I must be dreaming," he said. "Or drunk."

He let his head fall back against the wall and opened his mouth like he was going to say something else. Then he shut it. I stared at him trying to puzzle out what he was thinking. Gradually, I became self-conscious. Dropping my gaze, I started thumbing through the magazine. Ten minutes later I was blinking and yawning, struggling to keep my eyes open.

Rubber squeaked on tile and my head jerked up. A skinny nurse curled one finger. Johnny and I followed her starched whites down a long hallway. Every ten feet there were purple arrows on the floor. I wondered what they were pointing the way to.

We turned left at the first intersection and she opened the first door on the right. I followed her in. Johnny's footsteps echoed behind me.

A row of beds, separated by curtains, ran down one side. An old man lay on the first bed. His mouth was opened and spittle ran down from the corners of his mouth as though he'd developed leaks.

In the second bed a Hispanic man lay on his back staring at the ceiling with one eye. A swatch of gauze covered the other. Something very sharp had sliced his face. Skin was layered back and blood oozed through the bandages. As I walked by, he moaned, calling softly for his madre.

Herb was in the third bed. One leg lay on top of the sheet, the foot covered in a plaster cast. His eyes were closed, but they opened as the nurse pulled the curtain back. A single plastic chair was wedged into the corner of the cubicle. This one was orange. Somebody must have gotten a deal on ugly plastic chairs.

I looked at the chair and then at Johnny. He shook his head and leaned against the wall. In the yellowish light he looked like an old man. I felt like one, so I sat down. It was three fifteen and I was way short on sleep. Herb rolled his head on his neck and stared at Johnny and then at me. His eyes were bloodshot and swollen. He looked like hell. But then, I felt like hell.

"Took your time getting here," he said out of the side of his mouth. His lips moved only a little when he spoke.

My blood warmed up in a hurry and I forced myself to look at the floor until the vein quit throbbing in my temple. Somebody had slid most of a bedpan under my chair. Staring down I could see a distorted reflection of my face. It was that sort of night. Time and space, reality, felt distorted.

"It's raining out there and I had to swing by and pick up Johnny."

Herb twisted on the bed and stared at Johnny. Pain flared up in his eyes as he moved. It faded slowly, and remained glowing, banked like embers.

"I called you, Glotzback. Why did you bring him?"

"I didn't have enough money, Herb. Don't keep that much cash lying around."

Johnny snorted loudly. "Yeah, Henley, nobody who works for you has any money just lying around. Takes every damn dime we make just to get by. You suck up to all the bosses and we just end up sucking the hind tit. If it wasn't for Ray I sure as hell wouldn't have come out in the middle of the night just to bail your ass out." Johnny pushed off the wall then and leaned forward. For a second I thought he was going to spit in Herb's face.

Instead, he leaned even closer, so close to Herb that their noses were almost touching. "Get this straight, Henley, and don't ever forget it." Johnny's lips curled back from his teeth. He was missing one on the left side. "I hate your guts. Your attitude disgusts me. It's so far removed from reality that you don't have a fuckin' clue."

Johnny straightened up and walked across the room. An orange and lime poster was taped to the wall. Something about washing your hands. He stared at it.

Herb grimaced and rolled over and made a face like a man who has just swallowed a dose of castor oil. I looked at him then. Stared straight into his eyes. They were brown and moist looking, like a dog's I'd had when I was twelve. It was the first time I'd looked Herb in the eye. He didn't say anything, only breathed rapidly out of the corner of his mouth. His eyes were open, only I didn't think he was seeing anything.

The room grew quiet. Now and then the Mexican moaned and once I heard two nurses talking about the man in Room 107. The guy wasn't going to make it. I thought about the dark and the rain coming down outside and dying on such a night, surrounded by diseased and dying strangers. I wondered then about God. Then I came back from that dangerous zone and leaned forward.

"When are they going to let you go home?"

Herb closed his eyes and swallowed. His chest rose and fell. Finally his eyes came open slowly, warily, like he'd been having a bad dream and was afraid that it was real. "Whenever we pay them."

I nodded and told him I'd be back soon. I pushed my butt out of the plastic chair and. strolled down the hallway to the cashier's station. Except for a guy waltzing with his IV the hallway was empty. He was wearing one of those hospital gowns that never quite cover everything. The guy had a bony ass.

A woman with fake black fingernails took my money while she read me all the checkout regulations in a monotone. I paid up like a champ.

When I got back to the room Johnny was sitting in the plastic chair and Herb was staring at his palms like he was a gypsy reading fortunes.

"They're bringing a wheelchair. We can go as soon as they get here."

"I don't need a wheelchair," Herb said without lifting his eyes. Johnny just sighed. I leaned against the wall. This night seemed like it was never going to end. For once I'd be glad to see daylight come.

I stood there listening to the night grow older. Seconds metronomed inside my head. I thought about Donna and her hungry mouth. In certain ways that was worse than wondering about God.

Out in the hallway a cart rolled by. It sounded like it had a wheel loose. Herb pressed the call button.

An ambulance wailed out in the rain. It sounded close. Probably pulling up out front. Herb's head had jerked at the sound, but then he sighed and raised himself up on one elbow. "Hand me my pants."

I studied the cast on his foot. "We'd better wait on a nurse. Have to roll you out, regulations."

"Damn," he said, and pressed the call button again. He said something else but the loudspeaker went off just then and all I heard was for Dr. Jahan to go to the ER.

I looked at Johnny. Behind his magazine he was grinning. Then I glanced at Herb. He had dropped the call button and was laying back, his head pressing into the pillow and his eyes closed. With his eyes shut he looked older. Maybe not as old as the night, or as old as I felt, but older than I'd ever seen him look.

The ambulance had quit wailing and in the windowless room I couldn't hear the rain. There was a clock on the wall, but the hands hadn't moved since I'd gotten there. Shoes squeaked in the hall. As the squeaking faded the room grew quiet. I could hear the shush of a ventilator. Then I could hear the Hispanic guy moaning, long and low and falling away like he was dying, or wanted to.

"What happened, Herb?" My voice was loud in the quiet.

Herb didn't say anything and I sat there watching the unmoving clock hands, wondering. A minute later he cleared his throat.

"It was like this. I was lying there on the couch, trying to get sleepy, watching some stupid movie about these Japs on an island. Guess it was during the war. They were in uniform anyway. And I started getting hungry. Had a craving for some good barbeque. The kind with Memphis sauce they serve at that shack over on Campbell Court."

I shook my head. I wasn't a big barbeque guy. Ate it only when the guys went to a place just down from the shop.

"Anyway, I love that pig meat when it just falls off the bone. Yeah, I know it was late, but that place stays open till midnight, so I get up and put my pants back on and drive my old Jeep clear over to Campbell. You know Campbell?"

"Used to go there years ago with my uncle. He always got his haircut there. Buddy of his was a barber. One-eyed guy, but he could cut hair."

"So you know that the street sorta curls around the side of a hill?"

"Right."

"Well, I backed into a spot at the rear of the lot and hopped out. Left the motor running 'cause I wasn't planning on being in there for more than a couple of minutes. What with it being so late and raining there just wasn't any crowd."

"Sure," I said, not quite sure why Herb had gone all the way to Campbell Court for barbeque. Campbell was halfway across town from his two-story. I couldn't remember the name of the street Herb lived on, but it was in the Clifton neighborhood. Most of the guys in the plant had grown up there, or just beyond. Herb was the only one I knew who'd never left.

Herb was mumbling now and I had to ask him to repeat himself. He took a deep breath and sighed, as if life was a horrible burden sometimes.

"Damn, Glotzback, can't you pay attention? Don't you realize I'm in pain?"

"Just tell me what happened, Herb." My head felt hollow and cold. I wondered what Donna was doing.

"Okay, so I go to hop out, only I've got on my loafers, see, and they're slick on the bottom and with the rain the pavement was wet, see, and I slipped. Tried to catch myself and..."

His voice faded away as though he was floating across the room. Turning my head, I studied his face. It was very calm, but his eyes seemed to be looking far away, or inward.

"What happened?"

I watched his throat work. "Somehow I half fell back inside the Jeep and I don't know how it happened, but I must have hit the stick 'cause the next thing I know the damn thing is rolling backwards and is going over my foot."

"Bet that hurt."

"Broke three bones, the doc says."

"Damn."

"Exactly. And you wanna know the worst of it, Glotzback?"

"What's that?"

"Naturally, I'm laying there hollering for help with the rain in my face and my foot hurting like hell."

"Surely somebody heard you."

"Sure they heard me, the bastards. Two of 'em came running out right away. This fat black man wearing an apron and this white kid, smiling, real friendly like. Remember his teeth were extra white. Too white, if you ask me."

"See that all the time these days, Herb."

"Well, I don't have to like it, do I? Anyhow, the old black fool starts carrying on and runs off. Guess he must have called 911, 'cause an ambulance showed up in a little while."

He paused and licked his lips and took a deep breath and let it out. "The kid though, he stayed with me, fussing around like my mother used to, patting my face and asking a bunch of questions and helping me sort of sit up against this other car so the rain wouldn't be in my face. Kept twisting me this way and that and talking like a parrot on speed. Damn him, anyway."

"What are you mad at the kid for, Herb? Sounds like he was only trying to help."

"Just shut your flapper, Glotzback, and I'll tell you. I'm getting there. Don't rush me. Can't you see I'm hurtin'?"

Johnny mumbled something then, but I didn't catch his words.

"So anyway," Herb said, "the ambulance finally comes and hauls me here. Guess the doc and the nurses were okay. At least they gave me a pain shot, but when I go to pay, guess what?"

"What?" I said, wondering where that wheelchair was.

"Well, here's the straight and short of it," Herb said, screwing his face up like he'd been sucking on lemon rinds. "While I was lying there in the rain with a broken foot somebody stole my damn wallet. Probably that damn kid. And him a white kid, too. Could have been my own son, see. Just don't understand kids these days."

I heard a sound then and I turned and looked at Johnny and he had his face in his hands and his shoulders were shaking. For a second I thought he was crying, but then I could see that his face was flushed with laughter. Then the laughter exploded across the room and Johnny kept on laughing until tears filled his eyes and trickled down and dampened the stubble on his jaw.

Herb's face was red by now and I was sorta embarrassed for all of us.

"What the hell is wrong with you, Turner? You're one sick son-of-a-bitch. Only a sicko would laugh at a man with a broken foot who has been robbed." Herb shook his head. "You disgust me, Turner."

Johnny looked up then, smiling. "Then we're even, Henley. Of all the assholes in the world you're the biggest, and the most perfect. And now I've got a question for you, old buddy."

I hoped Herb would keep his mouth shut, for once. But that was asking a lot out of a night that wasn't long on charity.

"What that, Turner?"

Johnny leaned forward and smiled at Herb. "I just want to know, Herb, old buddy, old pal, if you still think America is the greatest country on earth?"

Herb's face got so red then that I thought he was going to have a stroke. The top of his nose quivered.

"Fuck you, Turner, you miserable bastard."

Johnny only started laughing again, louder than before. Somehow Herb rolled over and grabbed the clipboard hanging on the rail beside his bed and threw it at Johnny. Johnny ducked and the clipboard clattered across the floor. The Mexican screamed and I turned and walked out of the room to see if I could find out what was keeping the wheelchair.

Out in the hallway you could hear Johnny laughing and Herb cussing and the Mexican shouting. The guy with the bony ass was walking toward me. He walked like a zombie straight from a 50's horror movie.

My head was throbbing again. Taking a deep breath, I turned right and started following the purple arrows again, thinking about Donna's hungry mouth and what had become of America, and where Herb's wife was, wishing for daylight to hurry.

TRICK OR TREAT

IT WAS HALLOWEEN, LATE in the afternoon. We were sitting in the kitchen, drinking coffee and the last of the beer and chatting about things that no longer mattered and things that never had. She had come in just before daylight and slept till four. Last night she'd netted over three hundred dollars. She wasn't working tonight.

My legs had stiffened up and I wandered over to the window and peered out at the narrow strip of grass between the chain-link fences. Three finches fluttered around the feeder. Only an inch of black oil sunflower seeds remained. The day had been quite warm for so late in the season, and even after five o'clock sunlight still flowed across the ground like an amber flood.

"I'm going to go feed the birds," I said.

"Fix me a drink first," she said.

I turned and looked at her. Since I'd moved in on the Fourth of July she'd been drinking hard and eating slices of pizza like they were candy. Her stomach pooched out like she'd swallowed a watermelon. Her lipstick was smeared like somebody had punched her in the mouth.

"What do you want? We've got half a bottle of wine left."

"No, I drank too much wine last night. Give me whiskey. A good shot. Two ice cubes."

I fixed her drink and carried it over. As she took the glass I noticed her hands were shaking. Her face had that bloated look drunks get just before they start the really deep slides. It was a look I'd seen before. Mostly in the mirror.

She stared at the whiskey. Then, suddenly, as if she had a train to catch, she lifted the glass. I watched her throat work. When we first met she'd a lovely throat.

"Oh, that's better," she said.

"Rough night?" I asked, just to make conversation.

She took another hit. Lights in her eyes ramped up. "Couple of blow jobs down on Sinclair, then a quickie for an old fart, and then a gang bang for a bunch of assholes at a bachelor party." She put the glass down and bent over and rubbed her calves. "Damn," she said, "I'm tired."

"Whoring is hard work."

"Shut up, asshole. It was wearing those heels."

"Sure," I said, and nodded.

"Go to hell," she said.

"Think I'll go feed the birds instead."

She mumbled something but I was already headed for the door. The bucket of sunflower seeds was on the sun porch and I picked it up and stepped outside.

The air was intensely still, as though the earth was holding its breath. I could hear the wooden steps squeak beneath my feet and the finches fussing at me from the locust tree and a dog barking down the block. I stood beside the feeder with the last good daylight warming my face. Someone was grilling out and the meaty aromas reminded me I hadn't eaten lunch. The dog quit barking and I listened to a car roll by on Madison. Then a phone started ringing. It went on ringing for a long time. The call wasn't for me.

Sunlight was warm on my face, making me feel almost young again and I had the sudden urge to dig out my old catcher's mitt and stroll over to Findlay Park and see if there were any kids around who wanted to pass ball. It was a pleasant notion and I stood there thinking about it for some time, remembering the old days. It had been so long since I'd felt that young that the scraps of memory seemed to belong to another man.

I got tired of holding the bucket and filled the feeder and went back inside. She'd moved to the living room and had the television on with the sound turned all the way down. She had slipped on one of my old long-sleeve white shirts and hadn't bothered to button it. Her belly drooped over her panties. Flab was starting to gather in her thighs. Not that I didn't understand. Aging and drinking and sitting around was a sure way to pick up pounds. I'd found a few that way myself.

She lifted her head and struggled to focus her eyes. The skin on her face was flat and dull looking, like a smudged mask. There was a vacant look to her eyes, one that I remembered from the days when I'd loaded up on meds.

"Get me another drink will you? I don't feel like getting up." She waggled her glass at me and the glass caught the light from the television and shot random strands of light into the universe.

"Join me," she said as I rescued the glass.

"I'll pass."

"Piss on you. You're no fun anymore. Ever since you crawled back on the wagon you've been a pain to live with."

I didn't say anything. Just carried her glass into the kitchen and poured her another shot. Then I took it back to her. No use arguing with a drunken woman. Especially when she's right.

I handed her the drink and sat down beside her on the couch. Some game show was on television. Contestants were running around a stage trying to open huge locks on glass doors. Behind the glass were all these fabulous prizes. The contestants kept twisting the dial on the locks to different numbers, trying to figure out the combinations. I couldn't get a handle on how they knew which numbers to try. Maybe they had been given clues, or maybe there was some system I didn't know about.

Now and then the cameras would pan the audience. Almost all were waving their arms or jumping up and down. Just about all the audience members had their mouths open. They looked like they were screaming. It was funny watching them without any sound.

One contestant kept jumping up and down while she twisted the dials. She never opened even one of the locks. One woman did get one in, a big fat black woman, so wide her hips almost got stuck in the door. I watched until she squeezed through. Then I got up and fixed a pot of coffee.

When I got back a stock car race was on. While the afternoon grew old and died we sat there drinking and watching the cars go around and around and around.

She had two more drinks. I had another cup of coffee. After a while she snuggled up against me and I draped an arm across her shoulders. Two laps later she was snoring softly. Her breath was redolent with whiskey. Her body smelled of used sex and stale sweat. The race went under the caution flag and I quit watching the television and looked out the window.

A decrepit elm occupied most of the front yard. A squirrel was perched on a bare limb that ran like a dark snake toward the house. He was staring at me, or maybe his reflection. His eyes were bright. They looked hot. I stared back at him until the shadows converged with the gathering dusk.

The doorbell rang and she jerked like she'd been electrocuted.

"What the hell?" she mumbled.

"I don't know," I said. "Scoot over and I'll get up and see who it is."

It took us a few seconds to disengage and I hoped whoever was out there had given up. I tugged the door open. In the dusk it was hard to make out who it was. I flipped on the porch light.

A middle-aged man with a scraggly beard opened his mouth. "Trick or treat," he shouted.

"What?"

"Trick or treat," he said. "It's Halloween, buddy." He thrust an open pillowcase at me. It needed washing. So did his clothes. Something about the man seemed familiar. Tilting my head, I studied his face. He smelled like he needed a shower.

"I've seen you around."

"Probably. Usually sleep down at the mission on Grundy."

"Yeah, okay." I recognized him now. He was one of the men who hung around in front of the mission the Episcopalians ran, bumming cigarettes and pocket change. I was sure it was him by his accent. I'd spent a year in Oklahoma selling cemetery plots to veterans and had heard a hundred who sounded just like him. An Oklahoma twang a man remembered.

"It's illegal to panhandle door-to-door."

He grinned. What teeth he had left looked rotten. "I ain't handling. I'm trick-or-treating. It's Halloween. Saw that in the newspaper."

"You're too damn old to be doing that."

"Who is it?" she asked.

"Aw, come on, buddy, have a heart. Ain't you seen no hard times?"

"Who is it?"

"Yeah," I said. "A few. Hold on."

I turned, closing the door behind me. One Hershey bar was hidden in my sock drawer. I walked toward the bedroom.

"Who the hell is it?" she asked, grabbing for my arm.

"A trick-or-treater," I said.

"What?"

"It's Halloween."

"Oh," she said and subsided back on the couch.

I gave the Oklahoma Kid the Hershey bar. He thanked me like a schoolboy and toddled off down the sidewalk.

"We're out of candy," I said. "I've got to run down to Noonan's."

"Bring me back a bottle of Jack."

"Noonan's only has beer."

"Alright, a case."

I thought about the state of my billfold. "We'll see."

She said something else, but I was going down the steps. Outside, the air was cooler and it was pleasant walking down the street with a reason to be moving. The sky was growing dark and I could see the kids running from house to house. They were laughing and calling out to each other, disturbing the birds who were trying to roost.

Under a streetlight I glanced at my watch. Noonan's would be closing any time. I began to run. A little boy in a cowboy outfit was walking towards me and he gave me a look that made me wonder what I looked like to him.

By the time I made it back she had wandered out on the porch. The shirt was still unbuttoned and her breasts were visible in the porch light. I hadn't realized how flabby they'd become.

"You sure took your own sweet time."

"I wasn't gone ten minutes. Now get inside before somebody sees you."

"What's the matter, don't you like the way I look anymore?"

"Sure, you look great. But let's not let everybody have a free shot. Besides, there are kids out." I put a hand on an elbow and began to steer.

"I like kids, alright. You know I like kids."

"Sure, sure, now let's get in and get ready."

"Okay, but give me a beer first."

"Here's the whole damn six pack."

"A six pack, why you cheap..."

"Now, now, there are kids running around."

I'd hardly got her situated on the couch and the Snickers poured into a mixing bowl when the doorbell rang.

A little boy and girl were on the porch. Both wore skeleton costumes and held plastic pumpkins nearly full of candy. I tossed a Snickers into each pumpkin.

"Oh," she said when I'd closed the door. "They were so cute."

The doorbell rang again. It was a pirate with an eye patch, who was followed by a fat boy in a football helmet, a miniature ghost, a kid with a blue face who was almost as tall as I was, and two little blondes in ballerina dresses. After they left I looked around but didn't see any more little fartknockers. I closed the door.

"Well," I said, "guess that was our rush. Cute little yard apes, weren't they?" I put the mixing bowl down on top of the television and looked at her.

She put a can of beer down on the coffee table and pulled another one out. "Damn," she said. "Damn, damn, damn." Then she started crying.

"What's the matter now?"

"I'll never see my own kids again. I want to see my babies," she sobbed.

Before she started hooking and drinking she'd two kids. A boy and a girl. They lived with their father. He was a cop in Glendale.

Big fat tears slid down her cheeks and her body shook. Her stomach wobbled like a globe tilting off its axis and the flesh under her chin wobbled. She closed her eyes. She still had beautiful eyes. They were the color of a clear October sky over Portland, Maine.

I went over and sat down and put my arms around her. She cried for a long time. Twice I had to get up to pass out more Snickers. Finally I turned out the porch light and went and opened a can of beef stew.

She wouldn't eat, so I ate the whole can. Then I washed up the dishes and ate one of my leftover Snickers. Only three huddled at the bottom of the mixing bowl. They looked lonely.

I poured myself another cup of coffee and went back in the living room. She had stopped crying. Her face needed washing. She was smoking a cigarette. She hadn't smoked in months. She tapped the ashes into an empty beer can. "I love my kids, you know," she said without looking up. "I miss 'em like hell."

"I know," I said. "I know."

A baseball game was on the tube. I sat down in a leather recliner that had given up reclining and turned up the sound.

After the fifth inning she said she was sleepy. I told her to go on to bed. She was mumbling to herself now and once she farted. The bases were loaded in the sixth when she struggled to her feet, belching loudly.

"Can we go see them sometime?" she whispered.

"Go see who?" I asked without taking my eyes off the pitcher.

"My kids," she said. "My babies."

The batter struck out and the station went to commercial. I lifted my eyes. She was crying again, only silently.

"Sure," I said. "On Saturday, I'll call Joe and see what I can set up. Now go on to bed. You need some rest."

She stared at me then, right into my eyes, and she went on staring like she never intended to stop. Her mouth worked a little and I think she wanted to say something. But she couldn't bring herself to say whatever was on her mind. Or maybe that was the beer messing with her. She just stood there, swaying a little now like a storm was starting to blow. After a minute I got up and helped her to bed. She went to sleep still wearing my shirt.

The game went to extra innings and it was after midnight before I brushed my teeth and slipped between the sheets. A shaft of moonlight was falling through the curtains and her face was peaceful in the alabaster. She was snoring softly.

Before dawn something woke me. It wasn't a dream. I hadn't dreamed since my dad died ten years ago. A muffled choking sound was drifting through the darkness. After a minute I figured it out.

She was crying again. Crying with her eyes shut tight. Maybe she was crying in her sleep. Maybe she didn't want to wake me. Maybe she wanted privacy.

For a long time I lay there listening to her crying, trying to think of a few comforting words. They wouldn't come, so I gave up and slipped out of bed. I put on my pants and a sweatshirt and slipped my feet into the corduroy house shoes she'd given me for my birthday. Then I tiptoed out into the hall and pulled the door to behind me.

The air in the house seemed stale, as if all the good had been sucked out. Meandering outside, I sat down on the porch and thought for a long time without coming to any conclusions about her and her kids and all that crying and where I fit in the equation.

There was a stillness to the night air. I couldn't hear any cars or kids or dogs or birds. It felt like I was the only creature living after some cataclysmic event. I told myself I'd always been a survivor. Some people were. Others survived only on the generosity of the strong.

I wondered if she would remember all the crying in the morning, or if she ever thought about her kids when she was turning a trick.

I tried not to judge. I'd had my share of fuckups, and then some. Life wasn't easy. Not for anybody. That much I'd figured out. Every morning you just had to get up and strap on the armor again.

Maybe if I had kids I'd cry, too. I told myself that if I ever had kids I'd never let them go. But then I tell myself a lot of things. Some of them are even true.

The moon was sliding down the sky now. A passage from the Thirty-first Chapter of Job came to me. "Or the moon moving in splendor."

I could see the man-in-the-moon through gaps in the old elm. Distance, or smog, or the angle of the light distorted his shape. It was like a gigantic, invisible vice grip was squeezing the life out of the moon. The limbs of the elm striped the face of the man-in-the-moon like prison bars.

SATURDAY SPECIAL

SATURDAY MORNING HAD SPLATTERED like a big hot pale yellow egg all over my world. I drug my carcass to the kitchen table, toting the first cup of coffee of the day. I sat down at the table and looked out the window.

The sun was up above the rooftops but it didn't seem to have much power. The sky looked washed out, as though it had been plastered above the trees and the roofs one too many times. The air was laced with heat, though. Sweat trickled down my chest. Last night hadn't been hot and I'd pulled an old quilt up over me. Things were always changing without warning me.

For a few minutes I sat on the wooden chair, sweating, sipping on coffee, trying to clear the dream webs out of my mind. When the sweat ran down the crack of my ass I got up and went around the table and tugged on the widow.

I tugged like hell with no results, except making my forearm hurt, before I remembered that the landlord had painted last winter. I dug a butter knife out of a drawer and ran it along the base of the window. After a couple of passes I'd pried off enough paint so that I could open the window.

Warm air drifted in, smelling stale, as though it had been bottled up for a long time. It seemed to stick to my skin. There was a fan in the kitchen. It was green and oscillated and sat on top of the refrigerator. I crossed the kitchen and turned the fan on. A band of cooler air blew across my face. Then it blew away. I walked back to my chair.

The coffee was tepid now and I drank it straight off. I got up and poured another cup, which I drank slowly, thinking about nothing more than what I was going to do that day. Most Saturdays I had to work. Sundays I usually visited my father in the nursing home. I sold shoes to women, usually women with cellulite thighs and odorous feet. Today, though, I wasn't working. Business had been off for weeks and Mr. Torrez, who owned the place, told me that only Bob Quincy was working today. Next Saturday would be my turn.

I must have dozed off, because all of a sudden there was a sharp pain in my neck and my head was lolling in front of my chest like some great hairy bell. Lately I hadn't been sleeping so good.

I felt refreshed and realized I was hungry. I fried an egg and toasted two slices of bread. I ate the egg at the kitchen table while I listened to a dog bark somewhere down the street. I couldn't remember hearing a dog bark on Roebuck Street before, not even on Sundays. Sundays always seemed to be lazy, restful days, even for dogs.

After breakfast I washed the skillet and spatula and my plate and fork. Then I took a cup of coffee into the living room. Small and dark, the room felt hot and the air smelled like the exhaust from a car motor. I took off my shirt and turned on the radio and sat down in my chair.

Music was playing. Dance music from an earlier generation. Music you danced to by holding your partner close. Only I didn't have a partner. Just a cup of coffee. That I held close and drank slowly as the music played.

After the song finished another dance tune came on. Then a commercial for a bank. The voice inside the ancient black Philco announced solemnly that the people at this bank really cared about you and your money. It wasn't my bank. I banked at the bank my father had used for fifty-seven years. I only had a small checking account.

After the bank commercial there was another song and then more commercials. I didn't actively listen to them. I was still trying to decide what I was going to do today. Having a Saturday off was special. I told myself I should do something new and exciting, something I'd never done before. Something to remember.

Yes, that was decided. What wasn't decided though, was what new, exciting, memorable thing I should do. I finished my coffee and picked idly at the stuffing coming out of one of the chair arms.

A man came on the radio and gave the news in measured tones. A garbage strike was threatened, a former mayor had died, the price of corn was rising. Then there was something about an art exhibit, but my mind was wandering again and I didn't catch back up until a different man started giving the weather forecast.

This second man sounded happy and excitable. He talked almost euphorically of hazy skies, the first heat wave of the season, and the prospect of drizzle on Sunday. I failed to appreciate his enthusiasm.

Following the news there were more commercials and then a baseball game came on. I turned the radio off. Sports were up there on the list of things I hadn't been good at. Basically, I was clumsy, slow on my feet. Funny, I thought, I was slow on my feet and sold shoes to women who were heavy on theirs.

After I turned the radio off I sat there in my underwear, sweating away Saturday morning, trying to decide. I began to think about my mother, wondering if she were still alive, and if so what she was doing on this special Saturday. She was younger than my father by four or five years, I couldn't remember which. For as long as she lived with us she'd been in excellent health. She and my father had been good dancers. I remembered them dancing around our living room. Dancing to music pouring out of the radio like a river. The same sort of music I had been listening to earlier. Then I remembered that it was the same radio.

When I tired of remembering, I got up and went to take a shower. I'd decided I'd take a long walk, stop off somewhere at a wicked looking bar and have a shot of whiskey, maybe two. I'd never been to a bar before and never drunk anything stronger than a couple of beers with my Uncle Fred when my father and I had taken the train to St. Louis to visit him.

After drinking my whiskey I would go see my father in the nursing home. That way I would not have to walk in the rain on Sunday. Walking in the rain was not my favorite thing. My mother had liked to walk in the rain. One day she'd taken a walk in the rain and had not come back. She'd told us she was going to go to a movie. A romance.

I hoped my father would be happy to see me on a Saturday. He was used to me visiting on Sunday. Perhaps, I told myself as I washed my arms, my surprise visit would make it seem like a special Saturday for him, too.

Usually when I went to see my father I walked down Roebuck, turned on Colston for one block, then hit 8th Avenue and took it all the way to where Merchant Drive intersected. The nursing home where my father stayed, Twin Oaks, was located there, on the corner.

Today though I swung down Meredith and then Ralston, finally curling down a street named Zaffer that was little more than an alley. I turned down Zaffer because a sign jutted out from one of the buildings about twenty yards down on the right that read *World Famous San Remo Bar and Grille!* The words were scripted across a red sailboat skimming across blue waters. The sails of the boat were so white they hurt my eyes. In the alley the stench of rotting fruit perfumed the air. A one-eyed cat peered at me from the shadow of a doorway. Old newspapers, yellowed and wrinkled, lay scattered about like dead soldiers. Sweat formed a line across my forehead and I wiped it off and pushed the door to the San Remo open.

After the sunlight the San Remo was a cave. Blind, I stood just inside the entrance and waited for my eyes to adjust. Behind me the door clicked shut. The click was the click you heard in those old black and white jailhouse movies from the 50's when the cell door shuts behind the hero.

Piano music floated across the darkness. It was a blues tune, heavy on the bass. The melody made my heart hurt. My eyes were starting to adjust and I could make out the piano player across the room. He wore a white suit and a dark Fedora cocked to one side. His profile reminded me of Boris Karloff. He nodded and I nodded. Then I maneuvered around a fistful of tables surrounded by chairs and sat down on a stool at one end of the bar.

Behind the bar the bartender was talking on the phone. As I sat down he glanced up and waved one finger at me. I studied the bottles behind the bar. The piano player began to play another tune, one that vaguely reminded me of a hymn that I'd heard long ago. Before I could put a name to the tune the bartender sidled over.

"What'll it be?"

I took another look at the bottles. "If that's whiskey, a shot of that," I said, pointing at a bottle on the bottom shelf.

The bartender looked down his nose at me, but he dutifully got the bottle down and poured a shot. He pushed the glass in front of me. "Two dollars," he said.

I dug two ones out of my wallet and laid them on the bar between us. I could smell the bartender's aftershave. He smelled like Old Spice. He sighed and picked the bills up and ambled over to the till. I took a sip of the whiskey. It tasted cooler than I expected and it burned a little going down.

I tipped the shot glass up and drained it. Then I waggled my glass at the bartender. While I drank the second whiskey, the piano man played a waltz. My mother and father had danced to that very tune in our living room. I tried to calculate how long ago that had been.

The piano player played another slow tune and I peered around the room. Now the room seemed pleasant. Cool and dimly lit, it seemed like a very peaceful place. Two women sat at the other end of the bar and an old man sat at a table near the piano. In front of the piano was a small dance floor.

Except for those three people I was the only customer. Of course it was still the middle of the afternoon. The place would probably grow lively after dark. Part of me wished I could stay.

I had the feeling that nothing could hurt me here. I drummed my fingers on the bar top in time to the piano. I wondered what time it was. Twisting my wrist I glanced at my watch. Plenty of time for one more. I nodded at the bartender.

While he was pouring the whiskey one of the women got off her stool at the far end of the bar and came over and sat down next to me.

"Buy a girl a drink?" Her voice was raspy and she smelled of stale cigarette smoke.

I'd never bought a woman a drink before, but I nodded. After all, it was a special Saturday. She gave the bartender hand signals.

"What's your name?" the woman asked after she'd taken a sip of her drink. A tiny umbrella floated in the glass.

"Charles."

"Mine's Joan." She smiled. She was missing a tooth on the bottom, but she had pretty lips. They were thick and in the lights from the row of tiny bulbs above the mirror behind the bar they looked as red as fresh blood.

"Cheers," she said and lifted her glass.

I lifted mine and we touched glasses. The tinkle was like the sound of a miniature sleigh bell. I closed my eyes and took a long drink.

When I opened my eyes she was staring at me. Her eyes were deep set. She was wearing eye makeup and it was hard to see what color her eyes were. I sipped again. Inside my head there was a faint buzzing. I thought I'd better get some air.

As I pushed off my stool the piano player switched to a tune that had been popular years before. Couples liked to dance to it. They danced very close together. I'd seen them dancing to the song on my Uncle Fred's television.

The woman stood up too and somehow we ended up on the dance floor. As we moved around the floor she pressed herself against me. Her breasts felt soft. I felt awkward. She put her head on my shoulder. Her neck smelled of violets. My legs seemed far away.

We danced two songs and my legs felt like they belonged to another man. It had been a long time since I'd been so close to a woman. Not since Betty left. Over two years ago. The woman had soft hands. They traced patterns I didn't recognize against the back of my neck. Somehow the bar had grown quite warm. When the second song ended she kissed me on the mouth. Her breath was thick with liquor and cigarette smoke.

Holding hands, we walked back to the bar. Holding hands wasn't something I had planned on. Holding hands was very special indeed.

We eased back down on our stools and ordered another drink. I wondered idly how my father was doing and how he would react when I showed up on a Saturday. Then I tried to calculate how much I'd spent, but my brain was moving sluggishly.

After our drinks came and we'd taken a good hit the woman kissed me again. The kiss started out as a light brushing of lips, but ended up with her tongue in my mouth. Warmth rushed through my body and I couldn't stop my erection.

The woman whispered in my ear but the piano player was hitting the high notes and I couldn't understand what she was saying. But then I wasn't hearing so good either. Probably because I wasn't used to drinking. All the sounds seem to be drifting away from me. To the top of the bar. To the sky. To Jupiter.

The woman's face was blurry. I blinked my eyes. "What did you say?"

She leaned closer and her hair tickled my ear. She giggled and her breath was warm against my cheek. "I asked if you wanted to go someplace more private."

I didn't know what to say. I tried to say something, but my voice seemed stuck in my throat. I nodded.

"Okay, sweetheart, just finish your drink and we'll take us a little walk. The place isn't far and it's cheap." Her fingertips stroked my arms. "You do have some money, don't you?"

I nodded again and downed my whiskey. Then I felt better, stronger, more in control of my emotions. "Sure, I just got paid yesterday. I have plenty of cash."

She kissed me again and rubbed her palms against my chest.

I'd forgotten about the sun and the light stabbed my brain. The air was hotter than before, but the sun was lower in the sky. Sunlight glared off the glass in the windows of an old warehouse across the street and it seemed to me that for a minute I was looking into the thousand eyes of God. Then we started walking and I forgot all about my Holy Father and my earthly one.

By the time we'd gone a couple of blocks I wasn't feeling so good. My head was threatening to split open and my stomach was starting to churn like an ocean before a coming storm. Our little walk was feeling like a forced march for an exhausted French Foreign Legionnaire.

At the corner of the next block I stopped walking and leaned against the building. I pressed my face against the glass. It was dusty. Inside there were dead people. Body parts were scattered everywhere. I blinked and the people and parts were only mannequins.

"What's the matter, honey?" The woman rubbed my shoulders.

"I don't feel so good."

"Oh, you can make it. Only a block or two now. It's a nice hotel. Each room has an air conditioner and a shower. Doesn't a nice cool shower sound good?"

I started to say yes, but my stomach was heaving a little and I clamped my mouth shut and nodded. We stumbled down the sidewalk, out of synch, moving slowly.

Dark spots danced before my eyes and I was sweating like a hard run racehorse, but the woman kept a firm grip on my arm and tugged me along when I faltered. Once, while we waited for a traffic light to change, I asked myself what was so special about this. I glanced up at the street sign, but the letters weren't holding still and all I could make out was an L.

The hotel was an old red brick, built hard against the sidewalk and we stepped over the threshold and tottered across the lobby.

The room was full of odors and dark paneled, dimly lit by an ancient chandelier and a pair of mismatched table lamps. I could vaguely make out a cracked leather sofa and some unmatched chairs scattered about. Except for the woman and me and the clerk behind the counter the room was empty.

A wooden-bladed ceiling fan stirred the air and I stood leaning against the counter with my face pointed at the fan. The cooler air felt good. It was good to get out of the sun.

The woman and the man were talking, but I wasn't listening. I was thinking about when I was younger, before I dropped out of college, and I had gone to the beach for the weekend. It had been a beautiful day and the sand had been smooth and brown and the water salty and green. For hours I'd walked along the edge of the surf, gazing at gulls and little kids squealing in the water and girls in their bathing suits and kites the older boys were flying.

Time had slipped away from me and it was almost dark before I started the long drive back. I'm not certain what time it I finally pulled into my driveway, but the night had carried that after midnight feeling and my head had felt hollow.

My head felt hollow like that now and I didn't want it to fill up again so I didn't listen to the hum of the voices or the thoughts that were crinkling the surface of my mind. Something was tugging on my arm, but I ignored it. It kept tugging and gradually I drifted back into the lobby.

"Honey, the man needs some money." The woman smiled with her lips. Her eyes were flat and dark.

"How much?"

"Twenty dollars, that's all. Twenty dollars for an hour. You've got that, don't you baby? Twenty dollars for a room and an hour with little old Joan?"

"Sure," I said, "I'm made of money."

I dug my wallet out of my trousers and fumbled with the bills. A few fell on the lobby floor. I tried to remember how much money I had. Over two hundred dollars, I thought. The woman picked up the fallen bills. My fingers found a bill, held it close to my eyes, then handed it to the man behind the counter. He had a smirkey look on his face and I felt like slapping it off. But the woman was tugging on my arm and we stumble-footed our way across the lobby. Once I bumped against a chair and staggered, but the woman had a good hold on my arm.

A long, curving, carpeted flight of stairs loomed. I shook my head. Inside the bones something shifted. I could not climb stairs. The woman steered me to an ancient, caged elevator. We rose like two decrepit birds. At the fourth floor the elevator stopped. We got off and she kissed my check and rubbed one hand up and down the small of my back. I couldn't quite get it clear in my mind what I was doing here.

Arm in arm, like some honeymooning couple, we strolled down a hallway framed by wallpapered walls. Roses climbed on trellises and there were women with pompadours and men in powdered wigs. The roses and the people had faded and were coming apart at the seams.

She worked a key in a brass lock and a door swung open. Her hips swayed invitingly. I followed them in. It had been a long time between women for me. Even in my condition desire rose and I remembered what I was doing in the hotel.

She crossed the room and turned on a window air conditioner. It rattled like it was breaking apart and shot out a cloud of dust and insulation. I sat down on the bed and watched her unbutton her blouse very slowly.

"Ooh, that's better," she said, standing in front of the air conditioner, revealing her profile, luxuriating in the cool air. She unfastened her bra and her breasts swung free. They weren't large, about the size of hens' eggs, but they had thick nipples.

"Why don't you take a shower, baby? Get cooled off and cleaned up. I'll be waiting for you. She patted the bed and parted her lips. Her hair swung across her face. In the light from the window it shimmered gold.

A shower sounded good. Since I'd been sitting my stomach had quit quivering and I floated to my feet.

"Take off all your clothes for me, baby. Do it right here. Let me see you undress for me. Oh, you've got such a nice body."

Even with all the whiskey sloshing around inside me I felt embarrassed as I kicked off my shoes, then took off my socks and shirt and pants. No way in hell was I going to take off my underwear and wobble my flabby butt to the bathroom in front of this woman.

She didn't seem to mind. She gave me another tongue kiss and squeezed me through my shorts. I was as hard as concrete. I wanted to go to bed with her then, but she pushed me toward the bathroom.

"Go on," she said, "you smell like an old sweathog. Get cleaned up and then come see little Joan for the time of your life."

Before I tottered off to the bathroom I bent my head and kissed each nipple twice. I made sure the door clicked behind me. Then I took a short piss and a long shower. The woman had been right. I smelled like a used t-shirt. Warm water felt good against my shoulders. Thousands of needles pricked my skin. I finished with a short blast of cold water and dried off. Then I studied myself in the mirror. My face looked pale, washed out, but I felt halfway human. Wrapping the towel around me I opened the door.

The air conditioner was still throbbing in the window and her perfume lingered like floating flowers, but the room had that same empty hollow feeling that had filled my head in the lobby. I looked around the room. It didn't take long.

The woman was gone.

It took me several seconds to remember her name.

In the wavy mirror above the dresser I could see myself. Pale, the color of a fish belly, my stomach protruding and my ass cheeks sagging. A nightmare believing in delusions.

My shoes and socks were hidden by the bed, but in the mirror I could see my shirt and pants. Something was strange about my pants. For a minute I just stood there, trying to figure out what wasn't right. Then I saw what was different. All the pockets of my pants were turned inside out.

It felt like a tumor had instantly formed in my stomach. I hurried over to my clothes. On the floor were my keys and handkerchief and a few stray coins. No wallet. I got down on my hands and knees and looked under the bed. Nothing but dust and a used rubber.

I pushed off the floor and sat down on the bed. Just like before my stomach churned. Only this time it wasn't alcohol. Weakness washed over me in waves. My mind felt like it had been jerked out of my head with pliers and pulverized with a hammer. Two week's pay gone. Broke as hell, except for the few coins on the floor and the twenty I kept stashed in my bedside table. I eased back onto the bed. The room swirled in ever quickening circles. I shut my eyes.

I came out of a deep sleep, sweating and shouting so loudly my throat hurt. I hadn't planned to sleep and had no idea how long I'd been out. Blinking, I sat up and looked out the window.

Daylight was slanting in between the buildings across the street, but the quality of the light had changed. A one-eyed pigeon sat on the window ledge outside my room. Where the other eye should have been there was just a hole. I felt as though I'd fallen into one and couldn't get out. The pigeon cocked his head and stared at me with his solitary eye.

For two minutes, or five, or even ten, I just sat there staring at the pigeon, trying to decide. Only my mind seemed stuck. Maybe I sort of passed out with my eyes open. I stared at that stupid one-eyed pigeon until the light begin to fade.

I took a deep breath, pushed off the bed and got dressed. Passing on the ancient elevator, I went down the steps, moving as quietly as I could. Maybe the desk clerk looked at me. I can't say. I kept my eyes on the door.

Outside the air was still hot and sticky, but the sun had slipped behind the buildings across the street and blue shadows lounged in doorways.

I had only the vaguest sense of where I was. Just guessing, I turned left. At the end of the block there was a street sign, Middleton Place. I'd never heard of it. I didn't feel like asking anybody for directions, which was good because the street was deserted. I just kept walking. Birds chirped and a heavy-throated freight moaned in the dying afternoon, but I just kept walking.

A half dozen blocks later I turned a corner and off to my left I could see the Winchell Tower. It was the tallest building on this side of town. From the tower, the nursing home where my father stayed was only two blocks west. My legs were coming back now and I started walking with a purpose.

The hallways of the home were quiet, the floors polished. My shoes squeaked. None of the staff members were visible. For that small blessing I was grateful. I wondered what my father would say. The door to his room was ajar.

He was propped up in bed, his supper on the tray before him. He wasn't looking at his supper, though. He was looking out the window.

Shifting my head, I let my eyes travel along his line of sight. There wasn't much to see. One scraggly locust tree, a couple of bushes I don't know the names of, a patch of grass, a concrete bench, and an angle of sidewalk. Birds were calling to one another, but I couldn't see them. Scents of boiled beef and Brussels sprouts smothered the usual aroma of bedpans and that raw medicine scent that plagues hospitals and nursing homes.

For a minute I stood there looking at my father. His arms were thin and the flesh along his neckline was slack. Bones poked at his skin. With eyes sunk deep in his skull and hair that was scarcely more than fuzz he looked like a refugee from a 1930's newsreel. Still, his face was calm and his eyes were open. But it didn't look to me like he was seeing anything in the room. I cleared my throat.

His head turned slowly, as though his neck muscles were tired. Without speaking he studied my face. I felt like an intruder. Then he smiled with his lips pressed together.

"Well," he said, "well, well. Hello, son. How are you?"

"I'm okay, Dad. And you?"

His smile softened and he shrugged. We just stared at each other. I could hear the birds outside in the tree and a cart squeaked in the hallway. I wanted to say something to make it all better. I couldn't think of one good thing.

Instead I crossed the room and lifted the cover on his supper. A pile of gray meat squatted between carrots, mashed potatoes, and Brussels sprouts. Everything on the plate looked artificial.

Around the plate was a piece of cornbread, a small bowl of soup, and a plate of orange Jell-O.

"Want some soup, Dad?"

"I'm not very hungry."

"Ah, come on," I said, "a little soup couldn't hurt."

My father closed one eye and gave me a hard look out of the other one. He didn't say anything. Then he closed his other eye and let his head fall back on the pillow.

"Today's Saturday, isn't it?"

"That's right."

"Usually you come on Sundays."

"I know," I said, "just felt like surprising you. Wanted to make it a special Saturday for both of us."

Out in the hallway the elevator dinged. My father opened his other eye then. I'd never noticed before that my father's eyes were hazel. I could smell my own sweat and the Brussels sprouts and my father's urine. It looked dark in the cath bag. My eyes felt like they had sand in them. Somebody, a nurse's aide I guess, had drawn a smiley face on the dry erase board beside the bed. Drawn it right between the times he was supposed to get a sponge bath and a diaper change.

My father tilted his face and looked up at me. I looked away. Down the block a police siren wailed. I could feel his eyes on me. My cheeks felt hot.

"Okay," he said, "let's eat some soup."

My eyes found his face. He was smiling. It was a tired smile, but it made it all the way to his eyes. I needed a cup of coffee. Instead I picked up the spoon. Somebody whistled as they strolled by his door. They had a cheerful whistle, only slightly off-key.

I fed him all the soup and half his Jell-O before he shook his head. Then I wiped his mouth. He kept a small radio by his bed. I turned it on. More piano music. Lilting was the word.

I walked around the foot of his bed and sat down beside him on the edge of the bed. Only the after wash of daylight remained. Sounds of birds and the distant hum of traffic highlighted the evening. Across the courtyard lights were coming on. An orderly slipped out of the building almost directly beneath us and walked down the sidewalk and sat down on the concrete bench. He pulled a pack of cigarettes out of a pocket, tapped one out and stuck it in his mouth. Smoke curled skyward. I could hear my father's breathing. It sounded shallow. I wished I knew how he really felt.

It was hard for me to look at him. I remembered when he had been a big man, vigorous and strong. I kept watching the courtyard. Two more birds flew in and fluttered down in the branches of the scraggly tree.

There was a sadness now in the piano music floating out of the radio. Yet, intertwined with the melancholy, was a sweetness. I felt my father's hand slide into mine. It was cool and full of bones. I lifted it to my lips and kissed the desiccated flesh. He squeezed my hand with his. I remembered when I had been a kid and he had squeezed my hand just that way.

I wanted to be a kid again. I wanted my money back. I wanted my Saturday back. I wanted my dad back, the happy healthy alive one; I wanted, I wanted, I wanted.

I didn't say anything. Just squeezed his hand gently and sat there on the side of the bed beside him, watching the light fade.